The Thinking Chair

Published by Gently Press, P.O.Box 2555, Inver Grove Heights, MN 55076
For additional copies, contact the publisher.

Publisher's Cataloging-in-Publication
   (Provided by Quality Books, Inc.)

   Brown, Audrey, 1926-
      The thinking chair : a novel / by Audrey Brown. --
   1st ed.
      p. cm.
      ISBN: 0-9719294-0-8

      1. Caregivers--Fiction.   2. Minnesota--Fiction.
   3. Montana--Fiction.   I. Title.

   PS3602.R677T45 2002   813'.6
                                QB102-701567

Cover illustration by Pat Brown
Book design by Dorie McClelland, Spring Book Design

The

Thinking Chair

a novel by

Audrey Brown

GENTLY PRESS, ST. PAUL, MINNESOTA

A heartfelt thank you

goes out to
My mother, Josephine, for believing in me,
My long-time friend, Marge, for encouraging me,
My diligent mentor, Jonis, for guiding me,
And my editor, Marilyn, for supporting me.

And, also, the many, many more family and friends,
who never let me give up.

Thank you all very much.

The Thinking Chair

My front doorbell rang out in several short bursts, its urgency shattering the quiet of the house. It startled me, even though I was aware it would ring any minute.

"She's here already," I cried. I took a deep breath and rushed to the door. "Well, it *is* time," I said, speaking aloud again, though now with much more control. But, upon turning the knob, my hand felt instantly weak. Damn nerves always interfering, I thought, yet I smiled with a determination and pulled the door open wide.

Dorrie stood on my porch, stiff-backed and expressionless. A moment lapsed, then her arm swept out in a grand gesture. "Your cah-r, Mah-dahm," she said, and bowed from the waist.

"A-ah, thank you." I stepped aside, inviting her to enter. "You're quite punctual." Then we broke into laughter at our stuffy pretense. It was easy to laugh with Dorrie. She'd been my truest friend since first grade when she'd offered me her barely-chewed wad of heavenly-smelling pink bubble gum.

"Oh! Hi, Lottie." Dorrie giggled then, bustling past me into the foyer where my small pile of assorted luggage stood ready. She reached for the largest piece, one spotlessly new and bulging. But, although she grinned, I still detected a slight quiver to her bottom lip.

"You go ahead, Dor, I can manage the rest. I'll be out in a few seconds."

"Good." Her grin was now just a crooked smile. "You wouldn't want to miss *that* flight."

I watched for a moment as she struggled with my heavy bag across the big open front porch and down the steps. Her long, straight, straw-blonde hair was sliding about her shoulders and it caught my eye. Such a color. Beside her I'd always felt my light brown hair to be just plain drab. And her skin was smooth and creamy-white, too, while I'd always had a splattering of large freckles across my nose. Besides that, she was tall, while I barely reached five, three and a half. We were an odd pair, all right, but nothing had ever threatened our close friendship since first grade, all those thirty-five years of growing up and living out our lives in Spencer, Minnesota. Nothing. Until now.

I was leaving Spencer this day, but only for a short time; only for an undetermined period of some months, taking a temporary job first, and, after that, an extended vacation.

I had turned then, hurrying to the kitchen where, by habit only, I stopped and peered out the sink window. The old house next door, separated from mine by a row of scrubby evergreens, was quiet—no one there to say goodbye to now. I looked to the sky. Drizzle had accompanied this particular September morning and a gloom had invaded my rooms as I'd finished packing my bags. But now the clouds had parted and the sun's brilliant rays sent sparkles dancing across the neighborhood. I felt an assurance in the warmth of the sunlight. Oh, yes. Yes, it is a wonderful day to travel. But then a sudden shiver ran through me and tears blurred my eyes. Oh, Lord, I thought, it really is time to leave, ready or not. I blinked quickly and shook my head.

Without plan, I snatched a tumbler from a shelf, filled it with water and ran to the huge Boston fern billowing over its pedestal in the living room. Here you go, pal. Father and I both loved you, you know. I gave it a good drink and left the tumbler nearby, trusting my new renters would treat the plant kindly also.

For a few moments I surveyed my clean, orderly rooms. Then I grabbed up my remaining bags, and, with a pain twisting somewhere in my heart, I stepped out onto the big, open front porch of my family home, the house where I'd spent the majority of my forty-one years. I pulled the door hard behind me, the lock making a hollow clack as it caught. Well, you've done it, Charlotte Foster, you've actually done it. My thoughts were almost accusing.

At once my eyes fell to my father's old white wicker rocking chair sitting in its same honored place to the right of the front door. His thinking chair, he'd often called it.

And, with one foot as I passed I gave it a loving jolt that set it into motion. I smiled a little then for I could almost see him in it, yet I soon felt a pang of guilt. No, not guilt. Fear, maybe. Yes. Some fear. I had to admit to some fear, some nagging apprehension.

Dorrie opened her trunk and we loaded my bags into it. "Crimony, Lottie, you must have all the clothes you own in here." She juggled the pieces around in the limited space.

"Well, I do—just about." I laughed and tilted my chin into the air. "After all," I said, "I have to be prepared for all sorts of climates, you know." I shrugged, adding more fake nonchalance. "Montana for the fall, California for the winter." I laughed again, but I couldn't conceal my nervousness any longer. Dorrie threw a curious glance in my direction as she slammed the trunk lid. I quickly got into her car.

After we'd both settled in and buckled up, Dorrie turned to me and asked, calmly, "Well, Charlotte Foster, do you have everything? Your instructions? Your funds? And your courage?" She pursed her lips and waited.

"Yes. Yes to all your questions." I answered, but then I had to look away and bite my lip for a moment before my composure returned. "Now, to the airport, puh-leeze, driver." Although I'd used a haughty tone, tears began to fill my eyes and my throat tightened. I couldn't swallow, it hurt so.

Dorrie started the car, shifted and eased it away from the curb. I glanced back, averting her eyes, and, through a mist, I saw my father's chair still rocking as we drove off. Oh, God, I thought, I hope he understands.

Dorrie really had come up with everything she could think of to change my mind about going. Not about the vacation, just the job part of it. She'd warned me I didn't know what I could be getting myself into. Well, I admit it wasn't like me to go off on a whim (her word) such as this, and she had cause to wonder. But I'd felt I'd given it sufficient thought and it was a whim no longer.

I swallowed hard and my throat felt better. Then I managed a determined set to my shoulders and pitched my chin upward, this time with a serious mind. I'll show her I can handle this, and I'll show that Mrs. Hilken a thing or two, too.

Funny how Mrs. Hilken'd popped into my mind. It was just a month ago at my father's funeral when she'd come up to me, hugged me hard, and said, "My, Lottie." (Father'd always called me Lottie since the day I was named, telling Mother that Charlotte took too long to say.) "Oh, my, whatever will you do now in that big old house all by yourself?"

"Mrs. Hilken," I'd said, "I really don't know." And I didn't.

She'd kept one arm around my shoulder, crushing me to her. "You've gone through so much, dear girl, losing your husband and your mother like you did," she spewed, wheezing and inhaling a deeper breath. "That dreadful accident. And now your father. My, dearie, you're so brave." And all the time she talked her huge, stone-encrusted broach kept jabbing me in the shoulder.

I wanted to push her away. I wanted to say bravery had nothing to do with it when Mr. Kelly, our fire chief, and his wife literally rescued me from her. He'd put a gentle arm around my shoulder then, and in his soft growl, said, "Take heart in your son, Lottie. You've done a fine job raising Kenny. Old Doc was mighty proud of him."

Everyone had called my father Old Doc for he'd been our town's only veterinarian almost until he died. His clinic was right behind our house, making it easy for him to keep working, and harder yet for him to retire. And it was difficult for me to believe now that it had been only two years since he'd closed his business and sold the building to a young photographer.

"Thank you so much, Mr. Kelly," I'd said, and during the rest of the funeral I'd kept Kenny nearby.

Now the present gripped me again when I sensed Dorrie's Oldsmobile gearing down as we made our way up the entrance ramp to the freeway. But it would be a fifty-mile ride to Twin Cities International Airport. As we rode up to a higher level, I glanced over my shoulder. I could see roofs, chimneys, treetops, and—the grain elevator. Goodbye, Spencer, Minnesota. Goodbye, everybody, I thought, see you in a—a—well, whenever I come back.

I was feeling almost flippant now, yet my stomach muscles tightened. This was my first-ever real trip away from home. Wow, even my first ride in an airplane. I tried not to think of that. Oh, I'd been on a few quick jaunts to Iowa to visit Kenny away at college, but that always by car.

Soon Dorrie had her Olds set on cruise and leaned back in her seat. I felt her eyes on me. "Oh, kiddo," she said, "I still can't believe it."

"I know." My teary eyes had improved enough I dared look at her. "Oh, Dor, but if you only knew what it's been like for me. I'd been feeling so damn down lately, so miserable—empty-like—ever since the funeral. And seeing Lena again, with Tom, well, it really set me to thinking. I've spent hours in that old rocker. Sometimes I even felt like I got some sort of vibes from it." I looked at her for some sign of understanding. She did glance to me and nod.

Lena was my twin sister, older by four minutes, but always the leader, the outgoing one. She was christened Charlene, but Father willfully shortened her name, too. Mother must have been too tired caring for us and our two-year-old brother, Larry, to object, I was sure.

Lena married her high school sweetheart and traveled all over the world as he pursued a career in the army. And their three girls had all been born in different countries. I envied her life; I pictured it exciting and glamorous, and always devoured her postcards and snapshots and letters. Yet they sometimes left me feeling a bit dull and uneasy, and, yes, even a little sick-to-my-stomach with jealousy. But, oh, how I hated that feeling.

Dorrie interrupted my thoughts. "So Lena's moving again?"

"Yes, to Hawaii this time. They're still in San Antonio, they do love it there." I sighed heavily without realizing it, and immediately hoped Dorrie didn't notice. I glanced at her; she hadn't seemed to. "Hawaii, yet," I said. "What next? It can't get much better. Oh, well, at least I might be able to visit them there, sometime." Then I added, skeptically, "Now that I'm—ah—ah— (I could hardly get myself to say the word now) free." I suddenly felt a whole lot better.

"Yeah, kiddo, that would be super. You might even get to be a perpetual tourist." She reached over and gave my shoulder a little push and grinned.

"Well, they're not moving 'till after our family reunion, after our great big get-together at Christmastime." I smiled now, thinking how hard it had been for them to convince me to join them all in California at Larry and Joyce's for Christmas. They'd said we'd never been together for the holidays, and we never had—not since we were teenagers.

Larry had gone to California right after his graduation to study marine biology. No one could ever figure out why he chose that field, but he met and married a fellow student there and stayed. They made short visits yearly and longer ones on the several sad occasions in our family. Sadly, too, they never had any children, but they'd decided not to adopt. They always thought nature might still find a way.

After Father's funeral, as emotions settled down somewhat, it was Joyce who convinced me to come, and she'd even connived with Dorrie to help me book a flight. But now, as it turned out, someone else had re-arranged my plans. Dorrie was seeing me off, though, and, Lord, how I needed her support. She mustn't know how badly I do, I thought; she must believe I *do* have the courage she'd asked about in the car in front of my house.

"That get-together thing sounds wonderful. I really envy you that part," Dorrie said. She concentrated on the traffic then, signaling and passing a rig carrying flattened, wrecked cars. After a moment she added, "Yeah, Lena sure has had her share of seeing the world."

I hadn't envied Lena so much when I still had my husband, Matt. It'd been really only since I lost him. Things would hurt so, then; there was such a void in my life. Lord, it's been eight years since he's been gone. There had been times I just wanted to die—but my son kept me going. I never told anyone how I'd envied Lena. Not even Dorrie. I couldn't tell my father, of course, he had his own problems, what with Mother gone, too. Oh, God, those were lonely times.

Father had always thought we'd worked well together— and we did. He had let me start helping him out at the clinic while I was still in high school, after Lena had taken a job at the drugstore. I'd never worked anywhere else.

We passed a tanker truck and then an older-model car "Oh, you'll have a great time in California," Dorrie said, while keeping an eye on the rear-view mirror. "Everything is so different out there. But do keep an open mind, kiddo."

She was paying close attention to the traffic and I didn't want to distract her. But I wanted to ask her what she meant by that; I wanted to know every last thing about California.

"Seacove is a wonderful town," Dorrie continued, "I remember that, even though I've only driven through it once years ago." (Larry and Joyce had a beach home near the little town of Seacove, a suburb of San Diego.) "Oh, you're going to just love it there." She reached over and gave my shoulder one sharp pat.

I laughed to myself. Dear Dorrie, she hardly remembers the place, but she's sure I'll love it. Then I felt a little perturbed. Darn, I thought, she doesn't say a word about Montana. Yes, I know, she's not crazy about my going there.

We were overtaking a train then and I watched it and it seemed to be racing with us. It excited me. That's right, I thought, I've never ridden on a train either. I should've taken a train to Montana, then a plane to California from there. But I was ordered to leave as soon as possible and the ticket was purchased and the arrangements were all made for me. There again, I didn't have much choice, really.

Soon we'd left the train behind us, and I thought once more of Lena. Being twins, Mother'd made one gorgeous, lacy wedding gown when Lena and Tom had gotten married. "It'll get double use," she'd said. And it did.

I turned to Dorrie. "Would you believe, of all things, I was just thinking about my wedding gown," I shook my head in disbelief.

"Why?" She threw me a furtive glance.

"Oh, I don't know." I shrugged. "I guess it was just another of those times I didn't get to choose for myself. Even though it was a beautiful dress, Lena had worn it first."

"But it certainly was a dreamy thing. Here I thought you were so lucky. We eloped, you know." Her mouth twisted into a wry grin.

"Oh, I hate myself when I think like that. It's so childish of me." I made two quick fists. "Well, anyway, now I'm free. I mean free to do as *I* please. Like this, you know, like now." I undid the fists and clasped my hands. "Do you understand what I'm talking about? It's so—so exciting!"

"Yes, Lottie, I do. I really do. And that's exactly why I bought you that magazine." She laughed and reached over and slapped the copy of NEW WOMAN that lay in my lap. "I can't help but worry about you though," she said, "going all the way out there—to a *ranch,* yet."

I crinkled my nose at her. "Well, I'm not going out there to round up cattle, you know—or anything like that." I was simply hired over the telephone to travel to Montana to take charge of a house and to care for a teen-age girl confined to bed with casts on both legs. Other duties were minor.

"I know," she said, "but s'pose that girl turns out to be a snip or a twit—or something worse. You'll be stuck there with her till you get to go to Larry's around Thanksgiving time."

"Yes, that's possible." I spoke slowly. "I don't know much about her, I admit that." I paused. "But I'll be busy," I said, forcing a confidence into my voice. "There'll be other people there, and I'm sure the country will be interesting. Hah, I understand her dad is a widower. Hmmm, who knows?" I crinkled my nose at her again.

"Yeah. Sure. Okay, smarty, I knew a few days ago I couldn't talk you out of it. And neither could John. So off you go to do your thing." She paused for a few moments. Then, "Seriously, kiddo, I'm going to miss you so damn much. We've gotten to be quite a habit, you know."

"Oh, come on now, Dorrie, it's not forever. I've only rented my house to those new teachers just for the school term."

"I know. But—write lots, okay?"

"Oh, yes. Yes, I will. Every detail. I promise. And you, too."

I had wanted to explain fully to her, then, how I'd felt like an emerging butterfly, wet and cramped, but wanting to stretch the wings and test them on the next willing breeze. And now this was the breeze that would take me on my first flight—all the way to a ranch near Red Hill, Montana.

But with my tears dried and my voice fully restored, I still couldn't find the words. I leaned over and patted her arm. She smiled to me then, all worry erased from her face, only a pleasant concern remaining.

[CHAPTER 2]

For a time Dorrie and I were silent and I gazed out the window, watching the Minnesota countryside pass by. The scenery was all too familiar, yet, oddly, it seemed like I was seeing it all for the first time. There were many grain fields shaved bare by their harvest, meadows browned from their last mowing and the recent hot days, but acres and acres of corn were yet to ripen. A giant patchwork quilt was forming and the quilt was dotted with faded red barns, white houses and glinting silver silos, while contented cattle grazed on the late summer's offerings. I leaned back in wonderment and sighed. Yes, I would miss Minnesota and its huge, rolling farmlands where I had lived all my life. And I especially loved it in the fall. I was bound to miss it; it was the only country I'd ever known. Yet I hungered to see new lands: ranches, mountains, beaches, ocean. Oh, yes, I was hungry.

Dorrie passed a motorhome and then a truck pulling a big boat. "Gotta get those things put away and get the kids settled in school. It started yesterday, you know. Time sure flies." She paused for a moment. "I was just thinking, what with my two back in school, I don't know what I'll do with my free time." She laughed and shot me a mischievous glance. "Oh, yeah, Lottie, I could keep an eye on John for you."

"No-o, sweetie, that won't be necessary. John has a perfect right to do as he pleases. We have an understanding, you see." I felt a smile pull my mouth upward at one corner, but a sad feeling hit me then. "Oh, he wasn't too happy about my going, at first, but it has to be this way—for awhile. We need some time apart, some time to think. He's agreed to that."

She sighed. "Oh, I know, but poor John."

John Cummings taught biology at our high school and I first met him when Kenny was a junior. We saw each other quite often; he had to walk past my house to get to his, which was only six blocks from the school. John owned a car but he preferred to walk, crediting the elements for his ruddiness.

In the beginning, when he would stop by, he always inquired something of Kenny, but finally he admitted, "It's you I want to see, Lottie, as often as I can."

A few people thought we should have married a long time ago, but he had an ailing mother to look after. Oh, Mama wasn't ill like my father had been with his minor strokes over the years. She did most of the housework yet, although she battled periods of confusion and depression. She could cry about most anything, and sometimes John didn't know which way to turn.

And, Lord, I didn't want to take on the care of his mother, not after the long bout of dealing with my father's illness. My father was never bad enough to need a nursing home, yet he was never well enough after his first stroke for me to let him out of my sight.

Oh, I wondered about marriage once in a while, but John and I just seemed to drift on and on, comfortable in our relationship. Well, I'd reasoned, affairs of the heart sometimes take a long time before they insist on an answer. And I was glad of that.

Traffic was sparse this Wednesday morning after Labor Day, making the trip to the airport a pleasant ride. We were at ease now with the situation and our conversation ebbed, but I think we both knew the lull couldn't last.

"That night of the big storm, Dorrie, remember? You had wanted to go to a movie."

"Yeah, to see Robert Redford, but you wouldn't go." She seemed irked still.

"Well—I'm sorry." A laugh escaped me. "Really, I was sorry I didn't go with you, but I'd thought John and I were going for a walk, to get a cone or something. He wouldn't have liked it if I'd gone with you."

"I figured that," she said.

"I should have gone, though. He never would actually tell me when he was coming over. He'd just drop by like I should always be expecting him. It was really starting to annoy me."

"Well, I can't say I blame you." Dorrie took the car

around a wide curve and had to adjust the sun visor. "But you were so good at being little Miss Patience."

"I know. But Mama had already called my house, as soon as she'd heard the first clap of thunder, I think, even before John had gotten there. So—you know John. He just hurried on home like a good boy. That's why I was all alone when the storm struck."

"You should have called me back right away."

"Well, I thought I'd just better get used to being alone in the house. But—I knew that night that something had to change." I laughed. "You actually did me a big favor by asking me to go. Because then when I turned you down and ended up alone, it gave me lots of time to think. I sat in the rocker on the porch, watching the storm building, and thought and thought about a lot of things." Suddenly I turned and poked her in the shoulder. "But who needs Robert Redford when you've got a mate like Jeff?" I asked, raising my voice. "Dorrie, you know you're Lady Luck, herself."

"Yeah—I know." She paused, as though thinking. "But Jeff had a meeting that night and I really thought you should've gotten out of the house more." Dorrie laughed aloud, then. Now look at you, going away all by yourself. I did it for you and you didn't even need it." She shook her head incredulously and laughed some more.

"Well, pal, it worked out just fine and I'm really grateful." I smiled to her then with a deep appreciation, just as I had, I felt, that day in first grade so long ago.

"No, I needn't have worried. You've taken things in hand quite nicely." She burst into laughter again. "You're on your way, kiddo."

Then she pulled into the left lane again and passed a huge trailer rig loaded with turkeys in their tight cages, feathers escaping into the wind. It made Thanksgiving pop into my mind, but I tried to force it out because I knew it would be really different this year. I will have had lots of new experiences by then, I thought, and—yes, maybe even a few disappointments, too. But I felt a new set to my shoulders; a new preparedness now for what the future had in store for me. Then the Minneapolis skyline came into view and a new excitement prickled my skin.

Dorrie was busy reading signs aloud, changing lanes, slowing and exiting, and soon we were in front of the airport terminal. We got out and hurriedly unloaded my bags, then she drove off to park the car. Suddenly I found myself standing alone amid my baggage. I started to perspire; I felt weak. Damn, damn, I thought, will I ever get over this fright of being on my own? Of being in unfamiliar places? Will I really be able to take care of myself after all these years so, so protected? Damn, damn, I *must*. I perspired even more.

I was relieved almost to the point of tears, when I saw Dorrie hurrying my way. And before long we were seated at the proper gate, my boarding pass clutched tightly in a sweaty hand.

Dorrie had explained everything to me, step by step, as we went along and although I felt like a real country bumpkin, I hoped desperately it didn't show on the outside. I noted my skirt and the jacket across my arm. Faded denim. Dorrie had helped me pick it out. And the shirt, a cotton print of green and gold fluttering leaves. She'd insisted it *did* something for my green eyes. I thought the gold added a new color to my mousy-brown hair. I admit I was pleased with my appearance.

I turned to Dorrie, brushing my bangs across my damp forehead. My hair was cut in a short bob, just to the top of my collar and it had enough natural wave to make it behave decently. I'd worn it that way for years. "Lord, it's warm in here," I said.

Suddenly I felt my heart beating a machine gun staccato and I began to fidget with my pass, rolling it and unrolling it. For a moment, it seemed, I was waiting for a sentencing to be handed down in a case where I'd not felt totally innocent. Maybe the flight will be cancelled. I've heard of such things. Wishful thinking, Charlotte Foster?

Dorrie folded her arms around her fake Gucci bag and leaned toward me. "So—this family—how much do you know about them?"

"Well," I admitted, "actually not much more than the woman on the phone told me." She'd said that the girl I was to care for was named Diane and was fifteen years old. Joanne, her only sister, was seventeen. No brothers. Both girls attended a parochial boarding school about fifty miles from their ranch home. But, of course, Diane was home confined to bed with her broken legs. I was also to help her with her school lessons, as well as running the house and cooking for three men. I turned to Dorrie. "Oh, God, I hope I didn't bite off too big a chunk."

"Oh, ho—you're capable all right. After taking care of your father like that for so long, I have no doubts about it at all," she said, "but there'll be others there to help you out, right?"

"Oh, yes. Yes, the woman said after she leaves another woman will come on weekends to help me catch up. You know, cleaning, laundry, stuff like that."

"Well, I sure hope you have some time for yourself. At least enough time to write me scads of letters. Oh, John, too, of course." Dorrie grinned impishly.

"Oh, yes. We went over things quite thoroughly on the phone." I gave her shoulder a nudge with mine. "Actually, I think it all sounds quite fun. Well, for sure, I won't be bored."

I glanced at my watch just as a voice blared, "Passengers on flight 601 may begin boarding for . . ." The words suddenly became indistinct to me, but I did hear the words, Jackson Buttes, Montana. Then the lump in my throat I'd thought I was rid of unceremoniously returned.

I jumped to my feet. "Oh, Lord, that's me."

Dorrie jumped up, too. "Take it easy, kiddo, you'll be fine." She grabbed me and hugged me and smacked a kiss on my cheek.

"Goodbye, Dorrie. Thanks. Goodbye. I'll write lots. Really I will." Then I was propelled by a crowd down a shaky ramp and onto the plane, almost falling into seat 9-A. I followed closely the procedure for takeoff, but still—I broke out in a cold sweat. Where's your strong chin now, Charlotte Foster?

❡[CHAPTER 3]❡

I laid my head on the back of the cushioned seat and tried to relax, but I stiffened when the engine noises rumbled throughout the plane. They reminded me of the thunder that deafened our neighborhood the night of that awful storm; the night Dorrie had wanted me to go to the Redford movie. I wanted to put my hands over my ears, but instead I rummaged in my bag for the gum Dorrie had given me, along with the magazine. I found it. "Chew it," she'd said, "It's good for the ears." And once more she'd added, "Don't forget, it was all your idea." Again her words rung in my ears.

I popped the gum into my mouth and shoved my bag, along with the magazine, under the seat in front of me. Then I held my breath for what seemed an eternity as the plane roared down the runway. Finally I sensed we were airborne. A strange feeling gripped me. Then I knew it—nausea. I swallowed hard against it and slowly chewed the gum.

My body became pressed into the give of the seat while the plane climbed into the sky. I dared pull forward to look out the window. I stared, unbelieving, watching Minnesota fade away into whiffs of clouds until it was out of sight. So, outwardly calm but with my insides churning, I leaned back against the seat once more and closed my eyes.

My thoughts took me back to the night of the storm. I'd been sitting in the rocker on the porch, barely moving, while the tips of my fingers traced over the deep cracks in its many coats of paint, always white. I had a wonderful view of the park across the street from my house, and the park bordered the river. But that afternoon the clouds above the river were bulging higher and higher in the western sky, and darkening. I'd brushed strands of damp hair off my forehead and wished for a breeze. My dinner was baking in the oven, heating the kitchen to an unbearable degree, and the porch offered the coolest spot to be found.

John had come rushing up the walk on his way home from school where he'd been readying his classroom for the beginning of the new term. No sooner had he settled himself on the top step in front of me than a splash of heat lightning colored the sky a striking pink. I let out a short squeal; John winced. Then the sky sounded a menacing rumble.

"Ah, yes, Mama will be calling any minute."

"She already has." I knew I sounded sour. "She said the sky looked scary."

"Then I'd best be getting on." He pushed himself to his feet and reached for my hand. Taking it gently, he squeezed it and I looked up to him. Weariness showed in his soft brown eyes and his smile drooped at one corner. I wanted to jump up and hug him, but something held me back. Something. I didn't know what.

"Goodbye, hon," he said, giving my hand a little pat.

No kiss, I thought? But then I was glad he didn't.

"Get the windows shut now," he added, dropping my hand, "and if it looks bad you'd better go in the basement."

"Yes, John—I'll be okay," I assured him, but there was a snippiness in my voice. For several moments we watched the skies darkening and the clouds tumbling against themselves. And not a breath of air stirred around us on my big, open front porch.

He turned and started down the steps. "Bye," I said. I watched him hurry down the sidewalk, and when he got to Mrs. Nelson's evergreens next door, he turned and waved. I saw him remove his brown tweed jacket with the leather-patched elbows, then he was out of sight.

Yes, you must be sweltering, John, I thought. So proper John.

All the while, I sat in the rocker letting the premature dusk close in around me. Something was making me feel uneasy. Then I realized I was peevishly muttering, "Yes, sir. Of course, sir. Damnit, John, I'm not your helpless mother." Then, with one foot, I furiously pushed the rocker to rock me back and forth. Push. Back and forth. Push. Back and forth. Push. . . .

But now in the plane, with my back still pressed to the cushion, I sensed again the back and forth motion, and the word *helpless* returned and seemed to dry in my throat. It was choking me. Now I will be forced to prove I'm *not* helpless—to myself—as well as the new family I'm on my way to meet. God help me, I never have to *eat* that horrible word.

Some time later a tasty lunch was served, and I was relieved all traces of nausea had disappeared. I lingered over warm sweet coffee. Ah-h-h. I felt pleased. Selfishly satisfied. I leaned my head back and my eyes grew heavy and I let them fall shut.

Well, the butterfly is actually flying, I thought, and the wings are strong. And on a full stomach, too.

Occasionally I would open an eye and I could see that we were going in and out of huge puffy pure-white clouds. I closed my eyes again and I could envision Kenny's face as a little five-year-old. We'd taken a long drive on a Sunday and we were returning home and he was tired. He looked up in the sky and exclaimed how the clouds looked like piles of mashed potatoes and he was hungry. Little stories like that are mine to keep, and I shall always treasure them, even though Kenny is twenty now, away at college, and already in love.

I was astonished then to hear the captain announce we would be landing in another eighteen minutes. We were about to start our descent to Jackson Buttes, Montana. Wow! Two states away and in such a short time. I felt my mouth fall open. See, Charlotte, you're not really as far away from home as you thought. No wonder Lena takes it all so in stride. Of course, *she's* the one that's been living in the jet age—not *you.*

As the plane descended I became a little light-headed, but once it touched the runway, the process of the speed and braking sent a new exhilaration through me. It taxied up to a building. I felt as if I'd just ended a giant carnival ride, but was ready and willing for another.

The departing began. I gathered up all my things, and, with my free hand I steadied myself and walked off the plane as if it were a daily occurrence. Then my heart began to pound as I thought of my next challenge. Would I be able to recognize the voice of Mary Kane, the woman I'd spoken with over the telephone? She'd merely said, "Oh, Charlotte, I'll know you."

Once inside the building, I searched the faces around me, attempting to match the one with the too few clues she'd given me. Some of the people greeted others, hugging and laughing, but most just hurried away. Soon a tall, slender, sun-tanned woman walked toward me. She was wearing a navy pantsuit with a white blouse, and her silvery hair was pulled back in a tight twist. She had a fine-boned face, accentuated by a heavy jaw, but when she smiled at me it became much less noticeable. Actually, I found her stunning.

She touched my arm. "Charlotte Foster, I believe. I'm Mary Kane." Yes, it was the same deep, mellow voice I'd heard on the phone.

"Yes. Hello," I said, attempting to conceal my excitement. "I'm so glad to meet you." What I really wanted to say was, "Thank God, I'm in safe hands in this new land." The firm handshake was gratifying.

A short, wiry man appeared from behind her, adding some to his height with the heels of dusty cowboy boots. He was wearing a wide-brimmed hat, jeans patched at the knee, and a bright red plaid shirt. Wow, I thought, a real cowboy. But of course, silly, you're going to a real ranch.

"Charlotte, this is Andy Wallace, our indispensable hand," Mary said, stepping aside. The man doffed his hat to me then, revealing a bushy head of salt-and-pepper gray hair.

I extended my hand. "Hello, Andy."

"Howja do, ma'm," he said, settling his hat down firmly on his head again. He gripped my hand and shook it hard. His grin was infectious and it set a sparkling in his pale gray eyes.

Then, gathering my luggage along the way, and making only small comments, we walked out of the building and into the brilliant sunshine of the late afternoon. I breathed deeply the Montana air and, for a moment, felt almost giddy. Well, I thought, the butterfly has landed intact, albeit somewhat wobbly.

Andy Wallace led us to a late model stationwagon, and, under the layers of dust, it appeared to be maroon in color. "Your next car, Charlotte. This is the one you'll be driving," Mary said, and she open-handedly presented the vehicle to me as if a gift.

"Oh, I thought she was s'posed to drive the old Jeep," Andy said, pulling his brows together. He glanced quickly from Mary to me and back to Mary. But I detected mischief in his eyes before he began to load my luggage into the rear of the wagon.

"Now, Andy, stop that teasing. Charlotte's too new here yet to put up with your sense of humor," Mary said, in a firm voice. She turned to me then. "Don't take him too seriously, it could ruin your day." The three of us broke out in laughter as we fastened our safety belts.

I liked Mary Kane. I liked Andy Wallace. Two out of two. Not bad, Dorrie would say.

{[CHAPTER 4]}

With Andy Wallace at the wheel, the highway soon drew us out of the city. Mary Kane and I occupied the vehicle's rear seat, so as not to disturb the driver, she'd said. Asking about my flight, she made only small-talk for a time.

Before long we were on open road. The land became stark, dry-looking, and visibly breezy. I viewed the terrain that was not a field, nor a lush meadow, nor a wood, but a harsh, brown, hilly country dotted with bushes and scrubby trees. I looked at it long and hard, little spears of apprehension jabbing at me. Mary spoke then and I felt instantly better.

She began a flutter of conversation. "We're, I mean, the Garner ranch, that is—it's forty-two miles from Jackson Buttes. Everyone here just says the Buttes. Oh, yes, we'll pass through Red Hill on our way to the ranch, that's the closest town. It's really OUR Ranch. I'd better explain. OUR is the Garner family's brand, but the letters are squeezed close together, touching each other. It's a nice looking brand."

"I'm sure it is," I said. "How clever."

"Yes, isn't it? Dan and his wife chose that brand when they first settled on the ranch." Then her voice faltered.

"I did tell you that Dan Garner is my brother, didn't I? I'm sure I did, but I know I didn't explain too fully on the phone. You see, ah—ah . . ." She turned away from me and I couldn't discern her words.

I felt I must say something. "You—you did mention that Mr. Garner is a—a widower—with two daughters." She seemed to be groping for words worse than I.

"Ah—yes. His wife died of leukemia over three years ago. Oh, she'd been very ill." Mary hesitated again, but then she seemed to find her voice and spoke quickly. "Of course, they were so proud of their spread out here in Peace County. He and the girls did have a rough time of it for a while, though. But they all seem quite well adjusted now."

"I'm glad," I said, softly.

She brushed the corner of her eye with a fingertip, then went on. "The girls really like their school over in Meadow Grand. It's just for girls. Oh, yes, I must tell you, it's over sixty miles from Red Hill."

"O-o-oh," I said, "things certainly are *spread* out." I giggled, adding quickly, "No pun intended." But my weak attempt at humor did seem to relieve the strain, and, in the mirror, I saw Andy grinning. "I've heard a lot about these wide open spaces—can't believe I'm actually seeing them." I looked out the window at the curious land. "I'm too used to plowed fields and hedgerows and woods, I guess."

"Oh, I know," Mary said. "I'm used to white sand and palm trees. Did I tell you that I'm from Florida?"

"Oh, really? And you came all this way to help?"

"Yes, I came as soon as I heard that Diane was coming home from the hospital. Dan needed me here fast. You see, he had to go up to our brother's place up in Idaho, on family matters, that is. I would have had to come later, anyway, to sign some papers about the old homestead up there. That's where we were all born. So I arranged to be able to stay a while. Thankfully, Phil is being wonderful about it. Phil's my husband."

"Oh, I see." I didn't know what more to say.

"Well now, I'll be leaving in about two weeks now that you have come. You know, I did a lot of searching for just the *right* person, Charlotte. We feel so lucky to have you here. Not too many people want to take on a job such as this."

"Oh," I said, then I realized I'd said it more like a question. I bit my lip, wishing I hadn't said it. But why don't they? I wondered.

"Of course," Mary said, I'm staying on to get you fully acquainted."

I smiled to her. "I appreciate that."

I'd no sooner said that when the wagon swerved and we were forced to lean with it. "Damned grouse," Andy muttered. "They're always jumpin' out at ya. They git their tail feathers scared off 'em sometimes." The bird flew ahead of us for a time before disappearing into the grass at the roadside. "Not too unlike home," I said, nodding agreement.

Mary seemed to ignore it all. "Dan should be home in about a week. He's spending a little extra time with his brother, a little hunting or fishing, I guess. I wished I could be there with them, but I'm enjoying the girls—and the ranch. Although now I'm getting lonesome for Phil; getting anxious to go home. I like living in Florida—no snow." She laughed.

I smiled; I knew snow. Now I was looking forward to discovering the climes of southern California I'd heard so much about, where people didn't have to dread being trapped by hard drifts filling the roads. Seems like only yesterday, I thought quickly, how Matt and I'd bought our little house out in the country north of Spencer soon after we'd married.

We'd spent almost twelve years there, twelve wonderful years watching our baby boy growing up. Many times we would follow the school bus into Spencer in our old Buick, letting the big bus tires break the crusts of packed snow on our way to our jobs, Matt to his insurance agency, and me, of course, to my father's clinic.

I was abruptly jolted back to the present when Mary said, "We never had any children, Phil and I, so you see, we're especially fond of my brothers' families." It was easy to detect pain in her words.

"Yes. Oh, yes, I'm sure." A tense moment passed, then I asked, "How did Diane get hurt so badly?"

"Well," Mary began, "Dan had taken both girls, along with two of their friends, on a short vacation just before school was to start." She took a sudden deep breath. "The girls were just climbing on some rocks in a ravine, but the rocks gave way. Oh, it was such a freak accident. Diane fell first, not far, but the other girls fell on top of her. She has nasty multiple breaks—both legs." I could sense Mary was near tears.

"Oh, that's terrible," I said, and shuddered, a sympathy pain clutching at my own legs.

"Yes, and Dan felt horrible about it because the trip was all his idea. He's worried, too, that she's missing so much school. But the teachers have put together lesson packets, and I'm sure she'll do just fine. Of course, you'll have to see that her work is done on schedule."

"Oh, I will. I'll . . ."

With that, Andy suddenly braked the wagon and we were thrown forward against our belts. "Sorry." He grumbled and shook his fist. "Stupid rabbit." I saw a white flash of tail streak into the bushes at the roadside. "You might not be so lucky next time. I'll git ya and the new cook can make stew outa ya." Then he guffawed and picked up speed again.

I felt my eyes roll upward, but I grinned.

"Oh, Andy, stop it. What will Charlotte think of us?"

Blood rushed to my face, leaving it hot, but I managed to say, "Oh, I'll get used to him." I grinned openly and looked to Mary. "You were telling me about Diane's lessons."

"Yes. Well, she's a pretty intelligent girl." Mary hesitated for a moment. "I guess that's where the problem lies."

"Problem?" I felt surprised—and a little irked. I did remember Mary hinting at something over the phone, but I had dismissed it as a mere misunderstanding.

"Well—it's—ah—possible," she said, clasping her hands and slowly wringing them. "The way I see it, Diane likes to blame her father for her predicament. Not openly, though. No, she's quite subtle about it. It seems she uses her situation to keep his attention all the time, keeping it away from her sister—and Helen, too."

"Helen? Is she . . . ?"

"Oh, yes—Helen, the woman who comes on weekends. She's been helping out for almost three years now. She's Andy's brother's wife's sister. Did I get that right, Andy?"

"Yep. She's kinda like a shirt-tail relative, if the shirt's tail is long enough."

I laughed.

"Clever, Andy, very clever." Mary suppressed a grin, but her clear blue eyes were twinkling. "Helen has a steady job now that she's divorced. She works in the mail order store in Red Hill. But she was able to come today, so you'll get to meet her, too."

"Oh, that'll be nice," I said, my pulse quickening as I mentally counted all the people I was yet to meet this day: Diane, the other ranch hand, and now—Helen, too. It would be impossible though, I thought quickly, for anyone else to take Dorrie's place, but it would be nice to have another woman to talk with now and then.

We'd been traveling for quite some time now and the stark hills had become higher and higher. But then we dipped down into a valley and the scene became refreshingly beautiful. Fascinated, I stared at the sudden greenery. I recognized some of the trees: cottonwoods and willows. Then I glimpsed a rippling stream, silver flashes playing on its surface. I wondered how this pleasant respite appeared in such contrast to the recent dry countryside. Then I knew. Water. The presence of water was like a miracle in the contrast it could produce. Birds flitted about on low branches, and I even caught sight of a rabbit dashing for cover.

Mary's deep, mellow voice invaded my silent appreciation of the beauty of the valley. "Diane's having one of her *off* days today," Mary continued, taking the scenery in stride. "She was moody this morning, I suppose because you were coming."

"Oh, really?" I cried, "I'm sorry. I thought she . . ." I thought she'd approved of me. I didn't say any more. Damn, Dorrie had warned me about a snip. Mary sucked in her breath and was silent and it caused me to stiffen.

Then Mary said, quickly, "Now, now, Charlotte, it'll be alright. Everything will be just fine. You'll just have to use your own common sense to decide when she's not using hers." Mary leaned back, almost collapsing, then took a deep breath and expelled it with a sigh. She reached over and gently patted my hand, and we offered each other weak smiles.

I remained silent for the time, although my mind began to whir. What did I get myself into? Will I be able to cope with a temperamental teenage girl? I've never had to in my life. Will I fail this nice woman who hired me and brought me all this way? Will I even like this strange land with its different lifestyle?

Lord, Charlotte Foster, maybe you should have listened to Dorrie. Maybe you should have thought things through a little longer and not have jumped at the chance to bring a little excitement into your life. There could have been other ways.

Whose advice did you seek? No one's. Well, damn, damn, it's too late now.

CHAPTER 5

We rode in silence for a few moments, then Mary sat upright, asking, "Didn't you say you cared for a bed-ridden father for a long time? You must have some idea what it's like for the patient."

"Yes, I did. I mean—I do," I said, my confidence returning. "It must be especially hard for a young person to be confined to bed when they're not actually ill. Yes, it has to be terribly difficult."

Mary sighed again, only deeper, a faint sign of tiredness escaping her. Then she slowly reached over and patted my hand again. "I'm sure things will work out just fine with you in charge, Charlotte."

We were out of the valley now and I heard Andy down-shift the gears and felt the pull of the wheels as we ground up a steep hill. And, as we came over the top of it, I could see the outline of a town in the distance. When we drew nearer. Mary smiled broadly and said, "Well, dear, take a look at Red Hill."

Andy chuckled and pressed harder on the accelerator. "Come on, hawse, step it up. We've got a visitor."

I laughed. I liked his comical ways.

And, as we neared the town, I grew anxious to view all the new sights. I could see short, squat buildings crowding next to tall, narrow ones, all in various stages of maintenance. Soon we were driving between them on, what I assumed, was the main street. It was bordered by walks of plank, with benches, also of plank, placed randomly alongside doorways. One bench that we passed was dark brown and shiny, a sign propped against it warning, "WET PAINT." And the vehicles parked about were mainly trucks of every sort. But it was the store fronts that I noticed most for they were wearing a wide assortment of colorful signs.

And the wind blew. A dust devil moved down the street in front of us, dancing with abandon. People seemed to ignore it and walked with heads down. They leaned into the wind, seemingly intent on their business only, while chain-held signs above them jangled in the gusty wind.

Tall trees swayed in tune with the wind; shorter ones resisted it. There were a few, however, that had given up the battle and stood, bent and rigid, most branches long since torn away. I hoped I wasn't gawking.

"You'll like Red Hill, Charlotte," Mary said, laughing, "that is if you don't mind the breezes." Then a serious note came into her voice. "It's a friendly town, really. Everyone knows everyone."

I smiled. "A lot like Spencer," I said.

"Now here's where we have to pick up our mail. We did that on our way in." Mary pointed to a small, gray building as we passed it. A flag jutted out over the plank walk, it's frayed edges flapping in the wind. "And there's Mitchell's General Store," she continued, "that's where you can pick up some things, but for serious shopping it's best to drive to Meadow Grand, where the girls' school is. Convenient that way." As Mary talked I observed the store building, big and square, it's white paint having been sandpapered away by the ever-present wind.

"And that's George's place over there," Andy said. "He's my brother." Andy pointed to a big building covered with glistening red paint, its sign above the door swinging mightily in the wind. But, as we passed, I did manage to read WALLACE and catch sight of a fancy saddle on it, painted in black and gold. "He sells saddles and stuff— makes 'em and repairs 'em, too. Best shop this side of the Rockies. People come from miles around." He turned, caught my eye and grinned.

"How interesting. Your whole town is, in fact. I like it very much." And I really did, but suddenly I felt a melancholy ache thinking about how it compared to Spencer. This town was on a hill, bare and bleak, exposed to the wind, all serious business. Spencer was neat, quiet, homey, sheltered by huge, old oaks and maples that stood guard the year around. Yes, I thought, a lump forming in my throat, Spencer was a nice town to call your own. But then, I had to be honest with myself. It had been closing in on me like the final curtain of a theatre production ever since my father's death. I *had* to leave.

We didn't stop anywhere, so before long the town was behind us and Andy eased the stationwagon down a long hill. In a huge, open area I saw a maze of fences, chutes and ramps. Men were working about, carrying lumber and hammers. I leaned to the window, straining for a closer look.

"Cattle-loading ramps," Mary said, in a casual manner, "round-ups are about to start. It'll be a mighty busy place for a while."

Well, I suppose she thought that I should've known what they were for, but given a little time, I think I would have figured it out. I found it fascinating and thought about it for quite some time.

We rode several more miles until we came to a crossroad. A big sign pointing to the east read "MEADOW GRAND," but we turned to the west. "Thank goodness, not much farther," Mary said. She sounded tired.

Soon we were driving in another valley, somewhat like the last one, crowded with aspen, willows and tall grasses. The road skirted a bubbling creek with little foamy mounds being buffeted along in its rapids. Here and there the sun's rays shot through the foliage and set the stream's swirls and ripples to glittering. It was lovely—fresh and green—again a pleasant contrast to the browning hills we'd just left. This was the kind of place I wanted to visit often, and hoped it would be walking distance from the ranch.

The road suddenly forked and we turned right again. "This is it," Mary said, somewhat excitedly, and pointed upward.

I caught a glimpse of a huge log chained above a narrow driveway, and on the log was chiseled the letters O-U-R, crowded together and painted a stark white. My pulse quickened as I felt the wagon's gears shift downward and pull us up the steepest hill yet.

Ranch buildings loomed in front of us as we neared the top. I saw the house, then, and blinked my eyes and gasped. It was built of rough woods, boxy, and with an abundance of windows. But it seemed to be built precariously over the side of the hill, clinging there by magical powers, I was certain. When I found my voice, "Oh, my," was all I could say. Then, as Andy circled the driveway within the cluster of buildings, I added, weakly, "It must have a fantastic view."

"Indeed it does, at all times of the day—and night," Mary assured me.

Andy stopped the wagon near a path leading to a porch, which ran the entire length of the back of the house. The porch, I thought, a wonderful similarity to the farmhouses of Minnesota. And my breathing eased. Relax now, Charlotte, you're in friendly territory.

As I climbed out of the wagon and stood upright, I became almost dazed with the sudden view of the mountains to the west. They unfolded in a glorious panorama before my tourist eyes.

"They are magnificent, aren't they?" Mary said, almost reverently.

The sun was beginning to sink behind the range and it threw masses of vibrant orange and red-gold colors across the sky, profusely staining the clouds. I took several gulping breaths before I could move. Maybe it's the air—too thin— way up here, I thought. I gathered my wits about me and took some of my things from the wagon. Well, Charlotte, look around, this *is* your new home for a time.

A black dog, not overly big, but with a wide muzzle and soft brown eyes, appeared from nowhere, demanding an introduction. Mary responded quickly, "Oh, Charlotte, I'd like you to meet Chase."

I offered him my hand to sniff. "Hi, Chase," I said, "Yes, I'm a foreigner—here for a visit. I'm from Minnesota."

"And that's *really* foreign, Chase," Andy said, as he hoisted my bags from the rear of the wagon. "It's not even on the map." He chuckled heartily.

"Yes, it is, Chase, and I can prove it. I have a valid driver's license." I laughed, too, and bent and roughed the long, silky hair on the dog's shoulders. He raised up on his hind feet as if wanting to play, and as he did, I saw a white patch, almost like a star, on a broad chest.

"He's our watchdog. He's always watching his food pan," Andy said, this time laughing at his own joke. "Really, Jed named him that. Jed's our other hand here. He says Chase was always chasn' somethin'—rabbits, gophers, birds, even snowflakes, sometimes. Aren't ya, boy?" He cupped the dog's head in his hands and rubbed his ears. The dog wheeled and jumped playfully into the air.

"Well, we're going to get along just fine," I said, giving the animal several pats on his well-padded rump. He licked my hand and I knew we were friends.

Then my eyes began to sweep the immediate dooryard and the driveway. It was a big loop, contoured by years of driving the same pattern. I see—easy access to the barns, the bunkhouse, the garage, and the house, in that order. A stand of pine sheltered the bunkhouse, while lofty fir trees towered over the house. Smaller trees and scrubby junipers popped out here and there in little, odd, protected places amongst the buildings and along the corral fences.

I turned to the east then, and saw the driveway disappear into the valley below. The last of the sun's rays were running over the treetops, transforming them into a variegated green blanket for as far as the eye could see into the dusk now enveloping the horizon.

"It's just grand—just grand," I whispered to my new friends. Then Mary and I walked to the porch. Andy followed, lugging my bulging, new bag, which contained almost all the clothes I owned.

⟨CHAPTER 6⟩

Once inside the porch, Mary opened the next door and held it wide, exposing a well-lit kitchen. Delicious, warm odors beckoned us in, and as we did, my baggage was placed in the middle of the floor. A woman stood facing the sink, and upon hearing us, whirled around. Instantly our eyes met and she fixed a steady gaze on me. She had large, dark eyes and I felt they pierced me through. My skin prickled. Quickly she dropped her eyes, shuffled her feet, and turned halfway about.

She was a small, amply-rounded woman, with black hair that hung to her shoulders in neat sausage-curls. She wore red pants and a black and white blouse of a bold flower print, and the fabric stretched snugly across her unnaturally-uplifted breasts. I felt I stared.

Mary took my arm and led me to her. "Charlotte, this is Helen Lucas. Helen, Charlotte Foster."

"Hello, Helen," I said, extending my hand, "I'm pleased to meet you."

"Lo," she said. Her dark eyes had narrowed somewhat.

We shook hands, but she quickly drew hers away. Her touch had been warm but limp. Is she that shy? I wondered. We can change that. Or is it something else? Maybe she doesn't like my coming here. Then, again, what if she doesn't like me?

Becoming uncomfortable, I glanced away, spotting my new luggage then, sitting isolated in the middle of the floor. They were the only familiar objects in the room and I wished desperately that they could share my anxiety. I felt so alone; as isolated as my luggage. Then, I heard again the clacking of the lock on the door behind me as I'd stepped out onto my porch to follow Dorrie to her car. It came as a loud, menacing echo in my ears. Only this morning, I thought. Damn, but why does it seem so long ago?

"I'll be taking Helen back to town in the jeep, Mary." Andy Wallace broke the awkward silence. "Now if you need me, just call me at George's place. I'll be back flat-out."

"Oh, thank you, Andy," Mary said. Then she turned to Helen. "We'll call you when we need you, Helen, but it won't be for a while. It'll really be up to you, Charlotte." She quickly looked to me, then back to Helen. "Sorry you have to rush. We could've had a nice supper together. Everything smells so good." She smiled to Helen, putting a hand on her arm.

"Thanks. Yeah, I'll come whenever she says." She wiped her hands on a small towel and carefully hung it on a bar. "Oh—Jed's been in to eat already. Gosh, he looks tired."

"Yes, I know," Mary said, nodding, "I've noticed."

"And Diane's had her supper, too. She's busy reading that big book a' hers."

"Yes, her English book. She calls it *Communications*," Mary said, nodding again. "We'll not disturb her for a while then."

Slipping on a dark jacket she'd taken from a pegged rack just inside the kitchen door, Helen picked up a small grip and turned to Andy. "I'm ready." She looked back to Mary. "Your supper should still be nice and hot. Goodbye." Andy opened the door and she passed through. "Goodbye, Charlte, was glad ta meetcha." As her clipped tone followed her out the door, she swung her head around, shaking her fat, sausage curls until they bounced on her shoulders.

A little wave of relief swept through me as she left, yet a mean feeling stayed behind nagging at me. That's not a good hair-do for a woman her age. Why, she must be at least forty-five. And she uses way too much make-up; those heavily rouged cheeks and those lips glossed in scarlet. Really! And the way she said my name—Charlte—as if all one syllable. That bothered me the most. Maybe I'll just ask her to call me Lottie. What sort is she anyway? Well, think kindly, Charlotte, you'll have to live and work with her for some time.

Long moments after the door closed behind them, a heavy, sweet smell of gardenia still waft in the air, mingling offensively with the aroma of recently cooked food. Wasn't the woman aware of that, either?

Mary took a slow, deep breath, like someone just waking up. "Well," she said, "let me take your coat. Oh, no, on second thought, let's go right to your room."

We picked up my things and I followed her through a doorway that led into a long hall. An archway to the left exposed a dining room, and we also passed two more doors on the right. She opened the next door and flipped on a light. "Ah, here we are. You'll have Joanne's room—close to Diane." I followed her into the room. "They share the bath," she continued, as she opened a door to a large room tiled in white, with a rainbow of colored towels hung about. Then she pointed to another door across the bath and whispered, "That's Diane's room in there,"her finger pecking toward it. Then she quietly pulled the door of the bath shut again behind her.

"Oh, that should work out nicely." I whispered, too. But why not meet Diane now? I thought. Why wait? I almost asked.

"Well, dear, you must be starved. In the time it takes you to freshen up, I'll have our supper on the table." Mary looked at me, studying me, it seemed, for a long moment. I felt a little uncomfortable, but then she smiled warmly and left the room. After a moment a calmness fell upon me.

I glanced around. It was a teenager's room, all right, quite bare, but a teenager's room, none-the-less. A small student's desk stood just inside the door, and above it, covering a large expanse of wall, were many high-school and college pennants. Then I spied the painting nestled among them. It was a vivid painting of a black and white horse in a rearing position. I studied it; it was really good. Then my gaze quickly moved about the rest of the room. Drapes of a gold and brown geometric print—earth tones, I thought—matching the spread on a fullsize bed. A mottled carpet of darker hues. Yes, comfortable. But my eyes drifted back to the painting. I shook my head to get my own attention.

Quickly, I hung my denim jacket in the closet, retucked my shirt, and smoothed my skirt. I caught my reflection in a full-length mirror. I liked what I saw. Lena's husband, Tom, always kidded me about looking like Doris Day. Hmmm? Well, nah. As quietly as possible, I re-entered the bathroom. I washed my hands and face and ran a comb through my hair. It perked me up. But the painting remained fixed in my mind and it excited me.

Thoughts of my own horse of years ago raced into the moment. He was a small, black and white quarter horse, a paint, he was called. I grinned to myself at the coincidence of the word. I'd called him Patches, for he was an all white horse, except for the few big, black, irregular spots on shoulder and rump. Matt had not cared to ride, but Kenny and I spent many happy hours traveling our roads and fields, he on his fat, speckled Welsh pony.

Now I found it tremendously exciting to be on a gen-uine ranch with many horses. I was even anxious to see wild cattle. Well, they must be wild, I thought, having never been confined in a barn. I felt a sudden renewal of the bond I had with all animals, a carry-over from my veterinary clinic years.

I quietly slipped out of my bedroom door and made my way down the hall to the kitchen. I found it to be a much larger room than I first noted, what with the focus of Helen taking my interest when I'd arrived. The room had a spacious bay window area bulging out toward the circular drive. A big table and six chairs filled the space. The table was nicely set with heavy stoneware of a blue-gray pattern. It looked enticing. And, best of all, the perfumy scent of before had given way to the bold aroma of paprika-roasted chicken, sharpening my appetite.

Mary placed a steaming, laden platter on the table and motioned me to sit. "I peeked in on Diane," she said, "she's fine, she's still reading."

I smiled, but couldn't think of anything appropriate to say just then. I did think, though, the situation was getting a little mysterious. I shrugged inwardly and called on patience.

"Help yourself now, Charlotte, please." Mary said, pulling up her chair. "You must be starved."

I began to eat, and as I did, I remembered with a jolt my recent taste of paprika-roasted chicken. It was late in the afternoon, just before the big storm, only about ten days ago, actually. I was in my kitchen, standing at the sink, rinsing and wringing a sponge, and wiping the counter over and over again. Forcing myself to begin my dinner, I placed the sponge at the back of the sink. Methodically, I took a piece of chicken and placed it in a baking dish and put it in the oven. No salt. Then I scrubbed a potato, pushed a baking pin through it and put it in the oven by the chicken. I started to snip some fresh green beans I'd picked from my garden earlier, but stopped, picked up the sponge and began again to wipe the counter. You did that already, silly, I scolded, Wake up! I was angry with myself.

I threw the sponge into the sink and stalked out the back door, slamming it behind me. "Intelligent people do not slam doors." Mother's words rang in my ears from some distant room in my past. Although she'd been gone eight years now, her lessons would stick for life. Sure, but she hadn't taught me how to cope with this. With being alone. *All* alone in this house. I'd lost most of those I'd loved, in one way or another. Lena and Larry moved away. Matt and Mother, both taken in a single accident. Kenny away at college. And now—Father. I put my hands to my head and began to pull at my hair. Damn this feeling; I've got to talk to someone. Tears stung my eyes.

I stood on my back sidewalk and looked to the sky. Thin, gray clouds were obscuring the late afternoon sun. Mrs. Nelson. Yes, I'll go talk to Mrs. Nelson. I walked across the lawn, ducking through her evergreens. I searched her yard and garden. She wasn't there. Of course, I thought, she naps about this time.

I went back home and climbed the steps to my front porch, plopping myself into the rocking chair. It groaned under me as I began to rock, and then I realized I was rocking with a great urgency. I wondered why the familiar creaking didn't comfort me for I'd spent many an hour rocking away the rough edges as I'd cared for my ailing father. Most of the time it'd been wonderful to sit there when I wanted to relax, or even daydream. It also helped when I wanted to scold myself or just plain think out a problem. But that day I'd felt a festering, a feeling denying a name.

I jumped up then, and almost ran to the kitchen. The baking chicken smelled good, but something was missing. What? That's it—it's too bland. The meals I'd had to prepare for my father in his last years were simple, almost tasteless meals, and I'd eaten them for convenience's sake. I was letting myself be influenced yet by his imagined presence. No more!

I opened the cupboard and searched for something—anything. I spied a box of cream-of-wheat. I shoved it out of sight. No! I found it again and threw it in the wastebasket. Then I saw the paprika. I doused the chicken with the spicy, red powder. Then I quickly snipped the beans and started them cooking, while I fried a bit of bacon to add to them, along with a dash of sugar and a splash of vinegar, to complete a dish my mother often made. I even went to the garden in search of some chives for my baked potato. I began to get quite excited about preparing a meal for myself—wholly for myself. It was an alien feeling, but I liked it. I even found a jar of pear chutney that Mrs. Nelson had given us, and actually decided to open it. Next, I concocted a wildly-original salad on my last scrap of lettuce. I was doing all this for myself, and only myself, I thought, and the alien feeling intensified. It felt wonderful. Then I accidentally spotted a bottle of white zinfandel. Why not?

When I finally sat down to my meal, I was at the height of a new exuberance. I thought of John. Poor John, you're really missing something. I *can* cook.

Now, sitting next to a nice stranger two states away, I couldn't help but thank that old, wicker rocking chair for helping me out of the rut I'd been in for so long. And I'd always thought Father had had some mysterious reason for calling it his *thinking chair.* Looking across the table to Mary Kane, then, I was compelled to smile.

We were nearing the end of our meal. "M-m-m," I said, "Helen certainly is a good cook."

"Yes, she is, and she's taught Joanne well," Mary said, "but Diane doesn't seem to like the kitchen, or any kind of housework, for that matter. But maybe she will—one day."

Then I told her how I'd always slipped out of the house every chance I got to follow my father around his clinic, until one day he finally put me to work in it. All the while, my sister would hang around the kitchen, pestering Mother, I'd thought. We reasoned together, laughing, how young people always seem to follow their own whims.

At least Diane and I had that much in common, I mused,

trying to find a degree of mutual ground. Although I'd learned the kitchen arts fast after marriage, I knew Diane still had a lot of time to grow. Well, maybe I can help.

We had a pleasant conversation and I relaxed in Mary's presence. She was a sensitive and perceptive person and I admired her gentility. But my mind was filled with questions about Diane. What's she like? Will she like me? Will we be able to get along with each other—in the same house for almost three months?

I began to worry. After all, she was the reason for the frenzy in my household for the past week or so, the reason for my long, gallant (my word only) journey here. But I still didn't probe. Patience, I decided, just better be a virtue.

Mary had removed our plates and returned with dessert. "Yum," I said, "blueberry pie, my favorite."

"Sorry. It's huckleberry."

My eyes widened.

"Notice the color? This pie is redder than your blueberries, but they are quite alike." Mary seemed delighted to be introducing me to new things, and I was amused by my mistake, which added to the enjoyment of the tart treat.

After we'd finished our coffee, Mary sighed, raised an eyebrow to me, and calmly asked, "Are you ready to meet your charge? I believe she's read long enough."

"Yes, let's," I said, jumping to my feet.

⟨[CHAPTER 7]⟩

"Oh, wait a minute, please," I said, as we moved down the hall, "I have something for her." In my room. I retrieved a small, gift-wrapped package from my tote, then we continued to Diane's hallway door. Mary tapped on it.

"Come in," beckoned a little-girl voice.

We entered the room, and the girl in the bed, propped high on pillows, laid a book across her thighs, then looked up to us. Long hair the color of golden wheat fanned out across the plump white cloud of pillows. I don't believe there is such a color, I thought. Even Dorrie's hair can't compare to that. I stared for a second, then discovered blue eyes riveting mine, eyes blue as the summer sky on its clearest day in Minnesota.

"Charlotte, I'd like you to meet Diane. She's our patient patient," Mary said, with a rippling laugh. She went to her side and patted her arm, but the love in Mary's eyes was the more significant sign of affection.

"Hello, Diane." I stepped close and held out my hand. She shook it—gingerly.

"Hi," she said, but I barely heard it.

"I'm glad to be here." I handed her the gift. "I brought you something from my home."

I observed her as she picked at the wrap. I perceived, then, a small, rather pointed nose, and a soft, full mouth with perfectly defined lips, much like a cupid's bow. She looked more like a princess out of a fairy tale, I thought, Cinderella—or a really blond Snow White. How could this lovely child ever be construed as temperamental?

"Oh, it's pretty," she said, the wrappings falling away, "I like it." She peered into a small, glass ball filled with a bouquet of brightly-colored straw flowers.

"I'm glad. My neighbor, Mrs. Nelson, grew them and I dried them and put them in there."

"Thank you very much, Mrs. Foster."

How mannerly she is, I thought.

"Well, Di—honey," Mary said, "are you about ready to turn in?"

"Sure." She paused. "But then I want to read a little longer, as long as I'm into it."

"Into what, Diane?" I asked.

"Bronte—Charlotte Bronte—actually." She giggled.

"Good, then your book report will be done by Sunday so Joanne can take it back with her," Mary said, sounding relieved.

She went into the bathroom, returning with a basin of water and placed it on the table by Diane's bed. Diane dipped a cloth into it and wiped her face, slowly—delicately.

Mary went for a glass of water then, and Diane brushed her teeth.

"Such a nuisance," I comforted, "having to do all that from a bed."

"It's okay," she said, with a resigned air, but then she began to perk up. "Did you like your trip out here, Mrs. Foster?"

"Oh, yes, I did. I couldn't believe I got here so fast. We stopped once in South Dakota, but only for a short time.

"The ride was smooth and the food was good. And, I might add, it was my first plane ride—ever. I have to admit I was nervous, at first." I wanted to sound friendly, to put her mind at ease; I wanted to make a good first-impression. "Now I won't mind at all flying to California later on—and back home again."

"Aunt Mary flies all over the country," Diane said, her voice rising. "I never get to go anywhere. I mean, my sister and I never get to go any place anymore, not since Mom died."

I could see her agitation building, and Mary's eyes widened.

"She used to take us to Disneyland and Washington, D.C., and places like that." She tipped her head toward Mary. "She even took us to Florida to visit her once. But now we're stuck in that prison-school."

"Well now," Mary countered, "how about Yellowstone?"

"Oh, yeah," she snapped, "In a car! And look where it

got me. Cemented into this bed." She reached for a hair-brush on her bedside table, but it moved from her grasp and toppled to the floor. "Oh, damnit," she muttered, attempting to catch it. After it hit the floor, she flopped back on her pillow with a cry as if she were mortally wounded.

"Now, Diane, that kind of action is uncalled for," Mary scolded. "We're here to help you."

"O-o-h, I'm sor-ry," she moaned, "But I get so tired of being in this bed I could just scream."

I picked up her brush and handed it to her. She laid it on the bed and began fingering the tie at the throat of her peach-colored nightgown. The very color of it heightened the flush now appearing in her cheeks. She looked even prettier than at first, but her lovely mouth had twisted into a pout and she slumped low on her pillows.

"Now, sweetheart, it's not all that bad. Your father is doing everything he can to make things as pleasant as possible for you. And the school—well, he just thinks that's the best way to look after the two of you. Don't forget, he has his hands full running this ranch, besides all the other matters he has to attend to, like going up to Idaho to see Uncle Dave." Mary was beginning to sound quite irritated, herself.

Without thinking, I took a step backwards and clasped both hands to my cheeks. Immediately I wished I hadn't and quickly let them drop.

What must they think of me? That their agitation

upset me? That I can't handle this job? Poise does it, Charlotte.

Diane hoisted herself back up on her pillows a bit. "Oh, I suppose. I don't mean to gripe, but now I have to wear these ugly things for weeks." And she reached to a leg and gave the cast a good smack. She winced, as if her fingers were smarting.

I looked at the casts. They started at her toes and went all the way to her hips, with writing all over them. There was a cheerful message in bright yellow from Mary, one in pink from Joanne, while Helen's was purple. There was a quip from Andy in black and a large red heart with the word Jed written in the middle. I also saw a big, blue scrawl that read, I love you, honey—Dad.

"I see autographs, Diane. May I?"

"Oh, sure." She produced a vivid green marker from her table drawer and handed it to me.

I wrote, "We'll do this together, Diane. Best wishes, Charlotte."

"Thanks. Well, at least I'm getting a little color on them now," she said, "But they're still pretty ugly. Pretty ugly that sounds weird." She giggled softly.

"Okay, honey, I think it's about time for the old boat," Mary said, and went to the bathroom, returning with a bedpan.

"This is the worst part," Diane sputtered, "I hate that cold thing."

Mary slipped it under the sheet, while I busied myself

arranging some books on her desk. "Yes," I said, "doctors sure know how to ruin a person's dignity. But I have a neat idea. We'll just run some hot water over it—just before."

Diane's eyes brightened, and then she grinned, but Mary's mouth dropped open. "Well, I just never thought of that. See, Charlotte, that's why we need you here—you're experienced."

"Thanks," I said, but even though somewhat pleased with myself, I felt a little embarrassed for Mary. I looked to her, grinned and shrugged.

Mary retrieved the pan then, and handed it to me. I went into the bathroom, and when I came out, Diane was lying low on her pillows and the covers were smoothed.

"Good night, Mrs. Foster. Thanks for the tip. And thanks again for the glass ball—it's nice."

"You're welcome, Diane, and please—call me Charlotte."

"Okay. No," she said, quickly, "I think I'll just call you Auntie, instead. I really don't have many of them, and I'm sure going to miss Aunt Mary when she leaves."

Mary beamed and leaned over and kissed her forehead. "Good night, sweets, don't read too late now."

"Wait, Mrs.—ah—Auntie, I almost forgot," Diane said, and she picked up a small bell that had been partially hidden behind a box of tissues on her table. She shook it rapidly and a tinkling sound filled the room. "That's how I say I need you. But I've hardly had to use it." She smiled sweetly.

"Well, let's hope you won't," I said, "but I'm glad you have it handy. Good night."

Mary handed Diane the big book again and adjusted her bed lamp and we left the room. That wasn't bad at all, I thought. Yes, she can get a little snippy, but it doesn't seem to last too long. I'm sure everything will work out just fine. And I followed Mary back down the hallway.

CHAPTER 8

"Come," Mary said,"I may as well show you the rest of the house now." She gave a tap on the door of the room next to mine. "Guest room," she said, "I'm in there now, but it'll be shared by Joanne or Helen later."

The next door on the same side of the hallway led into a small study with a large, old rolltop desk against one wall, a dark leather arm chair pulled up to it. Half-empty bookcases lined another wall, giving it a stark, unused look. "Dan always carries his papers and ledgers to the kitchen," Mary said, "he says the light's better there. He just likes the feel of people around him, I know. But this has the makings of a very nice den—or office—whatever." Mary waved a hand about as we passed quickly through the room.

We went directly into a huge bedroom, then." Dan's room. It's taken on quite a different flavor since Carol's gone." She shrugged, gently, sadly. "As you can see, it needs a lot of work yet." Paneling was missing on two inside walls. "He just doesn't seem to care anymore if it gets finished or not. They had such dreams, you see, and they were interrupted so . . ."

I winced. Well, he wasn't the only one who's had dreams interrupted, I thought. I forced a slight smile, but something must have shown in my face.

Mary looked at me sharply. "Oh, Charlotte, I am sorry. I keep forgetting you've had a terrible loss, yourself." She patted my arm. "Forgive me, dear."

"It's quite alright. I've adjusted to it." But does one ever adjust? I wondered. Well, if it means putting things into a proper perspective, then—I contemplated for an instant— yes, I suppose so.

I glanced around the room. The furniture was of a heavy, burnished wood and the fabrics appeared dark, dull. No pictures on the walls, either. Leave it to a man to have only the bare necessities, I thought, and plain ones, too. All traces of a woman's touch were absent. An uncomfortable feeling nagged at me and I was relieved when we left the room.

Mary pushed open a door to a dressing room. We walked through it, and as we did, I noticed huge closets with doors still missing. "Dan will get to this sometime soon, I expect. Maybe this winter. But he just says it isn't important." Mary sighed as if she were carrying a huge burden on her shoulders.

It shouldn't bother her so, I thought. "A man does what he can," I said, shrugging indifferently.

"Well, at least this room is finished," she said, pushing

open an adjacent door to a bathroom fitted with almond-colored fixtures. As we passed through, she added, "Oh, it was a big project building this house—way out here. It took a long time before it was livable."

"It's a really nice home," I said, nodding. But my mind leaped backward the many years to when Matt and I had built our own little home several miles north of Spencer. Room to expand, we told the contractor, but we never got to do it. The new owners did, though; built ugly dormers on it and painted it a drab shade of gray. I never forgave them for that.

Mary opened another door and I discovered we'd stepped back into the kitchen. I drew in my breath with surprise.

"Yes," Mary said, apologetically, "the rooms lead one in a circle. Dan planned it that way, to have his room off the kitchen."

I looked around then, undisturbed by piercing dark eyes. I hadn't noticed the big dining booth near the back door. It was done in black leather with huge silver buttons making diamond patterns in the benches' cushioned backs. The table was black, too, in a material that shone almost like a mirror. Mary patted the high back of a bench. "The men eat here most of the time, Charlotte, especially when they're talking over chores, business, and the like. I call it their board room. Now, you can decide at the time where it's easiest to feed the crew." She laughed. "You'll get the hang of it soon enough."

We both laughed then. I'd begun to notice that Mary could have a unique sense of humor. I felt myself relaxing.

A pencil can and a chunky note pad stood next to a toaster where the table top joined the wall. Above it hung a huge calendar, a picture of a meadowlark on it with its head tilted back in song, exposing the brilliant yellow underparts. And every days' squared spaces were scribbled with numbers or words.

"A really well-appointed board room," I said, with a grin, "and so handy to the work place."

With that, Mary threw her head back and laughed uproariously Then, eyes rolling upwards, she said, "but Charlotte, make sure they clean their boots well."

At once, I envisioned little boys scurrying in for peanut butter sandwiches, never giving their muddy shoes a thought. I felt a camaraderie with men I hadn't even met yet, except one, and smiled inwardly.

"Really," Mary said, "they are quite good about it."

I noticed then, the kitchen floor was covered with a bluegray stone-patterned linoleum. A breeze to clean, I thought, just like home. But this floor was four times as big as mine. Oh, well, I'll have some help at times, when Helen comes. Then I didn't especially like to think of that.

Next, over by the bay window, Mary guided me through a swinging door into a spacious area ringed by windows on the two outer walls. Once past the dining room space, a living area was laid out in groups of dark brown leather couches and chairs of various sizes. But one could walk next to the windows all around the wall. Like rooms without walls, it seemed.

I turned then, and saw the fireplace. My jaw must have dropped. Built on an inside wall, it was constructed entirely of split rock, their exposed inner surfaces glittering and shining like so many jewels when caught in a point of light.

Rocks that had guarded their secrets for millions of years were blatantly exposed to the human eye by the crack of a mason's mall. Mary urged me to have a closer look. "It's a work of art," I whispered.

Then I looked down, sensing a softness under my feet. We were standing on a shaggy white fur rug. "Oh," I cried, thinking I shouldn't be standing there, like I was trespassing. I stepped backward.

"It's alright," Mary said. "It's—it's mountain goat taken a long time ago—by my father." She said it indifferently, but I knew their need for protection and it made me shudder. So beautiful.

I was suddenly attracted to a portrait above the mantel. I studied it. A lovely blond woman and a satiny black horse. It was signed "DIANE" in scroll lettering. I thought it primitive, yet there was an ethereal quality about it.

"Her mother," Mary said, simply, "It took her a long time to finish it."

"What a fine memorial. It's beautiful." But the eyes gave me a strange feeling and I was compelled to look away. Again, I felt like a trespasser.

As we retraced our steps to the kitchen, Mary began snapping off lights. "Of course, you'll have to hunt for things around here, like I did," she said, "but everyone will help you as best they can. Well, now—the rest can wait. Let's have some cocoa."

I watched Mary as she moved about the kitchen. I like her, I thought; I had liked her immediately. She's so genuinely honest, so straight-forward. Why, I feel like I've known her for a long time. It should be a snap—getting settled into this household. Your first instincts were right, Charlotte, remember how you felt so comfortable at the time of the interview? And you had thought, when you first spied the newspaper ad, that it would be so daring and adventurous to come way out here alone.

Mary brought fragrant mugs of cocoa, steam rising in tiny curls, to the table in the bay area where I was seated. "Oh, it's good to get off my feet, Charlotte," she said, easing herself down onto a chair, "I'm beat."

"Yes, it's been quite a day for me, too." And as we sipped our cocoa, our conversation slowed, until finally, I had to stifle a yawn.

While I collected the mugs, Mary rose and peered out the bay window. "I see Jed's lights are out," she said. "Helen said he looked tired. Well, we've all been under a bit of a strain these last days."

I rinsed the mugs and left them in the sink, the dishwasher already humming. I glanced around the area. A generous window stretched out the entire length of the sink's work space. Wonderful. I need a window there. Just like home, I thought, and smiled to myself.

"Peek in on Diane," Mary said, as we left the kitchen. "Good night, sleep well."

"Thanks, I will. Good night." And I padded on down the hall.

I peered into Diane's room through the bathroom door. She appeared to be sound asleep. Her hair, dark now in the dim glow of the nightlight, spread across her pillow, almost covering her face. I could make out the tip of her nose and the curve of her cheek. A lovely girl, indeed. But I'd learned already how quickly her disposition could change. Oh, Diane, I wondered, what will the days ahead bring?

I stayed in the bathroom long enough to complete my nightly rituals, then went back into my room, leaving the door ajar for the possible sound of a tinkling bell. I shed my clothes.

My pajamas were in my tote, but my slippers weren't. I dug for them in my large case. While rummaging around, I pulled out my new red bikini swimsuit. Lord, why did I ever let Dorrie talk me into buying this? Well, she said it was the *law* on California beaches. I held the bra over my breasts and giggled. Humph! Not me. I stuffed it back into the case. Maybe it will fit one of Lena's girls.

I shivered and quickly pulled on the pajamas. I've got to find those slippers; floors are always colder in the mornings. I poked around again until I found them, but at the same time I pulled out my housecoat, too.

It was the same housecoat I'd been wearing the morning I'd gotten the sad news about my dog. I winced, remembering.

Only a week after the funeral, my father's successor at the new veterinarian clinic had called to tell me that Pepper had died during the night. I had taken my little, black dog in there just a few days before. The doctor had said it looked like kidney failure. We had had her for twelve long years and the hurt bore deep.

Now, it seemed, I could still see the tear stains I'd gotten on it that morning, although it'd been washed at least twice. I bunched it together in my hands and stood, unmoving.

The coat was almost new, of a mossy green color, sprinkled with nosegays of white violets, their dark leaves tied up in white ribbons. And white eyelet ruffling set off the collar, pockets and sleeves. I hardly ever bought things so distinctly feminine, but Dorrie'd been shopping with me, and I would always hear the same thing from her, "But kiddo, the color green really does things for your eyes."

My thoughts jumbled. Darn, Dorrie, I miss you already. But why am I feeling so bad now? Yes, I know. Meeting that nice, friendly dog this evening has touched a really soft spot in my heart. This's too much, I thought, I don't need any sad memories now. The material of the coat felt as if it were stinging my hands. I threw it to the foot of the bed, and, with the same momentum, drew down the covers and turned out the lamp. I slid between the silky, cold sheets, pulling the covers all the way to my chin. Holding them with both hands, I shivered until my teeth chattered. Damnit, I muttered, almost like an oath, damnit, Charlotte, don't you dare look back now. It took me a long time to coax sleep.

❧[CHAPTER 9]❧

That night was marred by spells of wakefulness, but by early morning I must have fallen into a deep, restful sleep because I awoke stretching and yawning. I opened one eye and realized I was in strange surroundings. Then slowly I opened the other. My eyes roved around the entire room— the curtains, the desk, the painting. What have I done? I turned my face into the pillow, feeling self-abandoned. My mind churned. I lifted my head again and opened my eyes wide. My new luggage stood importantly in the corner.

Soon simple, clear thoughts prevailed and I realized I had a job to do—a really important job. A young girl's welfare depended on me. I looked at my alarm clock. Damn, I hadn't set it, and that Mary deliberately let me sleep in.

Dressing in a hurry, I splashed cold water on my face, whipped the brush through my hair, and, smoothing my simple corduroy jumper, I marched dutifully to the kitchen. Mary was seated at the table in the bay window area.

"Good morning, Mary," I said, as cheerfully as I could.

"Oh, good morning to you," Mary turned to greet me, smiling. "Did you sleep well?"

I took a deep breath. "Yes, thank you." It doesn't hurt to fib a little.

"Sit down, and have whatever it is you start with first." She pointed to an insulated coffee carafe and an icy pitcher of orange juice. "And relax," she said, "Diane has already had her breakfast."

"She has?" I felt my eyes open wide.

"Oh, yes, I must warn you, she's an early bird."

"She really must be," I said, quite surprised. A teenager an early bird?

"Well, she says she loves the view out over the valley when the sun spreads across it. The treetops change their image over and over. It is quite spectacular."

"Oh, I'll surely have to pay attention to that," I said, pouring a glass of juice. And the idea interested me greatly.

"You saw the painting over the mantel. She sketches, too."

"The painting is really nice. There's one in my room, also."

"Oh, she spends a good amount of time at it. It's a nice thing for her—now—in her predicament. And she even writes a little poetry now and then." Mary poured herself another cup of coffee and turned the carafe handle toward me.

I poured mine, took a few sips and leaned back in my chair. From the bay window I had a splendid view of the mountain range to the west, which was just beginning to be bathed in a flooding sea of sunlight. "My, just look at that. I can see Diane must have a lot of beautiful subjects."

Mary glanced out, too, nodding. "Oh, you'll surely enjoy the scenery," she said. "It's nice you're able to travel now, to see some other parts of the country."

"Yes," I said, but before I realized it, my thoughts had already slipped back to the week before when I'd taken an impulsive drive out into the country north of Spencer. Combines had gleaned most fields of grain, but the acres and acres of corn were still in the process of ripening, their leaves turning crisp and brown, rattling on their tall, sturdy stalks. And the ducks and geese had already been gathering on the marshy ponds, making their plans to follow the songbirds south.

But what I remembered most was a roadside stand where I'd stopped to look over the produce. Baskets and baskets of brown potatoes, white turnips with their purple blush, fall squash, some the darkest of greens, and bold-red tomatoes stood under shelves loaded with smaller baskets of yellow and green beans, glossy carrots and peppers in every conceivable shape. Odd, but I had thought, then, what a boon it would have been for the artist's brush.

I wanted to speak to Mary then, but I didn't trust my voice. Damn, why do I do it—think of home so easily? Quickly pulling my thoughts together, I asked, "Do you think Diane will choose art as a career?"

"Oh, she talks about it," Mary answered, "But she still

has three more years left at St. Anne's. She'll probably follow Joanne, though. She's going to the University at Jackson Buttes next year."

I poured another coffee and swirled the sugar in my cup.

"Joanne," I mused, "Joanne—what does she look like?"

"Oh, dear me, I meant to show you her picture last night, but it just slipped my mind." Mary rose and went through the swinging door, returning with a small framed photograph.

I examined it slowly, closely, expecting to see features similar to Diane's, but I found no resemblance at all.

"Surprised?" Mary asked. "Yes, there's little comparison. Joanne takes after her father, even in temperament. And you saw the woman in the portrait—Diane, all over again."

The girl in the picture was pleasant looking, with a rather prominent chin, and deep, wide-spaced eyes over high, handsome cheekbones. And hair near the coloring of my own. "Well, her eyes are as blue as Diane's," I surmised.

But Mary said, emphatically, "Not quite."

"Well, she's a lovely girl and I'm anxious to meet her."

I started then, seeing a sudden movement out the window. "Oh, a man," I exclaimed. Feeling somewhat foolish, I quickly added, "Oh, it must be Jed—there—by the barn door."

"Yes, that's Jed. He's probably just finished tending the horses. He'll be in for his breakfast soon. You'll like Jed, Charlotte, he's a grand person. Dan says he just couldn't get along without him." Mary got up and refilled the carafe and placed it on the dining booth's table. "I must warn you, though, he eats a lot. Four eggs and six sausages at a time." She smiled fondly, and retrieved things from the fridge.

There was a rough scraping noise on the back porch. "That's him now," she laughed, "he's cleaning his boots, all right."

A warning knock sounded, the knob turned slowly, and the door opened. A hulk of a man stepped in, almost blotting out the light of the morning in the doorway. "Howdy, Miz," the man said, and quickly removed his hat. His smile was full and instant, crinkling back heavy reddish whiskers. And I knew there had to be dimples lost somewhere in the thickness of the beard. "I'm Jed Simpson."

I reached out my hand, spontaneously returning the smile. "Howdy to you, too, Jed. I'm Charlotte Foster."

He took my hand and shook it soundly and I felt the well worked roughness of his touch. Jed was a big man, not too tall, but barrel-chested, with green eyes glinting above roundish, ruddy cheeks. He tossed his wide-brimmed hat through the air, and it caught accurately upon the pegged rack. It was then I noticed red hair, shades lighter than the beard.

I prepared the sausages and eggs as Mary suggested. And, at the same time, Jed made his own toast while guiding a tall glass of juice into the beard. He ate his food, seemingly enjoying it, but he declined the warm cinnamon roll Mary had offered.

He rose to leave, and, plucking his hat from the peg,

he twirled it in his hands. "I'd be right happy to show you around the place, Miz Foster," he said, grinning until crinkles showed at the corners of his eyes. "Course, the barns ain't much, but we have a fine bunch of horses down in the corral."

"Sounds good, Jed. I'll take you up on it right after lunch—uh—I mean, dinner."

After Jed left the house, I went to sit by Mary with the breakfast I'd prepared for myself. "How long has Jed been here at the ranch?" I asked, as I sat down.

"Oh, let's see." Mary's brows drew together. "It must be about eight years, right after he lost his wife."

"Oh, no." I felt a scowl pull at my forehead. "How was that?"

"Car accident."

I winced; I wished I'd bitten my tongue. "Sorry, Mary," I said, "I guess I'll never be completely free of it."

Mary jumped to her feet. I could see she was uncomfortable. "Take your time, dear. Rest a bit. I'll peek in on Diane." She left the kitchen hurriedly, smoothing her silver strands of hair into their proper places.

It was too late—I had to re-live the memories of how my husband was returning to Spencer, after so willingly picking up Mother at her club luncheon in the neighboring town of Simmons Point. He traveled a lot in the insurance business, and, coincidentally, was seeing people there that day. On their way home, just south of Spencer, a loaded dump truck blew a tire and hit our old Buick head-on. Death

took Matt and Mother instantly—and it was instant for
Father and I, too. Our lives were abruptly and totally altered.

It was a double funeral; a big funeral with nearly all the
townspeople turning out. I barely remember it, but I do
remember Father sobbing and saying, "Move back home
with me, Lottie. Kenny needs a man around, at his age.
Let's face it squarely, girl, we need each other."

So, I returned to live in my father's house and we
looked after each other—and raised my son. Kenny dearly
loved his grandfather, and, as the years progressed, he
spent more and more of his time in the clinic, just as I had.
Not surprisingly, he stood tall one day and stated, "Gramps,
I'm going to be a veterinarian, just like you." My eyes teared.

I ached for a long time after my life with Matt ended.
Then the ache changed to a new kind of hurt—loneliness
for a young man away at college. Then, the ultimate blow,
the disturbing presence of a new woman in his life, a lovely
girl with long, taffy-colored hair tied up in a saucy pony-tail.

It had all run through my mind again last week—in
the rocker on the porch—and it hurt. It hurt, too, that
she had green eyes, but I worked hard at reasoning it all
out. I told myself, flatly, "Life goes on." None-the-less, it
was still painful. I countered with thoughts of John—
steadfast, warm-hearted John—but even that didn't allay
the hurt, altogether.

I was abruptly brought to the moment when Mary
returned to the kitchen. She sat down and began to shuffle
the papers she was carrying. They were filled with notes.

Thankful for the distraction, I hopefully asked, "Instructions for me?"

"Oh, no, dear. It's a surprise—for Diane." But then she shoved all the papers under a mat holding condiments in the center of the table. "It can wait," she said, "I think it's about time for Diane's bath."

She got up from the table, but paused by the bay window, touching a side curtain. It was thin yellow gingham, faded and dingy. "Do something with these curtains, will you, Charlotte if you have time?"

"Oh, I will. Maybe I can sew some new ones." I felt a surge of enthusiasm; a chance to be creative with the girls, I thought.

We went to Diane's room, where Mary knocked three times.

"Enter," came a tiny voice.

"Hi, honey, back again," Mary said. "Oh, show Charlotte what you've been doing."

Diane smiled and handed me a sketch pad. I studied it. An ink drawing showed a chickadee in an evergreen bough. It was quite appealing.

"You do really nice work, Diane."

"Thank you. I just saw the bird outside my window."

I peeked out. I saw a shaggy spruce branch very near the window, and, as the wind blew, the needles brushed against the glass. "How convenient," I said, "to have your subjects come to you like that."

Diane's face brightened. "Yeah, I like that," she said, giggling little musical notes.

The morning bath ritual began. With only a slight assist from Mary, I helped Diane bathe and dress in a corn-flower blue gown, with matching bed jacket. And the blue of her eyes responded beautifully to the color. I changed her bed clothes in the process, proud that in the past years I'd become quite adept at not burying the patient in a heap of linen.

Mary had helped me shampoo Diane's hair, and, as it dried, I suggested I braid it and arrange it on top of her head like a crown. "That way you won't have to contend with lying on it."

"I think I'd like that," she said. When I finished, I handed her the mirror.

"Gosh, Mrs. Foster—I mean—Auntie—is it really me?" She giggled at length as she held the mirror in several different positions.

"Wow, Diane," Mary said, "what a transformation. Well, I must run. I have something mighty important to attend to." She exuded a smug air. "See you later, princess." She curtsied, blew her a kiss and left the room.

"So? What do you have in the lesson department today?"

"More English. This time it's essays," she said, "I hate essays. We have to re-write them and put them into paragraphs. It's a big waste of time." She sighed as though in total exasperation. "I hate it—but I'll do it."

Plumping her pillows, I helped her adjust to a higher position, placed a portable desk across her thighs, and collected the things she might need in her task. "I'll leave you to your misery then," I said, and laughed, giving her cast a gentle rap where I'd signed my name. I turned and moved toward the door.

"Thanks a lot," she said, and I felt a nip at my rear and saw an eraser bounce across the floor. "Skat," she added, then she giggled the loudest of all.

I walked smartly down the hall. Well, she certainly has a lively sense of humor. That should make it really fun being here. And Dorrie had said she could turn out to be a snip. Hah! I allowed myself the luxury of a smirk as I neared the kitchen.

{CHAPTER 10}

The breakfast dishes were cleared away, the dishwasher was making all sorts of wet sounds, and Mary was seated at the table, her mysterious papers spread before her.

"Should I start something for lunch—I mean—dinner?" I asked. I stood in the middle of the floor, looking around expectantly.

"Oh, yes, dinner. It'll soon be time. There's only Jed today, though. But the men do need a big meal at noon. Suppers can be big, too, sometimes." She laughed. "You'll have to decide that, day by day. Oh, there'll be lots of cooking to do, Charlotte. Yes, indeed." She paused and looked at her papers. "But come," she said, "sit down, this is going to be fun."

I dropped into a chair across from her, anxious now to the point of holding my breath.

"We're going to throw a party." She watched my expression. "I think Diane deserves a party—a big, noisy party—before her dad gets home. Don't you?"

"Oh, yes," I said, "I agree." But I wasn't quite sure what she meant.

"Well, Dan always promised the girls they could have parties, but then I guess he just didn't quite know how to go about having one," Mary said, "now the time has come. It'll be a pajama party, for the entire weekend, if they'd like. I've already arranged for their two friends to come home from school with Joanne tomorrow. They're the two that went on the trip to Yellowstone with them." Mary stopped to catch her breath.

"I see," I said, my interest mounting.

"Oh, it will be fun. You know—lots of music, as loud as they want, and junk food—whatever they desire. And they can do all the things their father's not accustomed to, like staying up all night." Her eyes were bright now, matching her mischievous smile.

"Sounds great to me. I'll help carry it off, if you promise not to report me." We laughed together. What fun, I thought, a real party. I ached, then, for all the parties Kenny never had. My father did not like "that loud trash," his idea of rock music. Father could be really opinionated at times, but then Kenny's youthfulness did produce quite a generation gap.

We worked on the party plans, with Mary revising her shopping list for the last time, she said. Then we hurried to prepare a dinner for all of us.

After the noon meal was over, I slipped on a windbreaker and walked with Jed toward a barn. The wind blew gusty and raw, robbing the warmth from the sunshine. But it streamed down, anyway, between huge, white clouds that billowed up to the heavens like mountains in their own right. I breathed deeply the clean mountain air, expanding my lungs to huge proportions, it seemed. And exhilaration ran through me.

Seconds later I sensed a movement behind me and felt the dog nuzzle my hand. I patted his head, but he soon went to Jed's side for more affection.

When we reached the barn, Jed swung open a large, heavy door and bade me enter. I was met by a musty, sweet odor and I knew it immediately as grain. A scattering of kernels covered the flooring and in the corner filled burlap bags were stacked in a neat pile. Jed patted one of the fat sacks. "Horse food," he said, "lots of it."

Another odor was present, then, but I adjusted to it without too much discomfort. "Yeah," Jed said, "better watch where you step." He chuckled.

There was an open door at the far end of the barn adding some light to the dimness of the interior. After my eyes became accustomed, I could see rows of stalls on either side of the entire length of the building. They were made of planks and rails, some uneven, with rails slanting downward from the back. "What happened?" I asked, instantly curious, "are they broke?"

Jed threw his head back and laughed. "No, no, Miz Foster, those rails are dropped on purpose, so's one can get a saddle on a stubborn mule of a horse. They do kick sometimes."

Well, you asked, and you learned something, Charlotte.

A front stall, opposite the grain pile, held stacks of saddle blankets, straps and odd pieces of gear. Several saddles rested on the top rail. Then I saw an open door nearby and peeked in. A well-filled tack room reeked with the strong odor of oiled leather, biting into my nostrils. But I sensed an excitement in the air from the very presence of the much used equipment.

I could see through the room, then, to another open door, and spotted the hitching rail out in the corral. But the door, itself, was swinging erratically in the wind, making a creaking sound.

"S'pose I did that. Left it open and forgot it," Jed said, going through the room and securing the latch. "The wind could surely wear out those old, rusty hinges pretty quick." He shook his head as if scolding himself.

Meanwhile, I'd looked around and spotted a nameplate above the first stall that had held all the gear. "Prince," it read, burned into the wood, the lettering in a scroll style. Diane's style, I thought immediately.

Jed noticed my interest. "Yup," he said, "that was the big guy's stall."

"Who?" I asked, quickly, anxious for an answer.

"Dan's wife had a big, black stallion. No horse has been in that stall since."

"Since?" I couldn't contain my curiosity.

"Well, it's like this," Jed said, "after Carol died, Dan never saddled Prince again." He kept up a monologue as we walked through the barn, out the rear door, and up a slope. "He had the freedom of the hills. He'd gallop and prance around just like he knew he'd always be free. But one day I missed him and went alookin'. He was way up there." Jed waved an arm in the direction of one distinct hill that was higher than the others. "I found him way up there, in a ravine. I just knew his leg was busted, and . . ." He shut his eyes and shook his head, "I sure didn't like what I had to do."

I bit my lower lip. "Oh, that sounds dreadful."

"Sometimes we think we still see 'im, way up there—there—on that ridge." He quickly turned on a heel and we strode back to the barn.

"It gives me goose bumps," I said, hurrying behind him. But Jed seemed not to hear.

We went around the outer corner of the barn until we could see the corral. It was empty, save for a large hay bunker with several missing rails. The bunker was empty, too.

"There they are," Jed said, clearly a note of pride in his voice. He pointed out a group of horses in a grassy meadow at the bottom of the slope. A creek meandered nearby forming a small pool in one of its bends, then disappeared behind a clump of willows. The horses grazed peacefully among the greens now touched with brown, their hides glistening in the sunshine.

"There—over there." A horse was standing alone. "That's Baron, Dan's horse. Handsome bay, huh?"

"Oh, yes—yes, he is." The horse raised his head and watched us for a moment, then resumed grazing.

"He's big, but not as big as my Duke. Duke's a sorrel, can't miss that big fella." And a giant of a horse, shining reddish-brown in the bright sun, began to walk toward us. He kept coming, picking up his pace until he was almost trotting.

"He likes you." I laughed.

"No grain, Duke," Jed called and held up both hands as if to prove it. Duke stopped. "That's the way we get hold of 'em to saddle 'em up. Just hold up a bucket and they know it's grain. Works every time." Jed chuckled deep in his throat. "He just hoped I had one."

"Miserable trick," I said, laughing along.

"Course, we usually grain 'em in the barn. They know where to find it when it's time."

Yes, years ago, I thought, I fed two horses. I knew about grain, especially oats. Now, here there are eight horses, and they're all so different looking. Excitement raced through me as my eyes darted from horse to horse.

"Those two over there are the girls' horses." Jed pointed to a black one with white stockings, and another one, white, with many distinct black spots. Joanne's horse, I knew—the one in the painting in her room.

Jed pointed out another. "And that's old Sal. She's pretty much retired now." He grinned. "Well, she doesn't have to do much anymore, 'cept once in awhile we use her for a pack horse. She's our old mare, mama to quite a few.

The girls' horses, I know for sure—I helped her." He had a proud air about him at that moment.

Yes, I'd gone with my father on many occasions, staying up all night, sometimes. Memories flashed back in an instant, like the night Hanson's mare had twin foals. It was a thrill. Then I thought, too, how the Hopkins' horses had gotten out one night, and one was hit by a car. We just couldn't save her. I'd cried all the way back to town that night.

Now, I gazed at old Sal, who was cropping grass contentedly. She was a piebald mare, more white than black. "She's a gentle old lady, she is," Jed added, with affection clearly showing. The mare looked up and greeted us with a whinny. I could've run to her and hugged her.

"There's three more over there," I said, not wanting to miss any of the animals. "They're off by themselves."

"Yup, those are the new ones. Andy and Joe—that's his nephew—they're trainin' 'em for cuttin'." Three chestnuts grazed at the creek's edge. "We haven't had 'em long." They feigned a disinterest in us, I thought, and kept heads low.

"Gosh, they are all so beautiful," I said, watching the girls' horses nip each other in play. "I had a horse once, looked a lot like the one with all the spots." It seemed so long ago, then, and I didn't want to dwell on it, so I turned and quickly walked away. See, you *can* control the melancholy, Charlotte.

We trudged into the wind, through the corral, and toward the other barn. I shivered and pulled the hood of my jacket up over my head, the gusts blowing hair into my face. I tried to brush it out of my eyes.

"Yup, that's what we got plenty of here—wind. You'll get used to it, I reckon'." Jed grinned and squinted into the stiff breeze, himself, his eyes crinkling at the corners. "This here barn's just for hay," he said, as we approached it. "We'll be gettin' a big load soon. Takes a mighty heap of it to get them cattle through the winter." We stood in front of a large, framed opening. "We can drive right through this one with a tractor and wagon." He put his arm on the edge of an empty wagon rack sitting in the entrance, as if suddenly tired.

I peered into the shadowy interior. "Yes, it'll hold quite a big load." I laughed. "You say some hay is coming soon?"

"Yup, in just a couple weeks or so. Have to have plenty on hand. Never know when there'll be a deep snow or a blizzard."

"Yes," I said, "I've heard Minnesota isn't the only state that has blizzards."

He chuckled deep in his throat again, and I saw the green of his eyes in the sunshine. It was easy becoming friends with Jed Simpson.

"Well, I'd better be agettin' at those old wagon wheels," he said, picking up a grease gun from a nearby tool box. "Gotta keep it ready to roll."

"Thanks for the tour, Jed, I really enjoyed it." I turned, waving goodbye, and started toward the house. "See you later."

As I neared the porch, I sensed being all alone. I looked for the dog, and found him laying near the wheel where Jed was working. Yes, Andy did say the dog was especially fond of Jed.

And, for a moment, I remembered a little, black dog that had singled me out of a diverse group of people for her very own. I held my bottom lip between my teeth to keep it from quivering. Lord, will the past always haunt me? Well, Charlotte, it isn't that long ago.

Only a month has passed since the new veterinarian had called to tell me that my dog, Pepper, had died in the night at his hospital. She was the last one in my life who really needed me, really needed my care.

I'd wrapped her dark, little body in Father's gold-colored heather afghan, the one that Mrs. Nelson had crocheted for him when he'd first become ill. And John had brought over a sturdy little box and we laid her down under my father's favorite plum tree back by the garage. We knew he would have liked that. And to me, just knowing she was wrapped in that comfy old thing was a buoy to my spirits at the time, like a healing tonic.

I shook my head quickly, swallowed the lump that had built in my throat and went into the house.

❦[CHAPTER 11]❧

Just before noon on Friday, Andy came back to the ranch in the Jeep. Jed was carrying in firewood and piling it in an iron cradle on the porch. Andy helped him, and they even brought a good supply to the woodbox in the living room. It filled the rooms with a pungent, piney fragrance and I was delighted by it. For a few moments I even longed for Christmases past and cozy winter hearths, and I had to shake my head to rid it of trespassing thoughts.

After our dinner, Mary announced, "Well, Charlotte, it's time to go for Joanne and the girls, and get all the party things. It'll take a lot of doing, but Andy's free to help you."

So, trading the Jeep for the stationwagon, Andy and I set out for Meadow Grand. "You drive, Charlotte," he said, "you may as well get used to it."

Once we were out of the hilly area, and heading toward Meadow Grand, the roads leveled and the driving became easier.

"The girls are really excited, and Diane said she could hardly wait," I told Andy. "She hasn't seen anyone but family since her accident. Mary asked Diane to pick out the music she liked best, and she put me in charge of junk food." Relaxed, I drove steadily, chatting. "So, Andy, give me some suggestions."

"Oh, shucks, when you say 'junk' I just think of some rusty, old buckets, or broken wheels."

"Fine help you are," I said, and we began to laugh.

Then I saw a blurry motion on my left, and speeding objects suddenly caught my eye, causing me to swerve the other way. I hit the shoulder of the road and my wheels dug into the slope of it and pulled me further off, nearing a narrow ditch. "Andy," I screamed, my hands freezing to the steering wheel.

"Easy," Andy coached, "easy now." And I managed to slow the wagon without braking too soon. "Slow up." He was in control. "Now stop."

I did. Then I let go my breath. I dared look out the window. A small herd of antelope scurried by, leaping and bobbing and flitting their white tails at me—tails laughing at me as they veered off further to the left. Then they were quickly swallowed up by the tall, brown grasses.

"Damnit, Andy, did you see that?" I wailed, shaking as if I'd just taken a dip in a cold stream.

"Shucks, Ma'm, it happens all the time around here. I s'pect you might as well get used to it." He patted my hand, still gripping the wheel. "Let's get right back on the road— them girls are waitin'."

It took awhile before I relaxed enough to enjoy the scenery. Then Meadow Grand came into view, and Andy directed me to the business district. It was neat and level and protected by many trees—cottonwoods, mostly.

We found the supermarket and approached it armed with Mary's lists. We followed them as best we could, and I snatched up bags and bags of intriguing junk. Andy even tossed in a bag of puffed pork rinds. I felt queasy and made a face at him. He just grinned. We filled the rear of the wagon with not only party needs, but endless supplies, too, leaving little room for the girls' luggage.

At last, we pulled up in front of St. Anne's School for Girls and stopped. Again, I felt unnerved. Come, now, Charlotte, three teen-age girls can't be that bad. But I'd had only one teen-ager—a boy. I took a filling breath, and ventured into the building—alone.

A young lady rose from her desk as I approached the principal's office. She was tall and slim, with long, black hair tied up in a pink bow at the nape of her neck. I was still admiring her prettiness when she spoke. "Hello. Mrs. Foster, I believe?"

"Yes," I returned quickly.

"I'm Janet Lonetree. We're expecting you." She smiled, creating apple-cheeks. "Please have a seat. I'll locate Sister Agnes."

It was only a few minutes when a figure in black seemed to float into the waiting room. "Hello, dear, I'm

Sister Agnes," she said, extending a hand. "And you must be Mrs. Foster. We're so glad to have you here."

"How do you do," I said, shaking her hand, my nervousness still building.

"The girls will be down soon. I do hope you had a nice trip. I trust you will find many things of interest here," she said, supplying small talk.

"Oh, yes." I was about to admit to the antelope affair, when I heard a symphony of giggling. Three young ladies then entered the room and Sister Agnes quickly led me to them. "Girls, this is Charlotte Foster. I guess you could say she'll be your foster mother for the next few days."

The girls burst into more laughter, Sister Agnes beamed, and my tenseness almost completely disappeared. "Mrs. Foster, I'd like you to meet Joanne Garner, Catherine Price, and Barbara Cloud."

I said, "Hello," to each one, shaking hands, and found them to be a well-poised lot. Then, I bumbled. "Oh, oh, I almost forgot, Sister. Here are Diane's lessons." I handed the package to her.

Then, after Janet Lonetree took them and left and returned with an even larger package, we all moved toward the door.

"Goodbye, girls. You know you have been forgiven any homework, so have a nice time. But you must be back by eight-o-clock, Sunday night." Sister Agnes waggled a finger at the girls. "Rules are strict, you know." That time she glanced at me.

After assuring her the girls would be returned on time, I left the room, and the girls, carrying their bags, trooped out behind me like eager soldiers. But, once in the wagon, they instantly transformed themselves into typical teenagers looking forward to an entire weekend of freedom from structure, I was sure. And the vehicle fairly shook with excitement as we headed out of town.

Joanne was a tall, slim girl, and much like her picture. She had short brown hair, quite straight, rather like my own. She didn't appear a likely sister to Diane, except for her expressive blue eyes, but there was a strong resemblance to her Aunt Mary, in the noticeably generous chin.

Barbara Cloud was Joanne's age, but not quite as tall. She had long, shiny black hair, and broad facial features, distinctly reflecting her Native American heritage. But Catherine Price was shorter yet, a plump girl with closely cropped auburn curls. She was the most quiet of the three, seemingly mature for her age. The perfect companion, I thought, for the active-minded Diane.

At first we drove along in a rather awkward silence, broken only by a whisper or giggle now and then. So, I decided to ask questions. "I saw a lot of yellow-breasted birds along the way. What kind are they?"

"Meadowlarks," Barbara said.

"Western Meadowlarks," Joanne added, "they're our state bird."

See, Charlotte, you just learned another new thing. "Is it true," I asked, "they really sing like a—a lark?"

"You bet." Andy joined in. "Stop the car once, you'll see."

I slowed to a halt. We opened all the windows and sat in silence. Soon song was heard, filling the crisp autumn air with a multitude of notes, still, an original piece never to be duplicated again, a symphony of nature's best. (Yes, Sister Agnes, there are many, many things of interest here.)

Once back on the road, I said, "Now, girls, it's your turn. Let's hear it, one by one, the silliest thing that's happened this entire week. It'll be a contest, and Andy can be the judge."

The girls squealed, Andy howled, and Barbara began. Andy never did get around to picking a winner, but it surely hastened the journey homeward.

We returned to OUR Ranch just as the sun was dropping behind the mountains. It was only my third sunset on the ranch, so I was still the awe-struck tourist. My oohs and aahs amused the girls. But I stood, almost reverently, and watched the golden brilliance, as it defied description, outline the dark, towering peaks, which were piercing the very clouds, themselves. I named them the Majestic Guardians of OUR Ranch, but only in my soul.

We all joined in to unload the wagon, then trooped, en masse, into the house with our burdens. Mary held the kitchen door wide, greeting everyone, even Andy and I, with loud salutations. Talk and laughter created a din within seconds.

"Oh, I'm so glad you thought of this, Aunt Mary. You're

just a peach," Joanne said, dropping her bags so quickly that one tipped and spilled some things onto the floor.

Unbeknownst to Andy, the bag of puffy pork rinds slid out first. After setting down his bags, he stepped backwards. Crunch! He spotted the flattened bag and his mouth twisted in mock disappointment. The kitchen rollicked with even more laughter.

"Well, girls, get on with it," Mary said, in a voice almost rent with joy. With a giant sweep of an arm, she motioned them through the swinging door, ushering them into the rooms without walls. They disappeared and only moments later we heard giggles and screams in all octaves coming from Diane's room at the far end of the hallway.

Joanne came flying back into the kitchen. "Pretty clever, Aunt Mary, putting Dad's mattress on the floor in there. Barb and I got dibs on that. Cathy gets the couch."

Cathy poked her head back through the doorway. "Sounds fine to me," she said, her reddish curls glinting in the last rays of sunshine coming through the bay window.

Mary called the girls together. "I need your help, We're going to carry Diane, mattress and all, to the party. She doesn't suspect it yet, but there's plenty of room for her, too, right here on the dining room floor."

Joanne squealed with delight. "I should've known you'd think of something like that. You're just super-terrific."

"Not so fast, Jo. It was Jed's idea. After he helped me move your father's mattress, he asked me why we couldn't move Diane, too. And I asked him, 'Why not?'"

So, after we'd accomplished the task of moving the patient, the party bloomed beautifully.

Mary spooned sloppy joe mixture on warm buns and laid them on a platter, a mouth-watering aroma quickly filling the air. I heaped bowls with potato chips, huge pretzels, and tiny crackers, and finished with a big, round tray of crisp vegetables with dip. The pork rinds were missing. Upon viewing, the girls soft moans told me my junk food splurge had been a success. Then Mary and Andy topped it all off by carrying in a large cooler of pop.

The girls already had the music's volume turned up to a questionable level, and, talking even louder, of course, they seemingly needed nothing further from us, so we retreated to the kitchen practically unnoticed.

Jed came in for supper, joining us at the big table for our share of the sloppy joes and all the rest of the party fare. But Andy, explaining it to Jed, expressed disappointment over the loss of the bag of pork rinds. Jed laughed. "Well," he said, "I'd just say I think it was a step in the right direction." He clapped Andy on the shoulder, but he winked at me.

For the most part, we ate our supper in silence, but we smiled an awfully lot.

[CHAPTER 12]

I had just finished preparing Jed's breakfast when Joanne walked into the kitchen, Cathy and Barbara close behind. "Good morning, everybody," they chorused.

Joanne turned to Jed, who was seated in the booth buttering his toast. "Oh, Jed, would you please keep Boots and Patches in the corral this morning?"

"Sure thing, Jo."

"Patches?" I set Jed's plate of food before him, my hand suddenly unsteady.

"Yes, my horse is Patches, the one with the big spots."

"Patches was my horse's name, too." I looked at Joanne, unbelieving. "What a coincidence." I was barely speaking above a whisper. "But then—I suppose there are quite a few spotted horses in the world named Patches."

"Well, it *is* a coincidence, alright," Joanne said, "Probably like an omen. Hmmm. Like it means you should ride Patches—again. Or something like that." They all laughed, watching me closely.

Ride again? After almost eight years? Yes, it'd been eight years since Kenny and I sadly gave up our horses to go back to town to live with my father.

Mary had been mixing frozen orange juice at the sink. She whirled around. "Oh, yes, Charlotte. Wouldn't that be fun? They're great horses."

Suddenly there were five pairs of eyes riveted on me. Well, kiddo, you haven't forgotten how, have you? I could just hear Dorrie's prodding comment. Of course not. I began to relish the idea and looked at Joanne. "You have a taker," I answered boldly and grinned. I felt a weakness hit me behind the knees.

Later, while clearing away the breakfast things, I watched Joanne and Barbara ride down through the meadow and up the east slope, heading for the high hill, but in a round about way. And Chase, true to his name, chased after them. Duke, Jed's big sorrel, pursued them, too, in a highly-spirited race for a short way before he circled back.

After a time I saw them returning and I rushed to my room. I dressed in jeans and sturdier shoes. And, with trepidation, I walked out of the house. A quick glance told me Mary was in the bay window. The dog, however, had returned to his cove under the bush by the porch. "Aren't you going to watch me, Chase?" I called to him. He took a few steps, then returned, settling into a big, furry mound. He'd had his romp.

I felt giddy and flushed as I hurried across the dooryard, speaking only to the heart hammering in my chest. "At ease! I shall conquer the wild beast!"

There was a stiff, cool breeze, but I ignored it completely; warmed by a rush of blood. My temples throbbed as I reached the corral. Joanne spotted me and dismounted, holding the reins. I approached the horse and slowly, gently rubbed her nose. "Hi, my name is Lottie, and I'm pleased to meet you." (I hadn't thought of myself as Lottie since I'd left Spencer.) I patted the horse soundly on her shoulder. "I plan on riding you around the corral, Patches, but I will need your cooperation." My throat felt dry and my knees turned rubbery.

"Go ahead, she's okay," Joanne said, and passed the reins to me. Now or never, I thought, as I summoned up every ounce of courage I had, and placed my foot in the stirrup. Then, heaving the other leg across her back in one swift motion, I settled into the saddle. Once astride, though, I felt comfortable, my nervousness eased, and I walked the horse around the corral several times, even trotting the final circle.

The girls had perched themselves on the hitching rail, and I rode up to them. They broke out in applause. Dismounting with a flourish, I bowed deeply, and said, with what little breath I had left, "Thank you very much, and you, too, Patches." I rubbed her nose and knew I would ride her again.

I watched as the girls unsaddled the two and turned them out to their pasture, then we walked briskly to the house. The wind blew in gusts, occasionally sending a dried weed tumbling across the dooryard.

The elements had turned Joanne's face a bright pink, but Barbara's had taken on a lovely, coppery glow. I wondered about my own. I felt strange—different, somehow. Thrilled? My scarf had slipped from my head and was now stowed in a pocket, while the wind whipped my hair about my face. I let it. Carefree's the word, I thought. I felt so carefree. I wanted to run and skip like a schoolgirl. What would Joanne and Barbara think of me, anyway?

Jed was standing on the porch when we walked up. "You look a little wild and wooly, Miz Foster," he said. He grinned behind his beard, causing his eyes to nearly shut.

"Well, thank you, Jed. I like that." I laughed. "Did you see? I didn't even get thrown."

"You done jus' fine. I knew you would." He patted my shoulder. But I felt as though he'd given me some kind of gold medal.

I felt an uninhibited pleasure then, earned because I dared—and did it. I could hardly wait to write letters home.

{CHAPTER 13}

Saturday sped by. I'd heard more music without stopping than I'd heard since Kenny was in his last year of high school. Father had always said to turn that noise down. He'd only wanted to hear the smooth, old, big-band sounds, if, indeed, he'd wanted to hear music at all. I realized now how music could excite the heart, while still putting the mind at ease. Feelings were strong as they coursed through me then, and I felt my life taking on a whole new dimension. I had just experienced a household resounding with joy, warmed with love.

It moved me to tears as I cleared away the supper dishes. Lord, how long has it been since I've had a semblance of real happiness. Yes, over two years—two years since my father's first stroke. What a short weekend this has been, I thought, and a heavy feeling fell upon me.

The girls were all packed, ready to leave. "Charlotte," Mary had said, "this time I want to drive the girls back to school myself. I'd like to spend a little more time with Jo. She's the one I've hardly had a chance to visit with."

"Oh, I understand. Of course." And I did understand the necessity of goodbyes, just as I had to go to Kenny's school last weekend to say goodbye to him. Although he'd been home for his grandfather's funeral, it was not the same. Last weekend had been *my* turn.

It had started with his phone call earlier the evening of the big storm. I'd been sitting in the rocker on the front porch, again, after indulging in my leisurely meal. But the blues had insidiously returned, what with all the recent events still pressing on my mind. Why did life have to be so complicated, I'd wondered, and with such heavy sadness, too? Tears had erupted then, and rolled down my cheeks. There was no way I could control them. I found a crumpled tissue in my pocket and dabbed at my eyes. My dreariness had just begun to lift a little when I heard the phone ringing. I clutched at my tangled skirt, pulling it free from my legs. Then I got to my feet and made my way into the house, somewhat confused, almost like a little child lost in a forest.

I picked up the phone. "H-h-hello." I couldn't help but sniffle one last time.

"Mom? Mom, what's wrong?"

"Kenny? Oh, I'm so glad you called."

"Mom, are you okay?" he demanded.

"Oh, yes. Yes, I'm fine—now."

So I told him how I'd been so undecided about what to do with myself; about how I'd thought I would try to get some kind of work, or maybe volunteer some time at the nursing home. (They'd been running ads.) Or just anything to help pull me out of the rut I'd been in.

"Yeah, I know, Mom. Uh, how's John?"

"Oh, he's fine. He stopped by a few minutes tonight. He had stayed late at school, setting up the lab. But a storm's coming and he had to hurry home. You know how Mama is."

"He's a great guy, Mom. Don't pass up a good thing."

"Now, Kenneth—mind your own business."

"I do. Her name is Beth."

So then he told me all about her; how he'd met her last summer working on her parents' farm near the school; how they both had many of the same interests; and how they could make each other laugh.

I knew he could earn extra money, and gain practical knowledge at the same time when he'd taken the job on the Bailey farm, but I hadn't bargained for a *Beth* when I'd agreed to the terms.

"Ah—Mom?"

"Yes?"

He paused, then, and I waited, the receiver glued to my ear.

"Come on, Mom, hasn't John asked you to—ah—don't you two ever talk about—well—getting married?"

"Kenneth!" It was a solid reprimand. "John has a responsibility to his mother, you know, and besides, I'm not quite sure . . ."

"Of what?"

"Never mind. Don't you worry about me. You just study hard—for Gramps—and me. Now, can I send you anything?"

"Oh, Mom, if you insist, sure—send money."

It was our favorite joke and I'd walked right into it. Then I said, "I will" and "take care" more times than was necessary and hung up the phone. Instinctively, I went back to the rocking chair on the porch to watch the incoming storm.

So, as you see, I was rather prepared to meet Beth when John, with Mama, drove me down to the Iowa college so I could say goodbye to my son. It was then I'd noticed something in their eyes that disturbed me greatly. You are losing him, Charlotte—you are losing him to another woman. It was a flat, undeniable statement to myself. I pondered it for a time, then common sense, alone, told me to accept it graciously. But, damn, why did she have to be so pretty?

Now, at the moment, the house at OUR Ranch was incredibly quiet. Diane had been returned to her room again on her magical "flying carpet." And she was in such a happy, relaxed mood she'd even agreed to read one of her assignments ahead of time. It was something by Edgar Allen Poe, and she'd said she hated Edgar Allen Poe. Diane was full of surprises.

I gave the kitchen a few final touches and hummed a tune along with the radio. I finished filling the dishwasher and punched the button. It started to make all sorts of gurgling noises, drowning out the music. I twisted the volume up a little, liking the music I'd found. Being alone just then, I tried out a new dance step I'd seen the girls doing, the rhythm beating a strong course through my body. Wow, John, I thought, maybe we can go dancing sometime and I could show you this one. I'll write to you—soon.

{CHAPTER 14}

The next two days passed quickly. Mary and I had been busy washing bedding and getting the house back in order. "Dan will never even suspect we had a party," she said, "but, of course, Diane will tell him all about it. Then she'll beg for another one." Mary bounced about the kitchen like an Olympic medal winner. Dan Garner would be coming home soon, and she would be leaving, but I felt confident now that I could run the home smoothly. I tackled my duties with pleasure, enjoying just being in a peopled houschold.

Jed had been in regularly for his meals; Andy having taken the jeep and gone back to Red Hill. The cook, whether Mary or I, was always complimented, even though Jed was not eating as much as a big man should. Well, I'll just have to try harder, I thought, and told him so. He just grinned; Jed always grinned.

Tuesday afternoon I felt the need for some fresh air, and decided to go out and explore the dooryard, and the buildings, and maybe beyond. Why not? I put on a sweater under my windbreaker and tied a scarf around my head, and walked down the driveway, quite the tenderfoot. (I'd only been out beyond the home place once since I'd arrived, and that was when I'd gone to Meadow Grand with Andy.) Chase had been lying by Jed as he worked about the tractor, but when the dog saw me start down the hill, he insisted on accompanying me, always ready to guard. I liked that.

Once at the bottom of the driveway, where the huge sign hung overhead, we paused and looked about. I remembered a fork in the road to the north, so decided that would be the way to explore first. As we trudged along the gravel road, I remembered a sign there, too, and I was compelled to read it. I began to feel uneasy, though, not having the homesite in view, but my curiosity pulled me on, fighting a winning battle with my reluctant other self.

A rabbit dashed from the bushes just ahead of me. I jumped backward, calling out, making a silly sound. Chase gave one loud yap and streaked after it. My knees quaked. My heart tripped. My, aren't we brave, I taunted, retaining just enough courage to forge ahead. I came to the sign, and read it. So that's where I am? Not in Red Hill, but in Peace County, Montana. County Road 19. OUR Ranch. I liked the sound of all of it, and repeated it several times.

I turned on a heel and headed back toward the driveway. Chase was at my side again, having lost interest in his quarry. I felt good then, really good. I felt like running. I felt like singing and shouting. I danced one full

circle and glanced up in the trees. Jays had begun to
screech at us from their lofty perches, then followed us up
the driveway, stirring other birds along the way. "Well,
protest all you want," I called to them, "I'm here to stay, at
least for awhile." But the jays just flew to higher elevations.

When we reached the dooryard, I saw Jed working
about the hay barn entrance. Chase left me then, bounding
to Jed's side, but all the time seeming to keep half an eye
on the birds. And I returned to the house in time to start
supper.

Diane had been buoyant since the party, digging into
her assignments with vigor and finishing many of them
ahead of schedule. Then Mary or I would find time to play
games, or watch her paint, or just plain talk. I felt comfortable in my relationship with Diane, and told Mary so.
She seemed especially pleased, and to me, the household
fairly hummed.

That evening Mary offered to play Scrabble with
Diane, so I retired early to my room to write long-overdue
postcards to my family, and Dorrie, and—John.

When I'd finished writing, I went into the bathroom.
Diane's room was quiet. I picked up my toothbrush and
began to squeeze the paste. Then I heard her voice, rising
several octaves.

"Well, you just can't make things happen, Aunt Mary.
You're not Peter Pan. And wishbones and first stars and all
that stuff doesn't mean anything. So just don't . . ." Her
voice faded.

I could hear Mary's then. "But, honey, I was . . ." Then her voice faded, too. I felt uncomfortable, almost guilty to have heard, but it'd been impossible not to have listened.

Was it an argument? Well, Diane sure sounded agitated. Oh, well, don't wonder, Charlotte, if it concerns you they will say so.

I was just about to drift off to sleep when a curious little voice within asked, "Isn't it strange, though, Diane raising her voice to her Aunt Mary?" I lay awake for a long time.

＊

Morning dawned especially clear. When Jed came in for his breakfast, he said the cool, early air was invigorating, and he pounded his chest with his fists and grinned. Jed's smile always brought joy to the day, no matter what the hour.

Mary had been in to tend Diane earlier, but when I took her breakfast tray to her, she seemed to be in a rather pensive mood. She looked beautiful, though fragile and somewhat vulnerable. The ugly casts were so visible; I wanted to cry for her entrapment. It's damn unfair, I thought, to ground a young fledgling so.

The curtains had been opened wide to the east, and I tried to make small talk about the treetops in the valley. They were shimmering in the morning breeze, their greens now turning to yellows and golds. I told her I could see lovely damsels dancing and leaping with abandon, pirouetting on tiptoe across the trees' cushiony crowns. I stretched my imagination beyond its self, but she would have none of it.

Well, people confined to bed do have their picky moments, I thought, remembering my father in his last months. Yes, I was well aware of that.

Later, during her bath, she still seemed cool and distant. "Cheer up, Diane, isn't this the day your father's coming home?" I had hoped to strike some kind of responsive cord in the girl. And I did.

"Yes. Yes, it is." She brightened considerably. Even a hint of a smile played about her mouth. I had my back to her when I heard her say, "Aunt Mary is a meddler." The words were low and soft; I did not hear more.

Reacting on impulse, I turned. "What, dear?"

"Oh. Nothing," she said, irritation beyond doubt in her voice.

Let it be, Charlotte, I warned, and promptly settled her into her lessons for the morning.

I was preparing dinner when I saw the jeep come up the drive, Andy at the wheel, and it circled the dooryard, stopping by the path. A tall, lithe figure leaped out and hurried to the porch. I knew Dan Garner was coming home this day, but I was not prepared for the actual happening. Instantly, I suffered a shortness of breath and my hands clutched at the opening of my shirt collar. Lord, Charlotte, relax, it's just your employer.

Mary had seen the jeep, too, and rushed to the door of the kitchen, pulling it wide open. A broad-shouldered man strode through the doorway, blocking out most of the day-light. "Hi, Sis." His voice boomed in the still of the kitchen. And then, he hugged her, picking her up and whirling her around one full circle. It caused his hat to fly from his head.

I stood like a pillar, waiting. It happened fast. "Oh, Dan, I'd like you to meet Charlotte. Charlotte Foster, that is." She had to wait for breath. "It's just wonderful having her here. She came last Wednesday. Remember I told you, the one from Minnesota." She took his arm and pulled him close to me.

I put out my hand. "How do you do?" I said, deter-mined to act with utmost poise. He took it, then, and I looked into the bluest eyes I had yet to see. I wanted to turn away, but it was not to happen. Again, I was a pillar.

"I'm Dan Garner. Welcome. Welcome to our home." He cocked his head to one side, sizing me, I reasoned. "Mary said she had a surprise for me, and, darned, if she wasn't right." He smiled and the smile grew bigger and bigger, but the—no words had come with a simple sincerity.

A little uncomfortable, I glanced to Mary. She stood motionless, beaming, her eyes shining like beacons. I was puzzled by the extend of her excitement. What is it, Mary? Let *me* in on it.

I stepped back, observing the man whose presence seemed to fill the entire room. He was wearing a tan rawhide jacket, which he quickly shed, then, picking his hat from the floor, he hung them both on the pegged rack. He gave his boots an extra shuffle on the big, rough rug by the door. "And how's my baby been doing?" He walked across the kitchen floor, but his footsteps told me he ran down the hallway to Diane's door. I heard a giggle, then a loud squeal, and then—silence. He must have been hugging the breath from her. Mary looked at me and I saw a glisten in her eyes, and my heart filled with joy at the reunion.

We'd set the big table near the bay window. Andy came into the house carrying one of Dan's bags, and Jed followed with the other. Both men had their shirts tucked in smoothly and their hair newly brushed. They sat at the table, waiting, faces eager as school boys. Dan joined them before too long.

Mary had arranged a huge platter with roast beef and vegetables and asked me to serve it. Suddenly I felt clumsy and feared I might spill it. I visualized the food sliding off the dish. I began to perspire. What ails you, Charlotte? You've always been competent enough, especially in the kitchen. I managed the heavy platter to the table. Then Mary asked me to slice more bread while she finished mixing the salad. Everything was a little disorganized, what with all the excitement of the homecoming.

I placed the basket of bread on the table and returned to Mary's side. "Anything else?"

"That, too," she said, pointing to the coffee carafe.

I turned slowly with it in my hand and saw Dan Garner looking squarely at me, while trying, at the same time, to butter a slice of bread. Quickly, I diverted my eyes to the table, but, too late, I felt the heat rise to my cheeks as I placed the carafe. Lord, I thought, I must be scarlet. Really, Charlotte, no need to act like a blushing schoolgirl just because the man is handsome. Mary and I seated ourselves across from the men, and, thankfully, I was opposite Jed. But I still felt the need to keep my eyes on my plate.

The men ate their big noon meal with gusto and talked of many things. Between bites and sips, I made out snatches of conversation: "Round-up next week . . . Jack Colby and his men . . . help them first . . . trucks all arranged . . . hope the weather holds . . . those chestnuts ready, Andy?"

"Yep," Andy replied, "they're in good shape. By the way, Diane told me she named them Larry, Curly, and Moe." Laughter rolled around the table.

Dinner over, the men departed, and Mary and I cleared the table. The big platter was empty. "So, looks like the roundup is next week," Mary said, "you'll have plenty of cooking to do to fill those men. Oh, but I hate to leave, round-ups are so exciting."

"Oh, I'm—I'm sure they are."

"Now, now, Charlotte, don't you worry about a thing. You'll do just fine. Helen is coming to help, remember?"

Yes, Helen is coming, I thought. It has to be.

That night as I laid in bed, I pictured, in a parade, the new people I'd met. There was Mary, Andy, Diane, Helen, Jed, and Joanne. The school people and the girls' friends.

Even Chase and Patches entered the parade. But they all seemed rather obscure when compared to Dan Garner. Those eyes, I thought, they're as blue as the fringy bachelor buttons in Mrs. Nelson's garden. Sleep came tumbling in, but, oh, how I wanted to hug Mrs. Nelson just then.

CHAPTER 15

My alarm clock roused me, and within minutes I was headed toward the kitchen. Mary was standing by the sink as I entered, her hands clasped together at her breast. "Oh, Charlotte, it's so good having Dan back home again." She was wearing a bright red, paisley caftan and her hair was done up in the usual tight twist. She looked striking, almost regal—and quite authoritative, too.

I think I stared. "Good morning, Mary. I'm sorry, but what was it you said?"

"Oh, I just meant I want to make Dan's breakfast for him—one last time," she said, with an air of possessiveness. "He's going to eat with Diane this morning." Then, in a low whisper, she added, "She'll find any reason to be near him. But he enjoys it as well, I know."

"Oh, I think that's really nice." I was trying to keep atune to her early morning exuberance. "But tell me, please, if I can help you."

"No, no, dear," she said, ushering me away. "Sit. Have your coffee."

I went to take up my morning station near the bay
window where I could watch the early rays of sunshine
creep up the hills and head for the mountains in the distance. But this morning the skies had clouded, creating a
dismal scene in all directions. It surprised me, and saddened
me a little, too. I poured a cup of coffee and watched the
steam as it rose from the surface, curling and twisting and
disappearing into the air of Mary's fragrant kitchen.

Then I looked to the little thermometer just outside
the window. Thirty-eight degrees. I gazed beyond and
watched the wind sway the naked aspens between the
barns, while a few dried weeds scampered across the driveway, then rolled out of sight. Beyond the corral a patch of
meadow was now as browned as the hills. Oh, it won't be
too long, I thought, before snow will come. I shivered just
thinking of it. My hands crept around my mug of coffee,
allowing the warmth to seep into my bones, and I sipped it
slowly, savoring every drop.

"Those two stayed up quite late last night," Mary
called, above the spattery noise of bacon frying. "Diane
wanted to hear all about her cousins and the old homestead. It's way up in northern Idaho, and she hasn't been
able to visit up there in a long time."

"Well, sis, we intend to find more time for things like
that from now on." Dan had appeared in the doorway of
the hall. Suddenly he turned to me, saying, "Oh, good
morning, Charlotte—if I may call you that?" His eyes
brightened as he spoke.

"Please do," I said, without hesitation.

"It's a nice name. It was my first grade teacher's name and I'll never forget it, I guess. She made quite an impression on me." A shy smile appeared, giving his face a boyish look. "She read lots of books to us."

"Yes, that would be impressive, I suppose." I smiled too and our eyes met, but only for a moment.

Then, his smile turned into a grin and spread across his ruggedly handsome features. I could observe him clearly now, not like in yesterday's rushed excitement. His was a face roughened by the weather, the forehead holding more than its share of worry lines. And he had a fine head of dark brown, wavy hair, quite recently barbered. It went well with his clean-shaven jaw—a jaw perhaps a bit more jutting than a handsome man's jaw should be. He was wearing a faded gray shirt and it softened the blue of his eyes, I noticed, when our eyes met once again—without plan. And Lord, he looked at me this time longer than was comfortable before he turned to Mary.

"Oh, let me," he said, stepping to her and taking a steaming tray from her hands. Then she picked up a smaller one and the two disappeared into the hallway.

The very moment they were out of sight I felt a void in the room. I sipped my coffee and stared into the depths of the mug. I knew I was smiling, yet curiously, I was asking myself "Why?" A bit confused, I started to rise.

Mary came back into the kitchen. "Stay right where you are, Charlotte, I have everything ready." She soon put a

plate of scrambled eggs and bacon before me, then placed
another for herself.

"Oh, thank you," I said, "but you shouldn't . . ."

"Hush now. You'll have plenty to do once I'm gone."

"I suppose. But, Mary, we're sure going to miss you."

"And I'm going to miss this family more than you
know." Mary dawdled with her food. She sipped her juice.
"I worry so much about them." She glanced out the
window while inadvertently fidgeting with her rings.
"Dan's a fine man, Charlotte," she said, "He loves his girls
and this ranch very much." Then she looked up, squarely at
me, and reached across the table and squeezed my wrist.
"But—well, he needs something more than that to
be—ah—complete." She was stumbling for words, her face
sober. "Maybe love will find a way." She looked at me then
with begging eyes.

"What?" I straightened in my chair. "Oh, no, Mary.
No, I didn't come here with any intentions like *that*." I
had burst out in a coarse whisper, terrified I may be over-
heard. "I needed a change in my life, and it sounded like
this girl needed me in return." Now I began to stumble
for words. "It seemed just right—ah—for the time—for
my situation." Then I blurted out rather loudly, "You see,
I expect to be in California with my family for
Christmas." I turned and looked out the window and fastened my eyes on the corral fence. Why am I explaining
this to Mary? How dare she . . . ?

"I'm sorry, dear. Oh, I really am sorry," Mary said, her voice thin and high. "But you can't fault me for trying." She bit her bottom lip and shook her head side to side. "That's me all the time. I just plunge right into things—like the girls' party—and then hope for the best. And, well, your resume sounded so ideal. I was hoping once you'd come . . ." It sounded like she was about to cry.

But I glared at her. Am I hearing her right? Did I walk into some kind of trap?

"Please forgive me, Charlotte. I'm truly sorry if I—I offended you." Her voice faltered and she rubbed and patted my hand.

It was an awkward situation. Damnit, I liked Mary Kane. She meant no harm; she couldn't have. She just couldn't.

"Mary, of course I forgive you." My free hand went over hers. "But you must understand why I came here." I felt a little like a pawn in a life-sized game of chess. My plate of food sat half-eaten. My coffee had lost its appeal.

I drew my hand away, but she touched it again. "No hard feelings, please?"

She meant no real offense to me, I assured myself, it was just wishful thinking. Lord, I couldn't blame her for wanting to see her brother remarry. "No. No hard feelings, Mary." I smiled to her, but it was a wan smile, to be sure. I got to my feet and began to clear the table.

Mary rose, too. "Let's pretend it never happened," she said, her voice timid.

I looked at her and saw a worried soul. I put both my hands up in front of me. "Okay, Mary, it never happened."

She threw her arms around me and hugged me hard. "I'd better pack," she said quickly, then pushed me aside and hurried to her room.

My irritation began to leave me and I started to giggle. It was all too comical to be true. Just what did that woman expect me to do? Flirt? Seduce? How preposterous!

I must have still had a hint of a smile on my face when Dan returned to the kitchen with the empty trays. "You're sure happy for such a gloomy day, Charlotte. What's your secret?"

I reached for the trays, avoiding his eyes as best I could. "Nothing. Ah, nothing, really." I wheeled around, my back to him then. Must I always get this scarlet feeling? My mind whirred with possible answers. "Oh, it was—ah—just a silly story one of the girls told last weekend."

"Good. You'll have to tell it to me sometime," he said, as he disappeared into his dressing room.

When he returned he was wearing a dark brown sheepskin-lined leather jacket and a wide-brimmed hat, curled smartly upward at the sides, and adorned with small, vividly colored feathers stuck all around in the band. It was quite attractive; decidedly unusual.

Oh, well, I thought, I suppose that's just what the well dressed rancher might wear. I realized then I was still a bit annoyed with Mary. She must think he's a real prize catch. Hah, Miss Matchmaker Mary. Well, now, Charlotte, it's not Dan's fault.

Then later, from the sink window, I watched him as he walked in long strides to the barn, carrying himself with a deliberate sureness. Jed was coming out of the horse barn, and Dan beckoned to him. Then I spun around and leaned against the sink, furious at myself for watching him so closely.

Mary came back into the kitchen and poured herself a cup of coffee. "It's such a chore to pack, but it's easier going home," she said. "Oh, well, just so it all gets stuffed in there." She laughed. Then, with her full cup, she left the room again. However, I did sense an uneasiness in her voice. Yes, I believe she's trying to mend a bridge.

Seconds later I heard the tinkling of Diane's bell. It surprised me. Up until now, she hadn't had to use it at all. I hurried to her room. "What can I do for you, Diane?"

"I need those notebooks. The ones over there on the desk." She seemed to be glowering at me. Oh-oh. Something was really irritating her.

"Will you need a pen or pencil?" I started rummaging for one.

"No!" she shouted at me. "I'll ring again if I do."

Poor darling, I thought, did she hear the voices and laughter from the kitchen? If she only knew the reason for the commotion. But she couldn't have heard. Something else was bothering her. Maybe her difference with her aunt last night. Sure. That's it.

So, I was really glad when Mary insisted on helping Diane with her morning routine. And she'd even helped her set up all her painting materials, Mary'd told me later when she'd come from her room.

I was pleased that I'd been the one to make Jed's breakfast. He was later than usual coming in that morning, but we chatted the entire time he was in the kitchen, about the horses, the pending round-up, and, of course—the weather. The clouds were thickening, adding just one more annoyance for the time. But at least Jed's smile when he left the house helped lift my spirits some.

I tidied the entire kitchen and even mopped the floor and shook the rug. When I finished I poured myself a cup of coffee and sat by the bay window and studied the curtains. Plenty of time to get to them, I thought, so I began reviewing a long list of notes Mary'd prepared for me. Lord, I'll soon be on my own; Mary is leaving tomorrow. I'd realized many times what a big responsibility I'd undertaken, but now I felt a real measure of apprehension. The heavy clouds that had formed seemed to be pressing down on me.

Don't worry, Charlotte, a voice reminded, Helen is coming to help. But the voice was Mary's voice reassuring me.

It was a crystal dawn the morning of Mary's departure. All the clouds had blown away, like a gift from the Montana winds. The sunlight had climbed the hills and was beginning to glisten the mountains. There was a tension in the house, though. Everyone seemed happy, yet the air was charged with an expectancy that almost hurt. Now it was Mary's bags lined by the kitchen door, and I heard the growl of the stationwagon as it was moved up to the path. I stood in the middle of the floor, not knowing quite what to do, twisting my hands together and taking nervous breaths.

Suddenly Mary breezed into the kitchen holding out two necklaces in her hands. "Which one do you like best, Charlotte?"

Assuming she meant for me to choose the one she should wear, I said, "Oh, the amber and green one. It's beautiful."

"Good," she said, "I want you to have it, a little remembrance from me." She popped the long string of sparkling beads around my neck.

"Oh, no." She had mended the bridge. "Well, thank you," I said, my hands fingering them with surprise.

"Yes." She stepped back. "Yes, they're just right for you. They do things for your eyes."

Suddenly Dan was in the room, the outer door closing swiftly behind him. "Yeah, that they do," he said. A huge smile broke across his face, minimizing his ample jaw. And his eyes danced blue.

It had all taken me quite by surprise and I felt embarrassed, not used to being singled out for attention such as that. Thankfully, it didn't last long.

Dan turned to Mary. "Ready, Sis?"

"I'll just be a minute," she said, and hurried down the hall to Diane's room.

I removed the string from around my neck, allowing my fingers to feel the many facets of the beads. I laid them on the table, then, realizing with a start that I was only marking time until Mary would return. Why was I allowing myself to be so bothered by the presence of my employer in the same quiet room? Where if your poise *now,* Charlotte? I taunted.

At once Mary was before me and I let go a deep sigh. Then I saw her eyes. Shiny teardrops oozed from the corners, but she quickly blinked them away. Her eyes brightened then as she put both hands on my shoulders and shook me gently and smiled. "Take care, dear, I'm counting on you." She hugged me then, but, while she patted me on the back, she whispered in an authoritative manner, "Give it a thought, though, anyway, Charlotte." She dropped her arms, stepped back, and looked me straight in the eye. This time, she winked.

"Goodbye, Mary. It's been so nice knowing you." But what I really wanted to say was, "Darn you, woman, you really did irritate me. Well, it was a silly notion you had, luckily, no one suspects." I backed away and smiled. "Take good care and have a safe trip." Mary Kane passed through the door and on out of the house at OUR Ranch.

Dan stopped in front of me then, Mary's bags in either hand, and fixed his gaze on me. "Well, you're on your own today, just you and Di. 'Course, Jed's around. Give him a holler if you need anything. I'll be back home around six—with Jo."

I looked up into his eyes as he spoke and became enveloped in a wrap of warmth. "Yes. Yes, I will." I held the door open wide as he passed through—so near to me. "Goodbye Dan," I said, my voice so low I hardly felt the words leave my lips. I closed the door with a firm hand, yet leaned against it for a few seconds.

Soon Chase let out several loud barks, then the engine's roar told me they were gone.

I rushed to the bay window just in time to catch a glimpse of the wagon as it rolled down the hill. Goodbye Mary. Mary, the matchmaker, I thought. I giggled to myself. Yes, I'll just pretend the whole episode never ever happened. I shrugged and walked unhurriedly to Diane's room.

❦[CHAPTER 16]❧

I tapped on Diane's door and heard a soft, "Yes?"

"It's just me," I said, entering the room. She was holding the little glass ball of dried flowers I'd given her when I'd first come.

"Oh!" she said, in a most disconcerting way, and quickly placed the ball on her bedside table.

"Well, shall we start the bath?"

"Yeah, I s'pose."

So, we went through almost the complete morning routine hardly speaking, and when we did it was in a too-polite a manner. At last, toward the end of the ritual, she began to brighten. "Ah—could you help me—ah—write a story?" It sounded like it was a real chore for her to ask. "I have to write a story that's supposed to be really exciting, or thrilling, they said. It has to have lots of action, you know—verbs."

"Hm-m-m," was all I replied, then waited. That's it, I thought, she needs extra help with her schoolwork.

"I just can't think of a thing, nothing exciting ever happens around here."

"Well, you could have written about your party last weekend." I laughed, attempting to be cheerful. "There must have been plenty of action by the decibel levels I heard coming from the dining room."

"That's not quite what they mean." She laughed too then. "It should be like an adventure, or something like that."

"Actually, now, I do have a story for you. At least my home town newspaper thought so." The bath and shampoo finished, I began to plait her damp hair, this time in French braids, and proceeded to tell her the entire story about the night when the big storm struck Spencer, Minnesota.

After Kenny had called me that evening, I'd gone back out on the porch to the rocking chair. I had a lot of thinking to do. The air was cooling a little and it felt good on my shoulders, bared by an old, yellow sundress.

Moments later a gust of wind ballooned my skirt and tumbled the pot of begonias I'd just watered right off the table next to me. Then a long, thin bolt of white lightning cracked the sky and thunder boomed. I grabbed the newspaper I'd had in my lap and dashed in the door just as leaves and twigs came sailing across the porch. I bolted the door behind me.

After rushing around shutting windows, I went to the couch in the living room. I sat down and shivered, unconsciously groping for the afghan that should have been there. I remembered. It'd been wrapped around my little dog for several weeks already. Habits are hard to lose.

I found an old sweater in the hall closet and slipped into it. I felt better. Let the storm rage, I thought. No, John, I don't think I need to go to the basement—the radio never warned of tornados. I tried to read the newspaper. Keep the mind occupied, Mother would always say.

I turned to the want-ad section to check on an ad I'd placed for some of my father's old things, but soon I was reading the help wanted section.

"And there was your Aunt Mary's ad, Diane. The bold print jumped right out at me. URGENT: NEED WOMAN TO ASSIST FAMILY." I remembered the rest of it then: temporary, must have nursing skills, housekeeping, driving, like animals. Send complete resume, references and picture to Box 18, Red Hill, Montana. Will reply by phone. "And that's how I came to be here now. If it had not been for the storm, I would never have read the paper that night." I continued to comb and part and braid her hair.

"So then what happened?" Diane asked in short breaths. "How bad was it?"

"Bad," I answered, and went on with the story.

Lightning slashed the sky, thunder rattled every door and window in the house, and rain pounded on the roof and gushed through the gutters and downspouts with a roar. Then suddenly one fierce bolt lit the evening sky like daylight. Its thunder was immediate. The hair on my arms bristled. I jumped to my feet and cautiously moved to the big window that looked out across the front porch and on to the lawn. Then I heard a howl of a wind and an ear-splitting crack. I wished then I'd gone to the basement. In the new lightning flashes I saw a big limb from the maple tree lying on the front lawn, the flagpole bent under it. And before my mind could even grasp that scene, the hanging basket of petunias that had been swinging from a hook in the porch ceiling broke loose and came crashing against the window, creating a huge star in the pane. I know I screamed and clutched myself.

Then, so quickly, the lightning ceased, the thunder quieted, and the rain became a patter. The storm was over. I'd become quite numb.

After a time, I prowled about the house, searching out windows, assessing any damage I might see. The corner streetlight shone on the front lawn, revealing a dark destruction. Well, at least we still have power, I thought, but with that, all the lights in the neighborhood went out.

The cloud-blackened sky began to turn a deep purplish-blue, with the last rays of a sinking sun forcing its way through thinner clouds, creating streaks of pink and violet. It was both beautiful and scary at the same time, and I kept thinking, God, how I hate to be alone. Moments later it was dark. Completely dark. I wanted to cry out, but felt it despairingly useless.

Candles. I'll get candles. I worked my way to the kitchen. I'm so thirsty. I'm glad I made lemonade this morning. I groped about for a tumbler. There's one on the sink, I thought, I'll use that one. I found it.

I wondered how Mrs. Nelson was faring in all this. I glanced out the sink window. A peculiar orange light filled her living room windows. Strange, flickering light. Flames! Eating the edges of her drapes. Fire! Oh, God, her house is on fire!

Upon relating that, I fumbled and stopped braiding Diane's hair. The comb fell to the floor.

She bolted upright in bed and her hand caught my wrist, her eyes huge. "Then what happened?"

"Well, I just stared for a few seconds, not believing what I saw." I told her then how I burst out my back door and raced across the lawn, through the row of evergreens, their branches ripping at my arms. I ran through her flower garden, where the rain had turned the beds to mud, and it sucked the shoes from my feet. But I ran on; I had to find Mrs. Nelson. Actually I knew her house as my own. Luckily the fire seemed to be only in the front part, in the living room.

I jerked open the screen door and turned the knob. The door opened. (She never did have the habit of locking them.) Smoke billowed over me. I dropped to the floor where the air was better, the acrid fumes tearing at my lungs. The heat stung my eyes. I didn't care; I had to find her. I knew her bedroom was in the back part of the house, far from the living room, and that she was a heavy sleeper who always retired early.

I squeezed my eyes shut and crawled across the linoleum floor. Then I touched her; I had touched her body on the kitchen floor. She *had* tried to escape.

I grabbed her arms and pulled. She didn't budge; she
was too heavy for me. There were crackling, popping
noises near me. Then I heard a choking sound. She's alive!
Dear God, she's alive. Desperation gave me strength and I
could inch her body along as I moved backward across the
floor. With my foot I felt the open door behind me. Standing
then, half stooped, I clasped my arms under hers and pulled
her out the door. We tumbled down the three steps of the
porch and lay in a heap.

She's breathing! Lord, I think she *is* breathing. I pushed
her off me and struggled to my feet. Shut the door! Smoke
was pouring out like a ghost in the night. Shut the door, I
thought, save her house if you can. I stumbled up the steps
and slammed the door, but pain flashed in my ankle and I
fell back down the flight of steps again. I sat up, dazed.
Go. Go. I hurt. Go. Keep going.

Managing a good grip under her arms, and, all the while
on my knees, I pulled and dragged her across her front
lawn and down the bank to the sidewalk. Lord, it was dark.
I had to kind of sense where I was. For a moment I lay
back and rested on the grass, thickly soft and cool.

Now she isn't breathing! My God, give her mouth-to-
mouth. Help! We need help. *I* need help! I don't think I
can do this alone. I wanted to wail.

"Oh, Diane, never in my life did I ever believe I'd use
those Red Cross lessons I'd taken." I stood motionless.

"Go on. Go on," she urged.

"Well, I worked and worked on her, forcing the words of the instructor over and over in my mind."

Tires screeched. Help's coming, thank God. A wave of relief pulsed through me. Two men appeared, barely visible in the faint glow of their car lights. Then an orange sheen from the fiery windows touched their faces. They looked like an apparition.

"The phone. The phone," I yelled, pointing, "my house—on the kitchen counter." One man rushed away while the other put me aside and continued the resuscitation. Moments later Mrs. Nelson began to thrash about, gasping for air. She started to breathe on her own then, in long, raspy waves.

"It sounded so good, Diane. Oh, it was wonderful."

"Then you saved her? You really saved her?" Diane's eyes were huge. She'd let go of my wrist, but grabbed it again.

I patted her hand. "Yes," I said, "yes, I guess I did."

I told her the rest of the story then, how I'd heard all the sirens—glorious sirens: police, fire, ambulance. And all of a sudden John was there and he put his arms around me, and, oh, it felt so good. I was beside myself with relief.

"John? Who's John?" Diane scowled, her eyes penetrating.

"Oh, just a friend, a neighbor, really." I abruptly turned my back; I'd felt the story ended.

"So, what did the newspaper say?" Diane wanted more facts.

"Oh, they sent a photographer out the next day.

Actually, it was a young man named Rod Price, the same man who'd bought our clinic building behind our house. So, of course, he had to take my picture and it ended up on the front page of our local paper. And the fire chief is to give me some kind of plaque at the fall festival. Hmmm, that's going to be in just a couple weeks now. Sorry, folks, I just can't make it." I grinned. Then Diane grinned, too, and I finished fixing her hair.

"So, did they save the lady's house?" I was glad she didn't ask more about John.

"Yes, in a way. But she didn't want to live there after that, so she went to live with her sister in the next town. A contractor bought the house and the day I left they were just beginning to gut it. They're going to rebuild it from the bottom up. She was sad about moving after all those years, but she knew it made more sense at her age to go live with her sister. They needed each other, really, and she didn't need that big house anymore. But I didn't think I could stand to have her move away. It was really sad."

"But weren't you sad to leave your house then?" she asked.

"Well, I thought I would be, but it's easier knowing I'll be back again before spring comes." I tilted my head and pursed my lips. "I really think, though, that that's what life is all about. Needs. People's needs."

"Yeah, I kind of know what you mean." She was quiet for a short time. "Well, you sure gave me some good ideas for a story. Guess I'd better get going with it." She had been reclining on her pillows and she sat up. "Oh, Charlotte, I'm not going to call you Auntie anymore. It's kind of childish. I never really wanted to, anyway."

"That's fine with me," I said. I piled all the things she would need for her task around her and moved to the door.

"Gosh, you were like a real hero, you know." It was like an afterthought.

I whirled around, facing her, and crinkled my nose before I left the room.

[CHAPTER 17]

The kitchen was silent, except for the humming of the fridge. No Mary, no Joanne, and—no Dan. At least Jed was somewhere out there.

I set about baking cookies, several kinds, and also preparing our noon meal. I tried to concentrate on the baking, but all the while my mind kept traveling back to the night of the fire. I thought now how all the events seemed to channel into one thing—my leaving Spencer, Minnesota.

I was glad Diane didn't ask any more about John, but I couldn't get him out of my mind. It seemed I just had to relive some of the last times with him.

Oh, he'd been very attentive from the moment he'd found me in Mrs. Nelson's yard. Seemingly out of nowhere he had knelt beside me. "Lottie, Lottie, honey, thank God you're alright." He had taken me in his arms. "I called and called. I just knew something was wrong."

"Oh, John, it was awful." I could hardly get the words out. He held me tight in his arms, stroking my hair, my face hidden in the curve of his neck.

The medics swarmed around us then, hustling me onto a stretcher. John had assured me that Mrs. Nelson was already in the ambulance, so I loosened the grip on his hand. He brushed the hair from my forehead and leaned close. "I'll be following in my car, Lottie—I'll be near."

I was relieved that, after an x-ray, the doctor said I only had a severely strained ankle, nothing worse. "Ice it, and I'll give you something for the pain," he'd said. And, before I left the hospital, I'd even spoken a few words with Mrs. Nelson, who was breathing now quite well on her own.

John drove me home through the darkened streets, his headlights picking up the clutter of twigs and branches and limbs. I snuggled close to him and he patted my hand. The stars, now tiny silvery specks, freckled the jet-black sky. The car's windows were lowered and cooling breezes played across my tangled, damp hair and glued some strands to my cheek. I brushed them off. Suddenly it seemed so romantic. I pressed even closer to John, wanting more assurance of his presence beside me.

The air smelled of raw wood, newly-split and twisted open by the anger of the winds. I breathed deeply, liking the odor—until we reached my street. I choked and shuddered; the air was reeking with smoke. Firemen hurried about. I turned my head away; I couldn't look at Mrs. Nelson's house. A lump filled my throat, hurting so I couldn't talk, either.

John didn't notice. He drove his car into the back driveway and up to the screened porch. It was awkward having to have him help me up the steps and into the house, but the pain was too much for me to bear walking on my own. I thought for a second the comfort of the wheelchair at the hospital, how good it felt.

Once in my living room, though, John eased me onto the couch, pulled up the ottoman and tenderly lifted my swollen ankle to rest upon it. He sat down beside me then, and took me in his arms, rocking me, slowly, gently, smoothing my hair and saying, "Lottie, Lottie, we've had such a scare." He kissed my temple, then proceeded to track light kisses all across my forehead. It felt wonderful. He cares. He truly cares, I thought. Its so nice to have someone who truly cares.

I shivered with a chill then, and waited for a sneeze, but it wouldn't come. "Well, look at you, still in this wet dress. Come on, let's get you out of it." He pulled me to my feet and helped me to the bathroom. I cried out several times on the way. "Next we'll put some ice on that big ankle."

"Yes, we should, I guess. Oh, John, there's a white terry robe on the inside of my bedroom door. Will you get it for me, please?"

Once in the bathroom, I closed the door and sloshed water on my face and wiped the mud from my legs, all the while letting my clothes, one by one, drop to the floor. The bathroom air had cooled and I felt goose bumps raise over my entire body. I quickly wrapped a towel about me.

When John tapped on the door I only opened it a crack. I expected a bit of teasing. What an opportunity,

John. But the robe was pushed through the crack and I heard his footsteps move away. That's John, I thought, always the perfect gentleman. I pursed my lips. Damn his perfection, anyway.

I slipped into the soft terry and snugged the sash at my waist.

My feet were bare and I saw then the swelling grotesquely misshaping my ankle. I winced and hobbled out of the bathroom.

John was in the kitchen looking out the window at Mrs. Nelson's house. He rushed to me. "Gosh, Lottie," he said, "the place is still smoldering." I didn't want to look then, either.

He helped me back to the couch, making me comfortable and packing ice about my ankle. It was throbbing. I took the pills the doctor had given me, and before long the pain eased somewhat. I let my head fall to the back of the couch. John sat down next to me and quickly put an arm about my shoulder, drawing my head to him. His hand slowly cupped my chin and I looked up to him. He kissed me and it was light and sweet and lingering. Musk cologne; always musk cologne. I'd grown to know it. I wanted to cry again then, but not from pain. Oh, John, darling, am I falling in love with you? Then I did cry—just a little.

Slowly he took his arms from me, pulling in a deep breath. "This is just hindsight, honey, but you really should have called for help before you ran over to that burning

house. You could have gotten yourself into a lot of trouble."
He looked at me unblinkingly.

"I know, I know." His sudden patronizing irked me.
"But all I could think of was making sure she was out of
there." I pulled away from him. "John," I asked quietly,
"would you call Dorrie for me? Maybe she'll spend the
night with me."

"Of course." But just as he started to get up, the phone
rang. "She heard you." He grinned at me then.

"Sure," I said. Sure, now you can grin.

He went to the kitchen. I could hear. "Hello? Oh,
Dorrie, I was just going to call you. Lottie has a problem.
She thought . . . You know? Of course, your husband runs
the newspaper." He listened. "Thanks," he said and hung
up the phone. He walked back to the couch. "She'll be over
in ten minutes."

I was so thankful to have a friend like Dorrie; everyone
should have a friend like Dorrie.

My mind had drifted for a long time and I was startled
to see movement out the window. The barn door had
opened and Jed stepped through and walked toward the
house, Chase at his side like a shadow. My thoughts were
catapulted back to the present. It was dinnertime.

{CHAPTER 18}

I had just finished taking the last pan of cookies from the oven and putting them on a cooling rack when Jed came in for his dinner. "Sure smells right good in here, Miz Foster," he said, and grinned until his eyes crinkled at their corners.

"Thanks, Jed, you just made my day." I smiled, feeling the joy of accomplishment.

After I'd served Diane, Jed and I had a leisurely meal. I sat in the booth with him and we talked of a wide variety of subjects about ranch life. He could make it all sound so exciting. And of course, I had a lot of questions.

When he was about to leave, he offered to build a fire in the living room fireplace for me. "It'll help take the chill off the place. Gettin' a might cool out these days."

"That's a grand idea; you build it and I'll keep it going," I said.

After coaxing the fire to a lively blaze, he refilled the wood box from the cradle on the porch. A fresh, woodsy odor filled the rooms, mingling with the aroma of ginger cookies. Oh, it smelled so nice. And, when Jed left the house, I handed him a tin of cookies still warm from the oven. His smile could easily have been the largest ever in Peace County. He had that little-boy aura about him sometimes. It was hard to keep from giving him a big hug. I was becoming really fond of Jed Simpson.

As the afternoon wore on I began to feel an urgency. I was preparing a beef stew for our supper, with lots of onion. Mary's notes said Dan liked lots of onion and I wanted to get it just right. It was my first day alone on the job and my excitement was reaching a high level. Lord, I hope neither Diane nor Jed notice anything. I relaxed a little after serving them when I realized they hadn't commented on my shorter breaths. Maybe it's just all in your mind, Charlotte. Oh, I hope so.

I had set two places at the big table in the dining room in full view of the glowing hearth. Joanne will like the intimacy of being with her father near the fire, I thought. She hadn't been able to spend much time with him lately and it pleased me to think I could be accommodating.

I'd found a nice, old blue and white soup tureen on a high shelf and decided to serve the stew in it. And the kitchen bragged of freshly-baked biscuits, too. Oh, I felt so capable.

I spotted the stationwagon coming up the driveway and my heart seemed to stumble and stop for a moment. And it wouldn't behave, either, as I watched the wagon circle the dooryard and stop by the path. I did so want everything to be at its best.

Joanne came into the house first, dropping her books in the booth. Dan followed, looking a bit weary, but grinning. After the initial greetings and banter, Dan went directly to Diane's room. Joanne followed, but returned moments later. She pushed open the dining room's swinging door and gasped. I thought it was because she was so pleased. "Oh, no, Charlotte, you're to eat with us," I flushed; I never presumed to intrude on their privacy. Quickly, she added another place setting, then, when Dan came back, she helped me serve the meal.

Dan nodded a silent approval, his too-blue eyes becoming quite aware. I couldn't help but notice, as he seated himself at the head of the table facing the fire, glints of flame dancing in his eyes. Charlotte, you're making much too much of this moment.

After we'd taken our places I moved the tureen to Dan. He began to ladle out a portion. "Jo," he said, quite relaxed now, "I talked with Ben Cloud and we can get all our hay from him this fall. He has plenty." He turned to me. "That's Barbara's father."

"I see," I said. "Would you like a biscuit?"

"Oh, good," Joanne wedged in.

"Dandy stew, Charlotte," Dan said as he ate, "I like the onion."

"Thank you." I didn't look up; I just reveled in the satisfaction that my first day alone on the job had been a success.

"Oh, Dad, that reminds me," Joanne said, "Barbara told

me she met Cathy's uncle today." She glanced to me. "He's from Minnesota."

My attention perked. Quickly, I glanced from Joanne to Dan, holding my breath as unnoticeably as possible.

"H-m-m," was all Dan replied, his mouth filled with biscuit just then.

"He moved here. He's studying somewhere."

Minnesota? See, I thought, people do leave their home state once in a while—if they have good reason. Suddenly I didn't feel like a defector anymore, and it buoyed my spirits even higher.

After Dan finished his meal, he excused himself and carried his coffee with him to Diane's room. Joanne and I remained, nibbling ginger cookies for dessert.

Before long we heard an awful clatter. "Guess they're going to play chess tonight," Joanne said. She grinned and shrugged. "That is, after Dad picks up all the chessmen from the floor." She leaned close. "That's one of her favorite tricks, I think, spilling the games. That way Dad has to stay longer and give her a little more attention." She shrugged again. "You'll get to know Diane, but you may never understand her."

"Oh," I said simply. It wasn't a question. We got up then and cleared the table, taking everything back to the kitchen. Then I shooed her away with her armload of books, and began to fill the dishwasher.

I remembered Mary's words then, spoken to me during our ride from the airport, about Diane being able to command attention. Spilling games? Is that really one of her ploys? Does seem rather childish. Well, she is barely fifteen. Lord, I wonder how many more tricks she has in her bag?

After setting the kitchen in order, I fussed with a pretty red gelatin dessert while listening to the radio. The weather reports told of clear skies and mild temperatures, but predicted a progressively colder trend. Just how far away can winter be? I wondered about a different climate. Already Jed had warned me of sudden storms, cold and snowy, but then warming quickly by the mild Chinook winds that would sweep in. Well, not too different from Minnesota. No, we don't have many Chinooks, but we do have our Alberta clippers and they can bring an awfully cold sting. I shivered from the very thought of them now, although I'd long since taken them in stride.

About to leave the kitchen for the night, I peered out the bay window for one last inspection of the dooryard. Two big lights flooded the area, showing things in good detail. I looked to the bunkhouse. Jed's windows were dark. Dear, thoughtful Jed. I was suddenly filled with a deep concern. Are you lonely out there? It would be nice if Andy stayed more often.

People need friends; they shouldn't be alone. They need friends to talk to. I was lucky to have a friend like Dorrie, and I suddenly missed her very much. My thoughts flashed back to her then, and, in my mind's eye I saw her rushing into my house that night after the storm had passed. She was true to the ten minutes time she'd promised to be there. Garbed in a red tank top and wrinkled white shorts, her legs stretched beautifully long beneath them. And her hair was tied up at the nape of her neck with a black shoe-string.

As she entered the room she stopped and stared at me. "Well, you look like you're still in one piece. How's the ankle?"

"Hurts," I mumbled.

"Crimony, Lottie, your yard's a mess. So's the street. I'm sure Rod's busy tonight with his fancy camera, taking pictures in the dark." Dorrie hardly took the time to breathe. "Mrs. Nelson's house looks ghastly. Firemen're still there. Some people watching yet, too."

"I know," I said, biting my lip to hold back the tears.

"Our place is okay. How's yours, John?"

"Okay, too," he answered.

"Oh, it just reeks outside. What a horrid smell." She had sunk into Father's old recliner and propped her feet up on the support. She paused for only a moment. "Poor Jeff's going crazy trying to decide what to cover first."

"Simmer down, Dorrie, the worst is over," John said, "here, sit here," He rose from beside me on the couch. "I've got to go. Mama will be pacing the floor. Take care, Lottie, see you tomorrow." He leaned over and patted my hand, then made his way out the kitchen door. I heard his car start, shift gears and leave the back yard. I wasn't sure if I was sad or glad.

Dorrie came over and sat beside me. "Sure was a hot one today," she said, and pulled the shoelace, letting her hair fall about her shoulders. "But it's cooled off now. So, tell me, how did you hurt your ankle? Jeff said you fell somewhere."

We must have talked for almost an hour, going over everything I could remember. Dorrie got up then and went to the kitchen. Before long she returned with a tray holding mugs of hot chocolate and graham crackers. It smelled nice, like a candy shop. "Just something to help you sleep," she said. Then she muttered, "There's not one cookie in your whole kitchen. What kind of a house-keeper are you, anyway?"

"Oh, Dorrie," I said, my voice rising, "One of these days I'm going to bake one of the richest pans of brownies you've ever tasted, and they'll be just lumpy with walnuts, and I'll invite you over for tea. How's that?" It was like a threat.

"No, you won't." She pretended to pout. "You'll invite John, instead. I just know it."

"Why do you say that?" Then I played at being miffed.

"Well, he's here all the time as it is. Next, he'll be asking for your hand in marriage." She batted her eyes at me, but was calculating my every response.

I gave her a solid push and laughed. "No, not likely." What is this, anyway? First Kenny, then Dorrie? Why the sudden interest in my marital standing? I was a bit annoyed.

"Oh, I see him, kiddo, the way he looks at you."

"Really? Well . . ." I almost chuckled, but instead, I sti-fled a yawn. "We can talk more of this affair in the morning." I yawned again, this time one that could not be stifled.

Dorrie helped me to my bedroom, clucking and scurrying around, and generally acting like a mother hen. After I was comfortably tucked in, she walked across the hall. "How do you like the new wallpaper, Dor?" I had just finished papering my father's room a few days earlier, turning it into a sunny guest room. And Dorrie was to be my first guest.

She flipped on the light. "Well," she said, "I'd say it's—ah—fresh-as-a-daisy." She laughed and went on into the room where I'd just put on rolls and rolls of paper sprinkled with yellow and white daisies. I loved to hang paper; it was almost a hobby with me. I'd papered my room last spring, just before Father's condition worsened. It was covered now, floor to ceiling, with huge, pale blue morning glories, and lots of vines twining up and over faint brown fences.

Oh, I had enjoyed doing it, but lately the morning glories had seemed to be closing in on me, boring me, threatening me. At times I could hardly stand to stay in the room. I even thought of sleeping in the daisied room. Even re-wallpapering.

I lie in bed, then, the pain throbbing in my ankle every time I moved. Lie still. I can't. The morning glories were growing and growing and winding around the slats of the fence, searching upward, higher and higher, for something more. I ran my hands through my hair.

Suddenly Dorrie was in my doorway. "Sorry. Smart me, I didn't even bring a nightgown."

I started. "Oh! Yes, second drawer down." I laughed then.
"What's so funny?"

"My long nightgown—it should come almost to your
knees."

She opened the drawer, pulled out a gown, flipped it over
her shoulder and left the room. "I'll learn," she said, laughing,
too. I watched her cross the hall and disappear into the
room, remembering the year she'd been homecoming queen,
and I'd been so jealous of her tall, blonde beauty.

Oh, I was happy for her, all right, but it made me so
conscious of my being short, my mousy hair, and—my flat
chest. But then she made me feel good again with her comments such as, you've got such a cute nose, I like the way
you walk, or—you've got the lips a man would die for. Oh,
she could be so much fun. "Thanks, Dorrie, for coming
tonight," I called out.

I brimmed with thankfulness at having a friend like
Dorrie. And now, all of a sudden, I wanted desperately to
hug her again, like I'd done at the airport. Just once.

Wiping a tear that had slipped down my cheek, I
turned away from the bay window, leaving Jed to his night
of rest. Sometime soon, Jed, I've got to tell you about Dorrie.

It was good to relax in my room; it'd been a tremendously exciting day. I knew the chess game was still in
progress and I was content that Diane's disposition had
bettered itself. Now is a good time, I decided, to get at my
letter writing. I sent a birthday card I'd bought at Meadow

Grand to Mrs. Nelson. It had yellow-breasted birds on it, so I told her about the late afternoon we'd stopped to listen to their song. And I wrote a short letter to Kenny to tell him that the roundup would be soon.

Then I wrote a lengthy letter to Dorrie, writing as fast as I could. When I finished, I laid my head down on my arms and before long my thoughts led me to the morning after the storm—and fire. Dorrie had helped me bathe and dress. My ankle was an ugly shade of purple, and I had sore spots all over my entire body. "Crimony," Dorrie said, "you must have taken quite a tumble."

I didn't like to think about it. We'd made our way to the screen porch on the back of my house where we sipped coffee at a rusty old black iron table, enjoying the early, warming sun. Pepper used to lay in a spot of sun right at the bottom of the door. It hurt when I looked down at her space, empty now for several weeks.

A shadow passed over the sun spot and I looked up. A man was about to knock. "Yes?" I asked.

"Mrs. Foster," he said, "I'm from the Greater Ohio Insurance Company. Mind if I ask you some questions?"

We talked briefly and he thanked me for my quick action. It was the fire marshall's belief, he told me, the fire started when lightning hit the television antenna and traveled down to the set.

"I did hear one tremendous bolt," I said, "sounded like it was right on us."

"That must have been the culprit," he said, nodding,

"Well, thanks again. We'll have someone out here shortly to secure the place."

After he'd left, Dorrie went into my kitchen and I could hear rattling and clunking around. She kept up a running commentary through the open door: "Your coffee canister is almost empty. Oh, here's a new can. You should see all the people down on the sidewalk staring at Mrs. Nelson's house. And there's that nosey Bertha what's-her-name."

Yes, I thought, it must be a curious sight.

"Only three eggs left, kiddo, I'll have to scramble them. Wait, here's a smidgen of ham—in it goes." More rattling. "Little kids down there gawking, too. Mouths wide open. Hope they learn never to play with matches. I'm sure I heard that big bolt, too."

I'll never forget it, I thought, it left me almost deaf.

"I can't find any OJ in the freezer, I'll have to use this powdered stuff. How about that rain last night? For awhile I thought we were going to have to build an ark."

"I know."

"You're almost out of bread. I'll go to the store for you later on." More clunking.

Dear Dorrie. I enjoyed her monologue even though I sat feeling totally useless. When she came back out to the porch, I bolted upright. "Wow, Mrs. Carson, you *are* fantastic." She'd set a large tray before us. Orange juice in footed glasses. Buttered toast cut in dainty little pieces with a smooth dab of grape jelly in their middles. Golden mounds of egg with bits of pink ham peeking out here and there. And a pot of coffee, its steam spiraling upward. It smelled heavenly and at once I was starving.

She sat down opposite me. "Lucky Jeff, lucky Jeff," I teased. "Oh, it's so nice to be pampered." How many times had I pampered and never knew what it was like to be on the receiving end? Oh, but it was especially nice to be breakfasting with someone. Father, in his last mixed-up years, grumbled aloud whenever I had company, so it seemed improbable now that it should even be happening at all. Just that simple pleasure was enough to bring a lump to my throat. "Dorrie, I can't thank you enough . . ." I couldn't finish for the choking.

"Oh, you're welcome. Forget it." She waved my words aside. "Where's last night's paper? I've got to show you the drapes in the Sears ad. I just love them."

"Still in the living room, I guess."

She left, returning with the paper bundled in her arms. "It's all messed up," she said, and proceeded to put the pages in order.

But the want-ad section slipped to the floor. I reached it, immediately spying the URGENT ad from Red Hill, Montana that I had circled in green ink. "Read this." I said, and passed it to her.

She shot me a quizzical glance and pulled the paper close. I don't think I breathed the entire time she took to read it.

"What?" She plopped the paper on the table. "Are you serious?"

I nodded.

"Lottie!" She looked me straight in the eye. "Would you leave Spencer? And this house? Would you leave John?"

"Maybe." I eyed her defensively. "Well, I've been thinking about getting a job, and it doesn't have to be in Spencer, you know. Besides, it might do me good to get away."

"But—for how long? Oh, Lottie, I'd miss you too much."

"The ad says temporary."

"But what about John?"

"What do you mean—what about John? Oh, you think there's something really serious between us, don't you? No, Dorrie, we're just special friends."

"Oh, hah! Lottie Mae, he's in love with you."

"Well, he's never said so. No, we're just really good friends."

"But everyone expects the two of you to get married now—now that your father . . ." She hesitated.

"Now that I'm free, you mean? Well, what about him? He's still got Mama to look after." I paused for a moment. "No, I don't think I could handle something like that again for quite a while."

"Well, I guess we just thought you'd be—ah—good at it."

"No, no." I shook my head emphatically. "Don't get me wrong, Dor, John's a dear, sweet fellow. He's so nice to be with, so—ah—comfortable, like an old shoe." I smiled, feeling a little wistful. "I always look forward to seeing him, even the few minutes a day until he has to run home to Mama. But love? Well, I almost thought so last night for a couple minutes. Then something always happens and I don't feel like it anymore. He just doesn't make me—ah . . ." I fumbled for the right words. "Oh, well, time will tell, they say, or, like the song—*que sera sera.*" I looked at her directly, then smiled and shrugged.

"Well, if that's the way you really feel, go ahead and answer the ad—and see what happens." Dorrie sounded disappointed, even a little irritated. "There are jobs here too, you know. The nursing home ran an ad just last week."

"I know, but I think I'd like a change of scenery. Maybe I didn't let on, but I've always envied Lena her traveling and living all over the world. She's seen so much. She's lived such as exciting life." I looked down at my coffee cup. I want something different, I thought, I'm so tired of waking every morning and seeing those same blue morning glories staring at me, challenging me. That's what they'd seemed to be doing lately. Damn, was my fertile idea being trampled even before it had a chance to sprout?

The phone rang, interrupting our little debate, and Dorrie sprang to answer it.

I read the ad again, slowly, word for word, imagining possible new adventures. I've never even been to the South Dakota border, let alone Montana. Fly? Me? I'll have to; I'll have to get to California somehow. The thrill of just thinking about it all warmed my blood considerably, and I knew then I was nearing a decision.

Dorrie came back out to the porch with a fresh pot of coffee. "That was Jeff, he's coming over. Oh, I just called the hospital, Mrs. Nelson's gone home already—to her sister's."

"Oh, good." I sighed; I could hardly bear to consider her trauma.

I was glad when Jeff rapped on the screen door. Dorrie jumped up and let him in. "Hi, sweets," he said, and kissed her quickly—on the mouth. He was carrying a pair of crutches. "Hello, gimpy," he said, turning to me then, "I thought you might be able to use these." He leaned them against the table near me. "They were Patti's, when she broke her foot last summer, remember?" (Patti was their teenage daughter.)

"Yes, I do. Thanks, Jeff."

"What the hell were you trying to do last night, get yourself killed?" His voice boomed. "Boy, you'll do anything just to get your name in the paper, won't you?"

"Thanks again, Jeff." I pulled the crutches to me. "Now please shut up." We laughed. Jeff had a strange way of showing affection to anyone—except his wife.

Dorrie sat down and Jeff moved close to her. He rubbed the back of her neck. I could tell she liked it. Lord, John never touches me like that. It would be kind of nice if he did.

"I won't be home until about four, hon. I'm going out to Perkins' farm with Rod. He's sure doing a fine job with that camera. The farm was hit hard. Terrible." He shook his head. "Some animals hurt, some even killed. We sure could use Grant's Clinic now."

His words saddened me, though I know he didn't mean to do it. "Yes, I'm sure," I said. Then I got up to try the crutches. "They're just fine." I leaned on them, staring at the worn floor boards of our old porch, seeing the hundreds of feet that had passed over them in time. I was saddened a bit more.

I stole a look at Jeff and Dorrie. So happy. So—married. They still had two teenagers at home. Active family—so busy. I hated myself when I envied, but a mist came to my eyes, and I blinked.

It was as if Jeff could read my mind. "We understand, kid," he said.

"What're our kids doing?" Dorrie asked, as she got up and followed Jeff to the door.

"Patti's been sewing on that—that thing for school."

"Jeff, it's a hobo bag. Girls just have to have one."

"And Mike's still eating. Does he *ever* stop?" He wagged his head. "He's going to football practice this afternoon." Then he pulled the door open. "See ya, hon." He reached out and patted Dorrie's behind, his hand lingering there.

Dorrie made a swipe at him and missed, then he was gone. "Never a dull moment with that guy," she said. But then she wouldn't look at me.

"That's okay." I paused a moment. "But you know, Dorrie, seriously, there are times I envy you so much." I just had to say it—to blurt it all out. "It's been so long since Matt's been gone. But I still miss the hugs, the kisses, the tender moments. And yes, sex, damnit. I miss sex."

Dorrie bit her lip, and again looked away.

"Even though I was busy with Kenny and Father, there were times I'd get so lonely I wanted to curl up and die." She had to have detected the tremor in my voice.

"Oh, Lottie, I know. Crimony, I've worried about you plenty of times. But, well, I thought—I hoped John'd changed all that." She searched my face, her eyes large, consoling.

"No, it's never come to that." Then it was my turn to look away. Damn, I thought, will John ever change? Doesn't he ever feel a—a need?

Now I just sat there and stared at the carpeting in Joanne Garner's bedroom. It had been hard on me to relive that time, all those words and painful feelings. But it helped me some to understand myself.

I adjusted to the moment and knew the chess game was still in progress in Diane's room. (Bathroom doors have wide cracks under them.) I quickly jotted a card to John then, a picture post card with racing antelope on it. Write him a long letter soon, Charlotte, cards are so impersonal. I do miss you, John, I'll write, sorry I haven't written sooner, but I've seen so busy here learning all sorts of new things.

{[CHAPTER 19]}

A new morning arrived at OUR Ranch, clear and bright. I helped Diane freshen up for breakfast, and we both watched, in an almost rapturous state, the sunlight spreading over the valley. The leafy treetops were brilliant golds and yellows now, the coloring so intense it hurt our eyes. I had to adjust the curtains before I left to tend the cooking.

Once in the kitchen, I set coffee to perk and browned some sausages laden with thyme. This has the makings of a cheery day, I thought, as next I poured pancake batter onto the grill and watched tiny bubbles appear in the cakes. The kitchen steeped in its mingling aromas, sending a surge of hunger through me.

But a trill of merry whistling startled me and I whirled around to find Dan standing in the middle of the room. First a rigidity gripped me, then just as quickly, I felt as though I were sinking in quicksand. The notes stopped abruptly. "Sorry, Char, I didn't mean to—ah—can I help?"

"No, not really, but—but, thank you," I said with a

gasp. I paused a moment. "Oh, I do have Diane's tray almost ready. Would you like to take it to her?"

"Oh, sure, I'd like that," he answered quickly, then stood too near me, for I could sense or imagine, maybe, his breath stirring my hair.

I finished the tray, picked it up and turned. I looked up to him, and as our eyes met, I froze. He was wearing a bright blue shirt and it intensified the blue of his eyes. And his eyes were smiling. I could not look away. I'm not sure if I breathed at all, but I felt my hands tremble for a few brief seconds.

"Looks good," he said, but all the time his eyes remained on me. Then he grasped the tray, turned and left the room.

At once I remembered Mary Kane's departure and her last words to me. I felt heat rise in my face. Damn. What is it, Charlotte? Embarrassed? Or charmed? His eyes had been like magnets, drawing my attention too easily. It disturbed me. No, it did not.

When Dan returned to the kitchen, he eased his tall, lean frame into the dining booth and poured a coffee. I began to heap his pancakes onto a plate when I felt my hands begin to fumble. The stacked plate tipped precariously—and my heart filled my throat. Charlotte Foster, where's your common sense? Then I swallowed hard and walked calmly to the booth and placed the plate before him.

Suddenly Joanne was in the kitchen, her greetings

filling the air. I was grateful for the distraction. "Don't make more for me, I'll just have one of Dad's." She fetched a plate and slid in the booth opposite him. Can't keep them waiting. We're going out to locate the herd today, and bring them down a way. Dad thinks they're up on the high hill." She wore an air of importance about her.

I nodded and left them to eat together, anxious for a break in the tension.

But, before long Jed came in from the bunkhouse, his hair still damp from a combing. And we ate up the last of the pancakes.

Later, I watched from the sink window as the three strode to the barn. Dan's arm was around Joanne's shoulders, their heads close together. They seemed indifferent to the wind that was blowing drifts of crispy aspen leaves about the dooryard. I watched, too, as they coaxed their mounts into the corral with grain buckets. The three chestnuts tried to join them but were shooed away. There was a bustling about the hitching rail as they saddled up. They swung into the saddles, disappearing behind the barns for a moment, then I saw them ride up the first hill. I watched it all with an envious tug.

On to your next task, Charlotte. So I went to Dianne's room, where I found her mood still as sunny as the morning sky. The bath routine took on a happy air as I brought a basin of warm water and towels.

Diane had tied a scarf around her head for sleeping and

was carefully undoing the knot. "Oh, I like my hair in French braids," she said, sighing, "it makes me look older, don't you think?"

"You want to look older? *I* always want to look younger." I laughed. "We women are never satisfied, are we? It's makeup and mousse when we're young, then wrinkle cream and hair dye when we're older." I dabbed dramatically at my face and hair as I spoke. "Really, it's all such a chore." I threw my hands in the air. "Maybe we get old too fast trying to stay so young." Diane began giggling and the time sped by.

Pleasant routines began to prevail in the Garner household. Diane was agreeable about all her schoolwork and Dan was busy making phone calls and plans, all in preparation for the coming roundup. He made several trips to Red Hill, too, for groceries, supplies, and—the mail.

One day he handed me a variety of mail. One letter postmarked Seacove, California, and forwarded from the Spencer post office, was from Joyce, my brother's wife. I sat down and ripped it open. It read:

Dear Lottie,

Larry and I have spent a lot of time thinking about you since we returned from the funeral. It was sad for us to lose Father, sad to feel an era ending. But we're happy to see you free of a terrible burden. We both feel you did a splendid job caring for him.

We hope you're seriously considering coming here for Christmas when Lena and her family will be here. They're staying for two weeks, then they're going to Hawaii. Tom was lucky getting transferred there. Imagine being forced to go to Hawaii?

We're hoping you will stay longer, lots longer after they leave. We talked about it, remember? There's so much we want to show you, we can't begin to say. If you start now, you should have plenty time to close the house, get your ticket—and a gallon of sunscreen, things like that. No, you can buy the sunscreen when you get here.

[Joyce went on to tell some interesting anecdotes about their work, all having to do with the ocean. It sounded so brainy and interesting. I began to feel anxious, yet things were quite interesting here on the ranch, and we hadn't even had the roundup yet. Lord, that's right, she doesn't even know that I'm as far as Montana already. Well, Lena must've told her by now.]

Let us hear from you soon and we'll start making firmer plans.

Love, Joyce

P. S. Can you put John 'on hold'?

I've got to write to her soon. Won't she be shocked to find out where little sister is? And with a red bikini in her bag, too!

It was exciting when someone brought the mail for we'd usually have several days mail at once. I'd gotten a hilarious, but short letter from Dorrie, wondering why I hadn't written. "Your's is on the way, Dor," I muttered.

Then I slit open the big, thick letter from my attorney, Martin Graves. I'd saved it until last because I just about knew the contents. I decided to have a cup of coffee to sip on while I went through the papers I was sure he'd sent. Thoughts tumbled about in my mind again, bringing me back to the series of events that occurred just before my leaving Spencer.

John had driven Mama to see her brother on the Sunday afternoon that I had written and mailed the resume to Red Hill, Montana. Days passed, and even though I'd talked to him briefly on several occasions, I'd never told John about it, not really expecting anyone to call so soon—or at all. And then when Mary Kane *did* call, and I actually accepted the job, I really had to hurry to get things done. Our communication seemed to be suffering some.

Dorrie and I rushed out and shopped for the entire afternoon. When she finally dropped me off at my house, she casually said, "Oh, yeah, Lottie, I saw John and Mama this noon at the drugstore. Crimony, I thought he . . ." She didn't finish what she was saying. I thought it strange, but at the time I was totally involved with collecting my bags of purchases. "See ya," she said, and drove away while I was still managing a thank you. And John never called all that evening either.

But the evening passed quickly for me, though, as I clipped price tags off plaid shirts, jeans, jackets, things like that. I even contemplated a few long moments on the sturdier shoes I'd bought. Then later, I sat at the dinette and scribbled all sorts of things that I wanted to talk to my lawyer about before drowsiness overtook me.

Morning came and I called Martin Graves' law office. "Charlotte Foster? Of course I'll have time to see you," he said, in a gruff, no-nonsense voice.

When I'd mentioned him to Dorrie while shopping, she'd said, "Not *that* Martin Graves?"

"Yes, why not?" I'd asked, exploding rather defensively.

"Crimony, I just thought since that messy divorce thing, you wouldn't want to do business with him." She stared, her mouth sagging a little.

"Really, Dor, he's always treated me nice. He solved a lot of problems for me when Matt died, you know. Now he's handling Father's will." I shrugged and pressed my mouth into a firm smile.

"Oh, I s'pose. But you know the talk that's gone around—puts the make on every woman that comes within six feet of him." She looked like she was sneering.

"That's just it," I said, "I think it's just that—*talk*." I felt my chin pushing out.

Then, as I dressed for the appointment, I noticed the

bright sunshine streaming through my bedroom window. Wear your new white cotton one more time, a voice nudged. You've hardly had it on since you bought it last spring.

It was a sleeveless, full-skirted dress, with huge pastel lilies on it—lilies strewn about as if blown by a wind. I remembered when I'd bought it how I'd smoothed the dress across my waist and watched intently in the mirror as I'd swished my hips from side to side. Charlotte, you still have a rather fit figure, you know. I'd felt good, excited, younger than in years. Hope John likes it, I thought. But it'd hung in my closet most of the summer for lack of any-where to wear it. Now I slipped it on, looked in the mirror and smiled. It was like putting on a *new me*. I felt a sense of being almost as free as the lilies, almost as if, I, myself, were being blown about by a like wind.

I studied my makeup, what little I wore, and gave my hair an extra brush to make it behave. It's my bangs, I thought, they're too long. Yes, Dorrie did tell me to get a haircut. Damn, she's always way ahead of me. I whipped the brush across my forehead one more time, then fas-tened a dainty strand of white beads at my throat.

I opened the closet and searched around for my good white heels. Something's missing here. Oh, yes. My old canvas slip-ons are still mired in Mrs. Nelson's flowerbed. No time now for looking back. So, snatching up my pret-tiest sweater, the lacy pink one, I left the house. But, as I pulled the back door shut behind me, I wondered curiously why I'd splashed on so much Lily-of-the-Valley. Oh, well, I thought, it'll fade.

When I walked into his office, Martin Graves smiled and jumped to his feet, his portly figure almost tipping his chair. "Charlotte—you look gorgeous." He rounded his desk to shake my hand, then held it for a moment too long.

I looked away, remembering Dorrie's scolding. "Thank you," I managed to say. I felt I must politely acknowledge the compliment. But my heart sent a strange new code of palpitations through me.

He soothed my sensitive edges though, when he quickly sat down, pulled a file and said, "Let's see now, what do we have here?"

"So you see," I said, after explaining everything, "I'd like to sell the old Pontiac, rent the house . . ."

His phone rang. "Oh, damn, right in the middle—Graves Law Office, Graves here." After a brief moment, he hung up the phone. "Char," he said, "I have to drive down to Simmons' Point to pick up some papers. Can we discuss this over lunch? It'll save both of us a lot of time."

"Of course," I said, but an inner voice cautioned, careful, he called you *Char*. My cheeks burned and I looked away, but I was committed.

The drive was uneventful, though, actually quite pleasant. Then, on the way back to Spencer, Martin swung his car into the lot at The Greenhouse, our area's most unique restaurant. I hadn't been there in years. It was filled with barreled fig trees, potted dracana, and hanging baskets with every sort of greenery cascading from their brim. Martin guided me as we followed the hostess to a secluded table by a window overlooking a large expanse of river. A heavy awning dimmed the sun. Soft music, white china, beige linens. It was very pleasant and I soon felt at ease.

After we'd ordered, Martin beckoned the waitress back. "Would you like something to drink, Char? I believe I'll have a beer."

At first I hesitated. "Yes, I will, too. Thank you." I hadn't had a beer in a long time, and when I sipped it, goose bumps rose along my arms, causing me to snug my sweater about me. I had a seafood salad, and Martin had a steak—well done. So it was, we were a long time at our meal, unhurriedly discussing my too-few problems. But I enjoyed the beer, the salad, the surroundings, and—Martin's attention.

He was a good-looking man, perhaps too bulging at the middle, but in his well-tailored suit, he was still suave in his own unique way. At times, though, his dark eyes would almost smother me, and once I felt a sort of *undressing*.

Charlotte, check your imagination, I scolded, but the flush was real. I couldn't decide if I liked it or if I wanted to flee. Then a sudden indignation prompted me to say, "Martin, it's been a lovely lunch, but we really should be going."

"Right, Char." And he signaled the waitress.

He called me Char again, and I liked it. Hardly anyone had ever called me that.

Just as we were readying to leave, I glanced to the foyer where several men were gathered. I thought I recognized the tweed jacket with the leather-patched elbows on the man with his back to me, his head obscured by leafy twigs. John? Down here in Simmons' Point? No. But—why not?

When we rose from the table, Martin took my chair and gave my elbow a slight touch. But just as I stepped forward, my heel caught on a bit of loosening carpet. I plunged ahead, but Martin's arm flew out and caught me. He held me for perhaps longer than was necessary. I'd cried out, though only faintly, never-the-less, I'd created a disturbance. My face grew hot and I wanted to hide.

When I'd regained my composure, Martin guided me to the foyer, and I found then that all the men were gone.

I wondered all the way back to Spencer if it actually *was* John. And what must he be thinking? *And* just why hasn't he called me these last few days? It's not at all like him.

Later, at Martin's office, we finished our business and I rose to leave. "Okay," he said, "I'll take care of everything and keep in touch. Don't worry about a thing."

"Thank you so much." I smiled and moved to the door.

He'd come around his desk then. "Just one more thing—promise me one more thing?"

"What is it?" I asked. "I have to know before I can promise." I giggled. Was I being coy or just honest, I wondered.

"Aw-w, Char, I've been trying to get up enough nerve to ask you out to dinner, ah—now that I'm—ah—free." He lied about the nerve part.

"Is this coercion? Or blackmail?" I swung my head around, nose in the air. "I'm afraid I'll have to consult my attorney." I struggled to keep a smile from my face.

"Nothing of the sort, Mrs. Foster," he said, with a perfect poker-face. "I'll even give you six months to decide." He took my hand and shook it, then covered it with both of his and squeezed it gently. He chuckled, deep and hearty.

"It's a deal," I said, smiling now like a girl being asked to prom. It's the dress, I thought. Lord, it's the dress.

And, while leaving the office, the door still ajar, I heard him call out, "Goodbye, gorgeous."

I smiled as I drove the old Pontiac down Grant Street and pulled it into my garage. It warmed me, still, to feel attractive to men.

My next task was to ready the house for new tenants. I was glad that Martin suggested renting to schoolteachers. "We'll have to hurry, though," he'd said. "School starts next Tuesday and you're leaving on Wednesday."

Well, I'm sure John will be so busy with his new classes, he'll hardly know I'm gone, I told myself. Now, I suspected, my conscience was playing tricks on me.

Changing quickly into my grubbiest clothes, I hurried to the garage. After I'd had the high school boys clean my yard of storm debris, it actually looked quite nice. So now, the chores were minimal. Put away the hose. Lower the storms. And dig those onions. You've put that off long enough, they're probably mush by now. I worked until late afternoon. Once in awhile John would cross my mind and I'd become irritated. He could have called; he knows I rarely call him. Okay, damnit. I will call *him*—tonight.

ॐ

The house at OUR Ranch was peacefully quiet, allowing me to think back in time with ease. I was glad Diane's bell had not rung. I gripped my coffee cup, sipping slowly now, remembering that evening in vivid detail, while holding Martin Graves' legal papers still folded in my hand.

It'd been very late in the afternoon when I'd re-entered my house, grimy and starved. I plopped the basket of onions, what few there were, on the kitchen floor. A hurried bath and clean clothes refreshed me and I was free to concentrate on a supper.

My food shelf had been gradually depleted, but I did manage a nice piece of sirloin from the fridge. I could broil it, make a stew, or even a soup. No, soup will take too long. A stew it is, I thought, spotting the onions again. I was busily peeling several small ones, when the front door bell sounded. Annoyed, I hurried to the door and pulled it open. "J-J-John." I backed up, staring.

"I hope I'm not interrupting your dinner, Lottie, but I've got to talk to you."

"Of course, John, come in." I was startled but calmed

enough to add, "I'm in the kitchen making a stew of sorts. I could use your advice." I knew I sounded flip. He followed me to the kitchen and sat down at the dinette. I picked up a carrot and began to scrape it, my hands unsteady.

"Dorrie told me about your letter to Montana, Lottie," he said, sputtering, "she thought I—knew."

Dorrie told . . . So, he did know. "But, John, I . . ."

"I guess I was just too hurt about your wanting to leave, I just couldn't call. Then, today I saw you with Graves." He thumped his fist on the table and shouted, "That womanizer!"

I whirled around to face him. "Now John, that's not fair. He's my lawyer, and a good one, too."

"But he has the reputation of chasing every eligible female he meets—and even some that aren't." His voice was shaking, and he thumped the table again.

"Yes, I know the talk. But he's been my lawyer ever since Matt was killed. I needed him then and he helped me—a lot." I turned my back to him, and, taking a knife, began chopping the carrot. "So I don't care all about this gossip, because he treats me just fine." Why did I feel the need to *defend* myself? *I'd* done nothing wrong. Wait. Did I give Martin the impression I'd date him when I returned from California? I doubt it. But, so what if I did?

I picked up the knife again and began to chop furiously at an onion. Fumes rose and began to sting my eyes.

"But his—his reputation . . ." John insisted.

"Well, maybe it's all lies." I shouted then, too. "Anyway, he's never so much as . . ." My display of temper surprised me.

"But I saw you at The Greenhouse today. You looked so damn pretty. That's all it took, Lottie, he couldn't keep his hands off you. I could hardly believe my eyes when he held you. . . ."

"Wait a minute. You have no right to imply . . ." I chopped at another onion, rage building inside me. Then the fumes smarted my eyes and caused a flood of tears to stream down my face. "Oh, damnit," I wailed, and squeezed them shut. The knife fell to the floor.

I heard John jump to his feet. "Oh, God. Oh, Lottie, honey. . . ." I felt his arms go around me. "I'm sorry." I heard his murmur in my hair. "I didn't mean to come here and do this. I don't have any right to be so hurt. It's just that—well, I love you, Lottie. I do love you." His breath was warm by my ear.

Oh, Lord, he's saying it. He's actually saying it, I thought. But, damn, why does he have to wait until I'm leaving?

He kissed me then—my forehead, my cheek, my tear-drenched eyes before he sought my mouth. I kissed him back, a strong kiss. But I didn't feel what I'd thought I would. His ardor increased, his arms strong and his hands moving.

Don't, John, please don't, I thought, my mind swirling. I pulled away. Oh, God, how I'd wanted this moment to happen, but now I wasn't at all sure. But you *always* thought you'd one day marry him, didn't you? He'd take good care of you, just like Mama.

But that was *not* what I wanted—I wanted to be free—to run, to fly, to feel blown about like the lilies in my dress. But he's good to you, Charlotte. He's comforting—and sweet. I cried. Lord, how I cried. Not only from the onions, but now from all the other pent-up emotions that had been dogging me since my father died.

Then I realized with a blow that my decision to go to Montana was sound and unbending, and some of the tears were for a new-found joy. My sobs subsided and I felt good, warm and relaxed, glad that it had all come to a head.

John held me close, tenderly close, for a long, long moment. Then he let me go and backed away to hold me at arm's length. "I understand, Lottie. I have no right to expect you to feel the same way I do. But I'm afraid I'm losing you. I'd always hoped we'd marry one day. You know, after our parents didn't need us anymore." He released my hands and fidgeted with his collar. "I thought, then we could spend the rest of our lives together."

I knew it. I knew it. He meant to go on like this for years, Mama coming first as long as she lived. Fine. I'll let it be that way. I'm just not ready for another . . . "I know," I said, and looked away. "There's no real reason to discuss it." I was silent for a few moments, then I turned back to him. "Oh, but I've loved being with you, John. I know I'll miss you a lot."

He stiffened. "Then you've already decided to go?" His eyes narrowed. He hadn't known I'd agreed with Mary Kane to fly to Montana the coming Wednesday. Oh, God, how our communications had suffered.

"Yes, I've agreed." I could face him honestly now. "There's a young girl that needs me. She has both legs in casts—and no mother. She really needs me."

"Or is it you that needs her?"

"I don't know—actually." I paused and took a deep breath, feeling a rush of new air in my lungs. It felt good. "I'll be back about the first of February, I think, after I visit with Larry and Joyce for awhile. We'll have lots of time to talk then, John." I reached out and patted his arm. I thought he flinched but I continued, "Lots of time to do things—together." I turned away to tend my cooking, the meat having begun to smoke in the browning pan. "Please stay, John, there's enough here for both of us. I have some wine. . . ."

But he'd already moved toward the door. "Sorry, Lottie, I told Mama I'd only be gone for a short time. She's not feeling well tonight, headache, you know."

I jabbed at the meat in the pan with a long fork, causing it to sizzle. Now, Charlotte, she *is* his mother.

"But I'm taking you to see Kenny on Sunday like I promised," he said. "Mama will enjoy the ride."

"Well," I said, shrugging, "I didn't think you wanted to since you hadn't called for days." I turned the meat and it spat at me, causing me to pull back quickly.

He took my arm and turned me toward him. "Now, look here, Charlotte Foster, you're not going to get rid of me that easy. Of course, I want to go." Then he planted the lightest of kisses on the tip of my nose and left the house.

Oh, John. I shook my head. I knew then love could not be made to happen at one's convenience. Well, maybe it will take root and grow once I'm back home again, I thought, with a smile—a satisfied smile.

Suddenly I felt anew the fat letter in my hand, the return address in bold black lettering—Attorney at Law. I finished my coffee, quickly poured another cup, and unfolded the crisp, sheets of legal forms. Martin Graves had rented my house to three schoolteachers. I just knew I'd read him right.

[CHAPTER 20]

One morning I accompanied Jed to the barn for a lesson on graining horses. The newly arrived sacks of feed were stacked neatly just inside the barn door, and I was immediately taken by the sweet, musty odor rising from them. It caused my heart to thud with remembrances of the little farm I'd once shared with Matt. Moments as this, I thought, can be a little bittersweet.

"Now you mix some of this here rolled oats with some of this here cracked barley," Jed said. He dipped into a bag with a big metal scoop and poured the grain into a bucket.

"Give 'em each about this much." I immediately felt better and peered into the bucket. "We feed 'em twice a day if they're working, once a day if they're not."

We filled the feed boxes in the barn, then Jed went out the rear door and thumped an empty bucket. The horses knew at once their breakfast had been served and eagerly tramped into the barn. We watched for a while as they munched and stomped and nickered their pleasure.

"Well, that should be easy enough," I told Jed, but I was already thinking how I would word it on a post card to Kenny. I'd found the perfect card, a picture of a beautiful black and white paint standing on an outcropping of rock, mane and tail being swished about by a strong wind. I knew he'd recognize it as similar to my own of years ago.

I didn't want to appear to be bragging to him, but I was thrilled about the chance to perform the graining chore whenever I could manage it. Trips to the barn, I knew, would allow me to reminisce about pleasant thoughts from a dim past, more often locked away. It would be my private time to wholly enjoy—away from the timer, the phone, the bell.

Chase had waited quietly outside the barn door and joined us as we trod back toward the house, the wind gently pushing against us. Jed turned to me and smiled faintly. Then his smile grew until it was a radiant glow, lighting up his entire face and causing his eyes to glint with a green fire. "I like the roundup days best of all, Miz Foster," he said with a burst of enthusiasm. Then he slowed his pace and looked out over the hills, his eyes coming to rest, it seemed, on the high hill. "That horse, that damn black stallion, he's up there. I seen him just the other day."

A gust of wind blew my scarf across my face and I brushed it away. What did he mean—black stallion? Did I hear him correctly? I remembered he mentioned a black stallion when I'd first come to the ranch. I turned to him. "What was that you said?"

He looked at me with a blank stare for a second. Then

he shook his head and I saw his eyes clearly focused on me. "We work the roundup with Jack Colby and his men—a fine bunch of fellas."

Quickly I dropped the thought of a black horse. "Oh, I'm anxious for the roundup, too," my grin matching his now. "It all sounds so exciting."

We neared the porch. "Yup, things are shapin' up for winter, too. Should be gettin' the first of our hay next week, I reckon. Hope so, anyway, before any big snow gets us." With that, Jed playfully roughed Chase's coat, causing the dog to bound up on his hind legs and give several cheery yaps.

Dan had been going to Meadow Grand every Friday night to get Joanne, and returning her to the school on Sunday for several weeks. She'd bring Diane's lessons, and, almost always, homework for herself. But she'd still very willingly offer to help Diane with her algebra lessons, for which I would secretly bless her.

On weekends, Joanne would ride Patches, and Boots, too. "He has to be kept used to the saddle or he'll get ornery," she'd say. "But Di will be riding by Thanksgiving, I bet."

And she would always bring letters to Diane from Cathy Price, letters Diane would quickly share with me. Lately her letters told more and more news of her uncle, the one from Minnesota. "I really like him a lot—he's fun," she wrote. "He comes with my dad all the time when he picks me up at school. And guess what? I think he's got a *thing* for Janet Lonetree. He spends enough time around her office, anyway." Then Cathy would doodle hearts and flowers and bows and arrows all around the edges of the page. I loved Cathy's letters, because I'd actually met her and counted her as another of my Montana friends.

I was beginning to feel at home at OUR Ranch and competent at tending everyone's needs. Even more, I loved the excitement of helping them prepare for winter, although I secretly questioned Dan's request to lay in twenty pounds of dried navy beans. Who in the world is going to cook all those beans, I wondered.

We hadn't needed Helen Lucas during September, but with the coming events, I knew things would change. At the thought of her, I puzzled. What would she be like to work with? I'd only seen her for those few brief moments when I'd first come to the ranch. Well, Charlotte, you'll soon find out. But I had to admit that I didn't especially like the thought of changes in our pleasant routines at OUR Ranch.

⁊[CHAPTER 21]⁊

October's first Monday arrived gloriously brilliant, but windy. The ranch was a busy place, both indoor and out, as we prepared Diane for her journey. It was now time for her legs to be x-rayed, time for the removal of the casts. Dan had made arrangements for her to enter the hospital in Jackson Buttes this day, so Andy had driven out from Red Hill in the Jeep with a stretcher he'd borrowed from a clinic there. The stationwagon had been backed up to the door and left warming.

I wrapped Diane in a wooly blanket and the men came and lifted her onto the stretcher, then slowly and gently trundled her through the house. I hurried ahead, carrying her bulging tote bag, and held the swinging door open for them. Once in the kitchen, they paused only long enough for me to place the bag beside her and squeeze her hand. She smiled to me, her clear blue eyes saucer-like with anticipation, clutched her bag with one arm and waved to me with the other. "See ya," she called, her smile now as bright as the morning. I opened the kitchen door and the three of them passed through the porch, where Jed had been tending that door, and then they disappeared into the brilliance.

"You and Jed take care of things now." Dan had tossed the words to me over his shoulder, his intentions funneled into one important task. They were all gone, save for Jed, who was somewhere out there tending his chores. It was a drastic change.

For the remainder of that day and the next it was unbearably quiet in the house. I'm all alone here, I thought, just like it was after my father died—and I don't like it. I would pace the floor, dust everything in sight, and use the phone, over and over, to make long-distance calls. It helped immensely to talk to Dorrie and Lena, and I even reached Kenny. It was a happy occasion to be able to track him down. I also ventured a call to John, but shortly after we began talking, Mama started to interrupt him, and we had to end the conversation. Damnit, Mama, I thought, you won again.

Luckily, Jed would linger after his breakfast coffee without being coaxed. Then I would throw on a jacket and race him to the barn to grain the horses. We'd almost quarrel, goodnaturedly, of course, about who would get to do the chore. Once I sneaked a carrot past the other horses, and offered it to Patches. She greedily accepted it and I glowed at the thought of winning another new friend. I felt warm the rest of the day.

But by Wednesday morning I was dying of loneliness.

It was then Jed said, as he nursed a cup of coffee, "How would you like to ride into Red Hill today with me, Miz Foster? We can get the mail, and shop around, if you'd like." And he flashed a smile, the kind that almost made his eyes disappear behind the ruddy cheeks.

"Super," I said, clapping my hands like a child, "I'd better hurry."

Arriving in Red Hill, our first stop was the small mail-order store where Helen Lucas worked. Oh, I thought, I'm going to meet her sooner than I expected. Jed pulled the door open for me and I stepped into the tiny room bulging with merchandise. Helen was sitting behind the counter working a crossword puzzle. She jumped up, shoving the papers out of sight under some others.

"Hello, Helen, how are you?" I offered the greeting with a smile.

"Hello, Miz Lucas," Jed called, warmly.

"Oh, hi, Jed." She nodded to me, then. "Hello, Charlte." She did smile, but the way she said my name again, with just one syllable, irritated me.

"We're just out gallivanting," Jed said with a chuckle. But then we did engage in a simple, matter-of-fact conversation about Diane and quiet days at the ranch.

At first she seemed happy enough to see us, but then she spent most of her time shuffling packages of long johns on a small rack, clearly bothered. We started to browse about, and Jed spotted some socks and stopped to examine them.

"Helen," I said, pointing to a stack of sale catalogs on

the counter, "I'd like to take one of these home with me. Can you spare it?"

"I s'pose," she answered in a crisp voice, pushing one across the counter to me. "But the sale's almost over." She shrugged her shoulders and moved away, her thick black curls bouncing on her collar.

I glanced to the corner of the catalog's front cover. There were still two weeks left before the expiration date of the sale. She's being a little rude to you, Charlotte. Oh, try not to mind, I thought, but it hurt—it really hurt.

"I need these here socks," Jed said, noticing and salving the gritty situation. "Are they wool?" He dangled them in the air like a matador in the ring.

"Oh, yeah, Jed, they surely are. Dan *always* buys those kind." Helen announced it, smiling with her knowledge, as she made the transaction and bagged them with care.

Does she know every personal thing about Dan? Well, I suppose so, I thought, fuming. She's been going out to the ranch for, what, three years? Still it irked me, the way she said it. Come now, Charlotte, actually—what do you care? We left, soon after, with curt goodbyes.

We moved up the sidewalk to Mitchell's General Store, our heels making hollow, clacking sounds on the wide boards. Jed pulled the door open, causing its big brass bells to jangle cheerfully. I stepped inside, feeling much better.

It was an all new shopping experience for me as I surveyed the large interior crowded with provisions, yet neat and orderly. Odors of apples, bacon and laundry products mingled pleasantly. One wall immediately caught my eye. It was lined solidly with numerous items such as oil lamps, dish pans, kegs of nails and grain buckets. Yes, general store said it all.

I'd brought an exacting list with me, but before long, I'd let Jed talk me into buying a basket of apples — for pie. It wasn't difficult.

Lastly, we stopped at the post office where we had four days mail waiting for us. A small man with a huge white moustache handed Jed a fistful of assorted pieces. He turned to me. "Wait, wait. Ain't you Mrs. Foster?"

"Why, yes, I am." Then I was taken aback when he handed me a rather large, but lightweight package. I was about to protest when I spotted the return label: Nelson, Box 122, Simmons' Point, Minnesota. I happily accepted it.

The Jeep bounced along the gravel road toward home, my excitement mounting. I tore at the heavy paper around the parcel until it exposed a cardboard box. I flipped the top open, and, as I loosened some inner tissue paper, a soft, pale green afghan puffed like a cloud from the confining box. I tugged at its intricately crocheted softness until it was completely out of its wrappings. Immediately swallowed up by homesickness, I buried my face in it and began to sob. I felt the Jeep slow.

Jed patted my shoulder. "Come on now, Miz Foster, don't do that." But I couldn't stop. I felt the jeep pull off the road and heard the engine stop. I was aware of Jed's arm going about my shoulder, but stopping the tears then was like trying to stop a burst dam. And when I felt his arm gently tighten about me, I collapsed against his welcoming chest. "There, there," he said, patting my back. "You want to tell me about it?" His voice was soothing, coaxing.

"Oh, Jed, I had a neighbor . . ." But I had to use a wad of tissues before I could continue. Then I told him all about my father, my dog, Mrs. Nelson, the fire—everything that had to do with a gold-colored afghan, now wrapped around a bundle of black fur and buried under the plum trees beside the garage on Grant Street in Spencer, Minnesota. I couldn't have been more specific. "You see, Jed, they all meant so much to me, I couldn't help the crying. I just never thought I'd get so homesick."

"That's okay, Miz Foster, you just plain go right ahead, if it makes you feel better." And he kept one arm about me.

Before too long, I pushed away, patting his chest quite lovingly. He brushed his eyes, cleared his throat and started the Jeep, pulling it back onto the road. But he didn't speak until we were almost home. Poor Jed, I thought, I didn't mean to make him sad, too.

Dan had stayed in Jackson Butte's until Wednesday evening, and upon returning, had much to tell. He'd arrived just as Jed and I were beginning our supper, so I quickly added a place for him in the booth. Jed and I kept our attentions glued on Dan.

"Doc said Di's x-rays looked real good, so off came the casts," he said, "you should've seen her face when she first saw her legs again. She let out a screech and yelled, 'They're not mine—they're too ugly.'" I started to laugh and I thought she was going to hit me. But then she laughed, too. Doc called her a good sport. She liked that. They'll be giving her therapy for a couple days," he continued. "I'll go back on Friday and they'll show me how it's done, and, hopefully, I can bring her home then."

I'd felt happily at ease sitting with the two men in the booth, but suddenly my spirits brightened even more. I saw it reflect in Dan's eyes and I felt my face flush some. I hadn't meant to draw in such an excited breath. His eyes stayed upon me and I could sense the compassion he was feeling for his daughter. I could clearly see a love in his eyes. I don't blame him, I thought, she's such a lovely girl. I felt warmly contented, sitting there with the two men, more so than I'd felt at any time since my arrival at the ranch. I wanted the feeling to last long, so I could relish the beauty of the moment.

But Jed broke the spell. He drained his coffee cup, set it down and rose from the booth. "Well, I'll be getting things ready for the morning, Dan." He turned to me. "We're gonna build those horsies a new hay bunker." He plucked his hat from the peg, gave it a few twirls, and left the house, our good nights trailing after him.

Dan quickly picked up the coffee pot and offered to pour some for me. "Thanks, but just a little," I said, holding up a protesting hand. He poured his cup to the brim. Did he want me to stay seated longer, I wondered? Okay, I'll gladly oblige.

"Well, Char," Dan said, softly, directly now, "first it'll be a wheelchair for Di, then crutches, then a walker. Hope it goes fast for her." His clear blue eyes cloudy then. "It's going to be real tough on everyone, I'm afraid. But Helen's coming to stay, you know, for just as long as you need her. It's all up to you."

I felt myself flinch, but grateful Dan didn't see. Oh, I thought, that wonderfully warm feeling is fading somewhat.

"The store manager's been real good about letting her have the time off. Don't know what I'd do if she couldn't come out here to help you out." Dan's eyes were cast downward now.

I stared at my empty coffee cup. Yes, Helen, come. I know it has to be. We rose, cleared away the dishes, offered our good nights and flicked the kitchen to darkness.

Later, as I lay sleepless in my bed, I pondered the new days to come. I tossed about, my mind grabbing on to all sorts of thoughts. Why, why, I suddenly wondered, did I feel that Dan had an urge to touch my hand as we sat in the booth with our cooling cups of coffee?

{CHAPTER 22}

The next morning I pretended to supervise, mostly through the kitchen sink window, as Dan and Jed went about building the new bunker. And, all the while, a flock of bold, jabbering magpies, dressed in their black-and-white finery and sporting long, greenish tails, observed it, too. I had never seen such birds before and I found them quite comical to watch for they chattered and scolded and stubbornly refused to budge from their haughty perches, all the bustling activity never daunting them the least. Sometimes the horses would even curiously crowd around.

A big truck came in the early afternoon loaded heavily with bales of hay. Andy had returned to the ranch in time to help the men transfer the bales into the hay barn. It looked as easy as stacking children's blocks, I'd decided and wished I could've helped, but I knew it was a job for the initiated.

Instead, I brewed fresh coffee and warmed cinnamon rolls, for they all trooped into the house for a repast when their task was finished. The men were in high spirits and

Dan quickly introduced me to Ben Cloud. "I'm so glad to meet you," I said, "Barbara is a sweet girl." He smiled and stood tall. I was pleased, then, to see the resemblance to his daughter, the same high cheek bones, the same blue-black hair, the same perfect teeth. He shook my hand with a gentle warmth.

But something about it bothered me. Yes, I realized with a strange pang, that I did not like meeting people thinking I would never see them again. After I'd finished setting out the big platter of warm rolls, I quickly excused myself and went to my room, leaving the men to their robust talk.

I sat at Joanne's desk, strangely confused, and arranged and rearranged every pen, pencil and paper clip. Now, Charlotte, I commanded, making a fist, don't stew over every little thing. Just tend to your duties.

So—when the men returned to the out-of-doors, I went back to the kitchen, cleared away the cups and things and turned on the radio, deliberately twisting the dial until I found some really upbeat music.

I began to feel much better, more a part of the accomplishment, when I went out later that afternoon to watch from the corral fence the horses re-action to their new *table* just baptized with fresh hay.

By Friday morning the excitement at OUR Ranch had become quite contagious as we prepared for Diane's return. I scurried about the kitchen, stirring up what I hoped were inviting aromas, as I brewed coffee, browned spitting sausages and squeezed plump oranges. I found myself humming a new tune. And when I heard faint, stirring sounds coming from Dan's room, it sent a race through my veins.

From the sink window I watched as Chase ran in tight circles around Jed as the two of them walked from the barn. As they neared the porch he attempted to pat the dog's head, but the dog pranced and bounced about with much too much energy. When Jed came into the kitchen we were both wearing a grin.

Then, almost as if rehearsed, Dan stepped into the room whistling a bar from *Oh What a Beautiful Morning*. He quickly stopped and both men slipped effortlessly into the booth, their sunny dispositions more so lightening mine. I placed their laden plates before them, tiny slivers of steam still rising from the food. The sausages were a golden-brown and the sunny-side-ups nearly perfect. They dug in with hearty appetites, murmuring their thanks in unison amid the clinking of their utensils. Again I was pleased my efforts were so appreciated.

I moved about the kitchen preparing a breakfast for myself, while the voices from the booth were like the chattering of the magpies of the day before, albeit a bit muffled by the food.

"After we get Di home again and all settled in, it'll be roundup time, Char," Dan announced then, loud and clear.

At the sudden sound of my name I quickly glanced to him. His eyes were on me, following me about the kitchen.

"Oh," I said, "Oh, yes." I felt as if I blushed, but I liked it.

"We'll be helping our neighbor first, that's Jack Colby, over to the north here," he said, gesturing. "Then, when we're done there, they'll all help us."

"That sounds like awfully hard work." I wondered what more I could say, but my mind asked a thousand questions.

"Oh, it's tough, all right, but we work well together," Dan continued between gulps of coffee. "We drive the herd up to the holding pens at the crossroads, then we cut out the ones we want to keep over winter and get the rest of them into the trucks that will be waiting." He paused for a moment, his eyes still on me. "Yup, it's lots of work, but it's what we wait for all year." His cup clinked on his saucer and he pulled in a hurried breath. "Well, Ma'm, that was a mighty nice meal," he said, his eyes twinkling, "I'll be leaving now. Di will be waiting anxiously, if not spitting fire by time I get there." He rose from the booth and hitched his belt over a full stomach.

Jed rose, too, and, taking his hat in his hand, he slapped his jacket over his shoulder and went out the door, grinning a merry lot.

I began to carry dishes to the sink when I sensed Dan's presence very near to me. "Helen's coming tonight with Andy, you know." There was a note of apprehension in his voice.

I started, then calmed quickly. "Yes, that will be nice."

"But I'm worried that the two of you will have your hands full helping Di get to walking again."

"Oh, she's a determined girl, I'm sure she'll work hard at it." I had to lift my chin high to meet his gaze. "I'm sure the three of us will manage just fine."

"Well, there's lots of cooking to be done, too, to feed all those men after the roundup." He smiled a broad smile, his teeth the whitest I'd noticed. "It's almost like a celebration, you know. Actually, it is a celebration. We're pretty darn happy when the roundup's all done and over with, Char." His eyes suddenly seemed to have acquired electrical qualities and for a moment I couldn't draw away. "You'll even have to care for the horses that are left here, you know. Andy will be with us."

"Oh, yes, I can do that. Jed showed me how."

"And don't forget the dog, too." He smiled again, only this time teasingly, as though the litany of chores was overwhelming me and he must lighten the load.

I tilted my head back and laughed, barely recognizing the sound as my own. Oh, but it was nice to be teased, to be paid attention to by so handsome a man in so intimate a moment.

I put up a fending hand. "Go, now," I said, with a giggle. "Everything's going to be just dandy, Dan." Then I couldn't stop giggling. Dandy Dan, I thought, sounds so silly.

He had started toward the door when he suddenly turned. His eyes sought mine again and held them fast. My heart began to thump. He started to put a hand out to me, but stopped and turned on a heel and walked again to the door. He pulled it open and went out, calling back over his shoulder, "We'll be home about six, Char. Make it a party. Di will like that."

The morning passed slowly as I did the routine kitchen chores, and gave Diane's room last minute touches. I even went into the guest room and smoothed the bedspread where Helen would be sleeping. Why, I wondered? Habits, I answered, and shrugged.

After Jed had had his noon meal, and the house was quiet again, I remembered Dan had said to make it a party, that Diane would like that. So I set about to prepare one.

Mary had noted some of the family's favorite recipes and one was for a chocolate cake. I paid attention to every detail.

It turned out to be three layers high, filled with a rich pudding, and covered with a fluffy white frosting that stood in peaks across the top. I hadn't baked one like that since Kenny's graduation party and it brought back a lot of memories as I'd swirled the icing about.

I thought about John, how he stayed late that night, how he helped me put away all the chairs and things, and take out the heaps of trash. How he helped me tidy the kitchen when the house was quiet and we could hear our hearts beat. And how he kept kissing me goodnight over and over, and chuckled, saying he couldn't remember whether he had or not. I missed John. I missed his arms around me.

❧

The late afternoon quiet gave way to the peals of the clock
on the living room mantle as it struck four times. Then my
heart's beat quickened when I heard the chugging of the
old Jeep coming up the drive. I was standing at the sink
washing vegetables for a salad, and I watched as it circled
about and stopped by the path. Andy sprang out on his
still-nimble legs and helped Helen with her various pieces
of luggage.

I remembered my manners, quickly opening the door
and holding it as they bustled into the kitchen. A few
cheery acknowledgements later, I put Andy at ease.
"Supper's as soon as they get here."

"Fine, I'll go and butt in on Jed for awhile, then," he
said, and slipped out the door.

"Let me take your coat, Helen." I reached out.

"Thanks, but I can manage." Her words were clipped.
She shrugged off a bright red coat and threw it over one
arm, and with her free hand, she pushed and patted her
thick, black curls about the nape of her neck. Then she
picked up some of her things, pulled her glossy red lips into
an upward curve and disappeared into the hallway. She
knew the guest room would be hers now, but I desperately
wished it was Mary Kane returning instead. Something
about Helen's arrival bothered me. I thought for a
moment. Yes—that's it—that's *her* room and she knows it.
She had slept there many, many times before *I'd* ever set
foot on OUR Ranch soil.

I remembered, Dan had said to Joanne to come home if she'd like, there would always be the couch. But she had declined, professing to have mountains of homework just as well done at school. Dan had commented to me at the time about his *sensible* girl.

I was distracted then by the tantalizing odor of garlic from the mutton roasting in the oven. Methodically, I reached for the hot pads, opened the oven, and inspected the meat, but my mind raced ahead with all the thoughts of the new events taking place in such rapid order.

I'm so glad Andy is moving into the bunkhouse with Jed tonight, I thought. Jed needs company. He's alone too much, poor man. What does he do with his long evening hours? Read? That's it, he must read. I wonder what books he likes best?

Helen appeared in the kitchen doorway, startling me back to the moment. She was wearing skin-tight, black jersey pants and a low-cut, black sweater, knit with a gold thread running through every row. Cleavage was very visible. She stood with folded hands, a question playing on her face, but she didn't say a word. Her dark eyes shot about the room, inspecting the changes I'd made, no doubt.

I quickly took charge. "Well, let's see, Helen, let's start with the table. There'll be six of us tonight."

Together we opened the bay window table and added another panel. And, at my suggestion, she set the table with a party flair, adding napkins printed with brightly-colored autumn leaves, napkins *she'd* known where to find.

After arranging the place settings with precision, she disappeared into the dining room, returning with a wicker horn-of-plenty filled with miniature pumpkins, ears of corn and apples, all glistening with a coat of shine. She arranged them carefully in the center of the table.

"Oh, that's lovely," I said. Sure she knew where that was, too.

"Thanks. Diane made them in an art class last year." Then she plucked the salt shaker from the table, gave it a shake and promptly refilled it. But she hefted the pepper shaker and replaced it on the table.

Oh, oh, I thought, she wants me to know she's in tune with this household, all right. Well, just wait until everyone sees the cake.

After a time, I decided we could work well together, but there didn't seem to be much comeraderie. I wasn't sure there could be much at all with only the short bits of conversation offered by her whenever I'd try to bring up a particular topic. How long have you lived in Red Hill? Quite a while. Do you ever travel? Sometimes. Love music, lively music. Do you? Yes, I do, too.

I was beginning to feel just a bit uneasy when I heard the wagon pulling up the drive, it's horn sending out a staccato of joy. I rushed to the window. "They're here, they're here," I sang out, clapping my hands like a child. I saw Jed and Andy fairly running from the bunkhouse. But when I turned to Helen she was looking at me with a slightly raised brow. It irked me, sending a quiver chasing up my spine. I rushed to the door and pulled it open, holding it steady as the crisp air sent a chill through my already goose-pimpled body. My excitement was almost out of control as Dan brought Diane into the kitchen, held high in his arms, both beaming. Jed followed, pushing a gleaming wheelchair, and wearing his usual large grin. He rolled the chair near the table's end and held it still as Dan lowered his daughter into it. I only heard a tiny whimper as he set about to make her comfortable. Her eyes twinkled with a blue brilliance and her smile was gigantic. Andy was in the house now, too, and we all set to clapping.

After a few rowdy exchanges, I begged them be seated, motioning Jed to sit by Dan, and Andy next to Jed. They began with a tomato juice cocktail and tiny crackers with a spicy cheese spread I'd concocted, giving me time to resurrect the platter of mutton from the warming oven. When I returned to the table with my *other* masterpiece, I was shocked to find Helen seated next to Dan, with Jed next to her behind the table, making Andy have to shift around to my side. Oh, sure, I thought, now it'll be next to impossible for her to help me serve the rest of the meal. It was a smacking blow to my ego, as I'd planned and worked for hours that the entire meal would be served with utmost order. Several times I had to go to the counter or fridge to retrieve various dishes, and each time I'd return to find Helen acting like the charming hostess, engaging everyone in some sort of trivia. I felt a scorching under my collar, but I had to ignore the hurts and get on with serving the meal.

Soon we were passing bowls and platters, large and small, amid jovial conversation. And I was right about the men appreciating the garlic-laden meat for they openly told me so.

But Diane laughed and huffed into her napkin, exclaiming, "Whew, I'm glad I don't have a date tonight."

The men chuckled, and for a moment I felt Dan's eyes on me. I looked away, overwhelmed with a sudden shyness. But I did detect a muffled snort from Helen.

As the meal progressed I couldn't help but wonder what an odd assortment of people we were, held here by a common bond—Diane. Our lives were crossing now but for a brief time, then soon to be taking new directions. But I liked being here. I liked being a part of a warm, caring group of people.

Then I winced slightly, reflecting on a reversal in time to the lonely last years of life with my father. I choked up for a second, had difficulty swallowing, and blinked back a swell of tears. Oh, Lord, not now, Charlotte. Good, no one seemed to notice. Then I realized they were tears of happiness and it was easier to control them.

When we'd finished the meal I cleared away the main dishes and placed the huge chocolate cake before Diane. A hum of ohs and ahs accompanied the act, but Helen sat like a forgotten ventriloquist's dummy, mouth agape. It was worth all the earlier slights.

I handed Diane the knife for the ceremonial first cut. Reaching for it, she brushed my hand and looked up to me, and I could see her lovely blue eyes had misted over quite thoroughly. That was all the thanks I needed, there—in one look.

I thought with clarity then of the joyous weekend get-together only a month before of the spirited high school girls. The house was alive again with many voices, only now there was a vast difference. Tonight there was the unmistakable reverberation of masculine laughter.

We partied late and Diane was exhausted. Dan wheeled her to her room. Helen followed. I'd insisted that Helen help Diane with her bedtime routine and I would clean up the kitchen myself. "Unpack and relax," I said, "that kitchen mess is mine. After all, I spent hours creating the meal that led to that chaos." She barely smiled.

Finally, almost midnight, I crawled into my bed. I curled and stretched and tried to find a comfortable position. I couldn't. What's bothering you now, Charlotte Foster? Oh, yes, I know. Why did Helen maneuver Jed aside so she could sit by Dan? And why did she wear that awful, low-cut black sweater with the gaudy gold threads in it?

I laid on my stomach and pressed my face deep into my pillow before I realized it was difficult to breathe that way. Damn.

{CHAPTER 23}

Diane's walking therapy began on Monday morning, the day the men left for the roundups. Helen and I would help her into deep, warm tubs of water, all the time coaxing her to move her withered legs as she was able. Then, as Dan had instructed—he'd spent time at the hospital working with the therapists—I'd massage her legs and ankles with well-oiled hands. It would be a slow process, they'd cautioned, but we were a dedicated threesome. And before long, Diane was relaxed and happy and guiding her wheelchair around the house with expertise.

But she could not pass through the swinging door from the dining room into the kitchen without help. Dan had propped it open and said he'd take it off if she liked. She declined, saying she could just as well use the hallway to get around. (A door at the far end of the living room connected with the hall next to her room.)

As her balance improved, Diane began the struggle to use her crutches to take a few labored steps, Helen and I at either side. Then she'd become exhausted and resort to the wheelchair again to move about the house.

Several days went by before I realized that Helen was persisting on spending more and more of her time with Diane, helping her shampoo her hair, smoothing the littlest wrinkle from her bed and adjusting the curtains to her every whim. It irritated me. "Diane," I finally ventured, "would you like me to braid your hair this morning?"

"No, that's all right—thank you," she said in a petulant voice. "Helen can help me put it in a pony tail or something."

That irritated me even more. So after I would finish helping her with lessons—that was one task Helen failed at—they would busy themselves in many ways and I would retreat to the kitchen. Diane didn't paint anymore after Helen came, so they had more time to play checkers and other games and talk—a good deal of muffled talk.

Most of the time I worked in the kitchen, if not the laundry, but I did find time to give the living and dining rooms an extra special polishing. Those rooms will shine beautifully in the sparkle of the hearth's flames when colder weather sets in, I thought. It will be something *I* can enjoy. For some unknown reason that idea pleased me. I whipped the polish cloth across the mantle. Then I knew the reason—I'll still be here—and *she* won't.

One afternoon Helen did help me wash windows so that job was finished in a short time. I was hoping Helen and I might get better acquainted during the chore, hoping we could melt some of the ice between us, but it didn't work that time either.

Diane had chosen to play her music at top volume. I'd found myself clenching my teeth to keep from scolding her. There's got to be something bothering her, something on her mind is not quite right, I just know it.

By the time we finished I knew I had to get out of the house for awhile, so I threw on my parka, went out the door, called to Chase for company, and went on a long walk—all the way to the fork in the road. It felt good to walk, relaxing—refreshing. Chase ran ahead, pouncing into low, thin brush, once raising several quail.

Past instances with Pepper floated through my mind, causing a lump to form in my throat. She was an entirely different type of dog, a lapdog, not a working dog, but I felt a friend is a friend, no less. It felt nice to remember her and the lump in my throat slowly left.

When I got back the house was quiet, so I slipped into my room, taking the mail-order catalog with me. Why did Helen suggest it was almost out of date? Can't she read? I grumbled. My new soft green afghan was laying on my bed and I took it and drew it around me and curled up like a snail. Oh, Mrs. Nelson, it's times like this I miss you the most. I closed my eyes and could clearly see her smiling. After a time I opened the catalog to the curtain section. Yes, Mary, I'll get to those bay window curtains soon.

Now the men had been away for three days already,

working the Colby roundup. And in three more days they would be coming home with a much smaller herd to tend on OUR Ranch. I hope the drive goes well, I thought, this house needs men's voices again, it's much too quiet.

Now, on the fourth day of their absence I began to prepare and cook the supply of food needed for the celebration. That's what Dan called it—a celebration—their big meal at the end of the drive, with all the men present. Well, they have good cause to celebrate, I thought, after the many months tending the huge herd, watching the cows calve and then watching the calves grow into fine young stock. Yes, it should be cause to rejoice. I smiled inwardly, then, and slapped and patted and smoothed loaf after loaf of pungent sourdough bread.

Early on the morning of the fifth day I went out again to grain the remaining horses. There was a strong sun but the wind blew cool as I strode to the barn, eager to see the friendly, whinnying creatures. But a sudden shiver ran through my body. I felt as if the air was charged with a rare, undefinable energy. It was a strange feeling, but by the time I reached the barn, I'd decided it was only an honest case of new-found excitement in all the happenings at OUR Ranch.

Chase was excited, too, for he'd followed, running in tight circles around me. He seemed starved for affection. Yes, Chase, your Jed will be back soon, I told him, trying to pat his head. But I only succeeded in nearly stumbling over him.

I had finished putting the grain in the feed boxes and was about to call to Patches, Boots, and old Sal, when I saw the sign which read Prince, the name of the black stallion once belonging to Dan's wife. I felt myself tremble and put my hands on the top rail to steady myself. Suddenly I was seized with a bitterness I found overwhelming. I gripped the rail. Tears flooded my eyes and made the nameplate disappear in a shimmering sea. I squeezed my eyes shut, lowered my head to my hands and stayed so for several minutes. Oh, Lord, I thought, life can be so cruel, so damn unfair. Yes, Matt had been taken from me, seemingly ripped from my arms—but instantly. No pain. No suffering for him. Just—gone. Dan's wife had died, too, only taken slowly, day by day, her blood devoured by a sinister disease.

But Charlotte, you had your father, remember? He needed you, too. The two of you leaned on each other. It was good. Dan only had a sister in a faraway place—and Helen. Oh, he must have depended a good deal on Helen. I suppose they have grown close. It would be strange if they haven't by now.

At that moment I felt a compassion, a tenderness for Dan that was almost unbearable. I walked over and sank onto the pile of plump sacks of grain that were stored in the corner of the barn by the door. I stared at the flooring, rubbing some loose grains under a foot. Then I buried my face in my hands and pondered the meaning of fairness. We know, don't we, Dan, what it's like to lose a loved one? We know the hurt, the pain.

A burst of wind slammed the barn door shut, shaking the very structure of the barn. I screamed. My eyes darted about. Where am I? It's so dark in here. Don't panic. But I'm all alone. I hate being alone. I hate it. Snap out of it, Charlotte. Don't be so dramatic. Remember, when you are no longer needed here you're going to go to California to be with your family for Christmas, and longer still. It's all arranged, you know. A real vacation. Sun-drenched beaches, warm sand, splashing surf. And shopping, too. Lots and lots of shopping. Oh, yes, I have to buy things for Kenny—and Beth.

I shook my head, trying to clear it, but it hurt. Then, with a great effort, I threw all the painful memories from my shoulders and left the barn, pulling the door hard behind me. I stalked toward the house, determined to get on with the tasks at hand.

I stopped abruptly and spun around. I ran back to the barn, flung the door open and raced through to the rear door. I called loudly to the horses. They were down by the stream, cropping the browning grass, but when they heard me they pricked up their ears and began to trudge up the slope. Old Sal whinnied. How? How could I have forgotten them, even for a moment?

Mid-afternoon of the sixth day Helen and I began to ready the food for the soon-to-be returning men. During a lull I sat down at the table in the bay window and sipped a cup of herb tea. The work and the excitement were taking their toll. Admittedly, I was nervous and needed a quiet time. I soon relaxed and gazed out the window, my eyesight roving about the hills.

Helen came into the kitchen, and, with her hands on her hips, stated flatly, "Diane's sure taking a long nap."

I looked squarely at her. "Oh, that means she'll probably stay up late now."

"Well," she snapped, "she gets tired out with all that pushing at her to get her walking again."

"Yes, I suppose so." I said, softly. But, damn, I get tired, too, I thought, and I don't like her radio playing so late at night. I turned back to the window but I felt my teeth clenching together.

"You'll know when those men are here," Helen said, dryly, "with all the whoopin' and hollerin' they'll be doin'." She made a humph sound and left the room. My teeth were still clenched and it took some time before I relaxed enough to sip my tea.

My eyes worked the hills again, finally resting on the high point of the north ridge. After a time I saw a cloud of dust billowing up, followed by the first line of cattle coming over the rise. I couldn't contain my excitement and ran to alert Diane and Helen. "They're coming, they're coming," I called down the hall.

Diane, bleary-eyed, yet smiling, and Helen joined me in the window to watch the men ease the herd down the south slope to their new winter area near the creek. I sensed their restlessness. Some hay had been scattered about in hopes of settling them. We could hear the young stock bellowing as they heaved against one another, some still bawling for their mother's assurance. They began to slow and mill about, their white faces now clearly visible.

Soon we could identify our men from the Colbys and I spotted Jed on his sorrel right away. Then I saw the tall, lean man on the giant bay, riding so upright in the saddle I just knew the roundup had gone well. My heart leaped to my throat, pounding with joy.

Helen scurried with buckets of warm water, piney-smelling soap, and an armload of towels to the bench outside the porch. I turned up the heat under the food. We hadn't known exactly when they would come, but it had been anticipated for such a long time that all the preparation went smoothly.

We carried heavy black kettles full of chili and thick beef stew, rich with onion—just the way Dan liked it—out to the porch where we'd set up tables the day before. The late sun streamed through the windows, warming the room, and increased the spicy aromas carried in the steam as we uncovered the pots. Big bowls of slaw and platters of pickles and fresh vegetables added more assaults on the tastebuds as well as the eye. I stepped back and viewed the tables, half scrutinizing them for something forgotten, and the other half in satisfaction for the accomplishment. Sweat trickled on my temples and my heart pounded.

After one last trip to the kitchen I began to set out baskets of glistening, crusty sourdough bread when Dan and another man entered the porch. He must be Jack Colby, I thought. Dan surveyed the spread of food, then turned and caught my eye. He moved close. His eyes shone with a blue fire and a smile burst forth like a sunrise. It all happened so quick I couldn't even think. He nodded and reached out and patted my shoulder, his hand resting there, lightly.

Jack Colby's attention was on me now and Dan quickly introduced us. "This is my helper, Jack. Meet Charlotte Foster." His hand slipped down my arm and eased me toward the man. I offered my hand to him while still wonderfully aware of Dan's touch. Jack Colby shook my hand and smiled. "Hell-o, hell-o," he said, "Dan's had nothing but praise for you." My knees began to weaken and I felt I leaned a little toward Dan.

"Thank you," I said, almost losing my voice in an attempt to become effaceable. I looked up to Dan. His smile was straightforward, unabashed. I partially turned away. "Everything's ready now," I said. "Please, ask the men to come in." I went into the kitchen, my face flushed. Attention and praise were too new to me. When I reached the counter I had to brace myself for several moments. My knees felt like they were nonexistent. What's wrong with you, Charlotte? I dared myself to answer. Maybe I'm just exhausted, we've all had so much to do lately. But it was a thrill to see Dan looking so happy, I had to admit.

Helen was at the counter, too, slicing more bread. "Would you please take the pots of coffee out to the tables? I don't know why, but I feel a bit shaky. I'd like to sit down for a few minutes."

She glanced sideways at me. "Sure," she said without another word. Her chance to be near Dan, I thought, and shrugged.

I went to the booth and sat quietly, my forehead in my hands, listening to much back-slapping and good-natured joshing before the loud voices ceased. I knew, then, that the men were intent on satisfying their ravenous appetites. I smiled to myself and closed my eyes. Muffled voices and jovial laughter, now, were scattered amid the clatter of utensils. Soon I rose and began to clean up things in the kitchen, and in less than an hour later Jack Colby and his men were gone.

Dan came in and thanked Helen and I again. She bustled about him, making all sorts of small talk. I tried not to notice, but I did see Dan pat her on the arm and smile at her. So? I asked myself.

Diane had been sitting in the bay window and Dan went to join her. They talked about her walking progress, her lessons, and other things in general, then he rose. "Catch you later, sport," he said, patting her back.

He walked to the door, but turned and looked squarely to me. "I'm going out to check on the horses. They did a great job. Worked hard." Then he was gone. I noticed that Diane seemed to be watching very closely.

Other than Diane's irritating attitude of late, all the things I had observed produced a positive feeling the year's work had gone well at OUR Ranch and a powerful joy entered my heart. Cleaning up the kitchen and the porch was easy.

{[CHAPTER 24]}

Late that night I sat at the bay window table sipping a cup of hot tea, thumbing through a recipe book and occasionally glancing up at the star-filled sky. I was tired, but not ready for sleep. Diane had been assigned a series of short stories to read, so she'd left the kitchen when the men did. Helen, also, had retired to her room as soon as the kitchen was orderly. The house was quiet, save for the humming of the fridge and I was beginning to give thoughts of going to my room, too.

"Not sleepy?" The voice was low, masculine, almost a whisper.

"Oh," I cried, softly, "Oh, no—not really."

"I'm sorry." Dan was standing near me. "These old mocassins don't make much noise." He had come from his room, his hair still moist from a shower. It was dark and curly with the dampness and it made him look almost boyish. The small chandelier above the table was of amber glass and it intensified a golden glow on his skin. Now a scent of cologne, new to me, waft across the table as he walked around and chose a chair opposite me. My pulse quickened, even skipping a few beats, it seemed.

He picked up the carafe and shook it. I heard a faint slosh, but before I could offer to make a new pot, he poured the scant amount into a mug. My pulse returned to near normal.

We talked, first of the roundup and the year's progress, then of Diane and her steady progress to walk again—unaided. He seemed relaxed and happy and tired. Long minutes passed before he leaned a bit and looked out the window. "Dark out—without a moon." Then he glanced toward the bunkhouse.

"Yes," I said, nodding, "the lights have been out for quite some time now. You must be pretty tired, too."

"Yeah, I am." He eased his chair away from the table. "I really didn't want that coffee, Char. I just wanted to talk to you, to tell you how grateful I am." His gaze was intense and I felt it slowly travel about my hands, my hair, my face. "I'm terribly grateful. I can't thank you enough for coming here." His eyes made mine their prisoner.

I thought I would just liquify. It was a wonderful feeling, hearing those words, and I wanted the moment to last and last but I felt I must say something. "I'm glad. I really wanted to come—once I'd answered the ad."

Dan leaned back then and yawned, quickly stifling it with his fist. "Yup—I guess it's time for bed."

I'd surprised myself by finding the power to speak,

then, gathering a bit more common sense, I rose from the table, taking the mugs with me. I went to the sink and deposited them there.

Quickly, I turned to get the pot and creamer. But Dan had followed directly behind me and we collided. He had the pot and creamer in his hands. I cried out in instant surprise and looked up to him. I froze. The bright light above the sink was full on him and his eyes were laughing, crinkling at the corners. "Sorry." He chuckled. "I'm so — so clumsy."

I backed and looked down. Cream was dripping from the tipped pitcher, spilling over his hands and onto the floor. I couldn't move, but felt my breath catch and hold. I looked up to him again, into those same captivatingly-blue eyes I'd perceived the morning Mary Kane left the ranch. Now her words came racing back to me and I felt, at once, irritated at her all over again. Well, damn, Charlotte, do something. And don't even consider her words. It was just a silly notion on her part.

But Dan was the one to be embarrassed now, with ruddy color clearly rouging his weather-worn cheeks. He grinned at me like a schoolboy who'd just accidentally dropped a little girl's books in the mud. "I was just trying to help," he said limply.

I quickly took the things from his hands and set them on the counter. Then, taking a damp cloth, I wiped the cream from his hands. They were warm, hard, roughened hands, and I ached when I touched them. He stood mute as I cleaned his hands, then he searched out my eyes again, saying, "I'm so glad you came to stay with us," His voice was deep, smooth and serious.

"Yes," I whispered. "Oh, yes, I am, too."

Suddenly I sensed another's eyes. I turned. Dan must have thought I'd turned from him, but at that instant I saw Diane peeping through the barely-opened swinging door, her eyes wide and unblinking. She drew back slightly and glared.

"Goodnight, Char." Dan turned quickly and disappeared into his room. I assumed he never sensed his daughter's presence or even my startled recognition of her. She had been there for just an instant and then she was gone, the door still moving slightly from her touch.

But why didn't she come into the kitchen? Why peek? It was almost ghostly. What could *this* be all about? I wondered. Her eyes had had a strange quality about them, first startled—then changing. Yes, they were accusing eyes. Yes, of course. She couldn't see the things in Dan's hands from where she was standing in the doorway across the room.

I shrugged. Well, I'm tired of trying to understand her. I dampened some paper towels, wiped the cream from the floor, and left the room, snapping off the lights behind me.

I went to my room, relieved the day was over, but was instantly startled by the sound of breaking glass coming from Diane's room. The door to my side of the bathroom was slightly ajar and I jerked it open. Her door was shut. I rapped. No answer. Cautiously, I opened the door and peered in.

Diane was standing drooped on her crutches, and the glass ball of Minnesota dried flowers lay in tiny pieces all over the floor. Our eyes met. We stared at one another. Then I saw tears glistening on her cheeks.

"You'll never be my mother," she wailed, her voice thin, pathetic.

"Diane—get into bed—now."

She hesitated for a moment, then turning, she eased herself onto her bed. I watched, never taking my eyes from her, lest she misread me. She still stared at me, but momentarily I could see her feistiness waning.

I stalked to the kitchen for a broom and dustpan. When I returned she was lying still in her bed, the sheet drawn over her head. I carefully swept up the shards of glass and bits of dried flowers, and, without speaking, took everything back to the kitchen. I emptied the dustpan into a paper bag, rolled it shut, and tucked it into the waste-basket. I returned to her room and sat in a chair. By then I was shaking.

"Now listen to me, Diane," I said, slowly, matter-of-factly. "I have no intention of becoming your mother. Wherever did you get that notion?"

Not a sound came from under the sheet.

"I came here because I really wanted to help. I don't

need the work. I have funds of my own." I used the most emphatic tones I could muster.

The sheet stirred. I heard a squeaky voice. "I didn't know . . . well, Helen said . . ." She was mumbling something more.

"I don't care what Helen said." So that's it, I thought, there's been talk about why I came here. What nerve! "I told you, Diane, the day I helped you write that story for your homework, that I feel a need to help people. And that's exactly why I came here. Besides, it's just about half way to California for me."

There was silence again, no movement from under the cover.

"I certainly didn't mean to impose on your personal life." I paused a long moment. "So—I'll talk to your father in the morning, and if he agrees, I'll leave on the first flight I can get." I rose to my feet. "Goodnight. I'll send Helen in if you need . . ."

She threw the sheet from her face and sat up. "No. Wait. Don't go. I'm sorry." She sucked in a couple short breaths. "But Helen said Aunt Mary asked you to come here and try to seduce my father. You know—make him marry you."

"Helen said that!" I cringed and sank into the chair again, pondering the past events with Mary Kane for a few moments. "Yes," I said, "Mary thought it would be a good thing to see your father remarry. She even told me she culled the applications, looking for just the right person, hoping it *would* happen. Mary was playing a game, I won't deny that. But that's a far cry from . . ."

"But Helen said Aunt Mary even paid you something before you came here, that it was all agreed."

I exploded. "She paid my airfare! *That's* what she paid!"

Diane was sitting up straighter now, her eyes large—and scared. "You mean none of it is true?"

"None of it! I swear!" A moment passed. "Besides, your father has a perfect right to lead his *own* life, to marry again if he chooses."

She dropped her head and there were a few moments of silence. "I'm sorry. Yes, I know he does."

I could hardly hear her and I didn't answer.

"I really am sorry." She was speaking louder now. "I don't want you to leave." She sniffed. "I kind of thought Helen was making it up. She always did like Dad, I could tell."

"Well, I guess she can if she wants to," I said, simply, "that's her business."

"But—well—but will you stay, Charlotte? Please?" There was a genuine pleading in her voice.

I sat quietly, thinking, Well, why should I let an impulsive teenager and a rejected woman run *my* life? I made up my mind in a hurry. "Yes, Diane, I'll stay. But it's a good thing Helen is leaving in the morning. I couldn't stand to be in the same house with her another day."

"Thank you," she said, her eyes downcast. "You must think I'm an awful brat, but I'm not—really I'm not." Then our eyes met.

"I know," I said, moving closer to her bed. "It's tough losing your mother when you're so young. And it's terrible to think of losing your father to a stranger." I patted her shoulder. "But you're not to worry, you hear?"

She put her hand on my wrist. "Don't tell my dad. And don't tell him I broke your gift. Promise? I'm sorry about the ball, I really liked it, too."

She sniffed several times. I reached and plucked a tissue from the box on her table. "It's okay, I won't tell." I handed her the tissue.

She wiped her eyes and blew her nose. "Thanks," she said, and plopped back on her pillow. She looked exhausted. "Good night," she added softly, and smiled ever-so-slightly, pulling the covers up to her chin.

"Good night, sleep tight." I made a tucking gesture with a bit of blanket. Then I made my way through the bathroom into my own room.

But when I thought of Helen the blood rushed anew through my veins, pounding at my temples. One piece at a time, I pulled off my clothes and threw them onto the bed. Sure. Helen's had a *thing* for Dan all these years, but nothing's happened. Then Mary thinks up a clever scheme and picks me to come here, to pit me against Helen, I guess, to maybe beat her at her own game? Oh, Mary wouldn't do that. Now would she?

I was chilled before I realized I stood naked. Damn! Now where are my pajamas? Oh, yes, I need fresh ones. I dug in the bureau drawer, seemingly forever. I found some. I jerked them on. I went into the bathroom, found my brush and yanked it through my hair. The nerve of that woman! Sure, she's had plenty of time to fill Diane's head with those lies. Damn. I wonder if I should confront her? No! I don't want to involve Diane again.

I brushed my teeth and by the time I had finished washing my face, I began to relax. I went to my room and turned down the covers and sat on the bed's edge. I reached for a jar of face cream, methodically opening it and putting little dabs of cream all over my face. Well, love is *not* a game, Mary Kane. You can't *make* things happen. I slowly smoothed the cream on my skin. But Dan *is* a handsome, pleasant man. Slowly, I put the cover back on the jar, slipped into bed and pulled the covers up to my chin. Yes, in a game of love, he could be an important player. I smiled to myself, then, thinking about the silly collision in the kitchen not too long before.

I thought of Helen's brash lies again, and punched my pillow into puffiness. But then I smoothed it over and lay my head down. I felt a little sorry for her, but, damn, I was glad she was leaving in the morning. I snugged the covers close and stretched long. Then the words of a song waft through my mind—whatever will be, will be. . . .

CHAPTER 25

Morning came quickly. Helen was packed, ready to leave, her bags lined by the kitchen door. She'd hardly spoken during breakfast. Had she heard the sound of breaking glass and the stern voices of last night? If so, she said nothing.

Luggage—a familiar sight, I thought, but this time I was elated. I wanted to open the door and kick them out. Charlotte, behave yourself.

Helen was putting on her coat just as Dan came from his room. He quickly helped her with it. "Thanks a lot, Helen, we really appreciated your being here," he said, and he patted her shoulder.

She pulled her curls from under her coat collar and looked up to him, still arranging her hair about her shoulders. "Oh, that's all right, Dan," she said, her smile dripping saccharine, "I was glad to help you. And just remember, if you should need me after *she's* gone," she motioned her head in my direction—"just you call."

She could've waited, I thought, and said that in the car.

"Well, I'll pull the wagon up by the porch and be back in for your things," Dan said, and with no further comment, he went out the door.

Helen hurried toward Diane's room. If she only knew, I thought, that Diane has told me the lies that she's used to get me to leave. Hah! *She's* the one that's leaving.

Then a saying my father often used popped into my mind: Let sleeping dogs lie. I would heed his words, but with some regret, nevertheless. I usually had mixed reactions when my father's sayings fit the situation too well. Again, I wanted to kick her tote bag like a football. Charlotte!

Dan came back into the house. I was loading the dishwasher and he came to the sink. He stood fairly close to me and reached for a tumbler. Our eyes met without intention on my part. I quickly sensed I was holding my breath when I heard Helen come back into the room. I breathed then and turned to her. She seemed to glare at me, but I calmly let my gaze rest on her. So what's she wondering now?

Quickly she snatched up her tote bag and left the house, flinging the words "Goodbye, Charlte" over her shoulder.

Damn, she never did want to say my name correctly.

I called after her, "Goodbye, Helen, have a nice day."

Dan had filled the tumbler, drained it, and placed it in the washer, brushing my shoulder as he did so. Turning, he looked down at me just as I glanced up. His blue-blue eyes had become bluer, still. I felt arrested—and happy.

"Bye, Char. I'll be bringing Jo tonight, remember?"

I had to speak. "Oh, yes. That's wonderful."

He burst into a big, beautiful smile, then turned, picked up Helen's large bag and left the house. The minute the door closed behind him, I whirled around and around the kitchen floor and I knew my smile was as big as his.

Diane began using her walker that same day, but she was having difficulty with it, so she would have to rest in her wheelchair for a half hour or so before she would test it again. It seemed her arms tired quickly. So we set up a mini classroom in the kitchen where we could work together, still trying the walker regularly. Therefore, most of Friday afternoon was spent studying pre-revolutionary Russia, Rasputin and the Czar.

Time passed quickly and soon it was dusk. Jed came into the house at his usual suppertime, but refused his meal, only wanting a thermos of hot soup. "For later," he said.

"Jed Simpson, I'm going to tell on you," I teased, half seriously.

"Aw, don't pay me no mind, Miz Foster, I'll be alright," he said, holding his hand in mid air as if to fend off the threat. And then the door closed behind him for the night. But I worried anyway when he didn't eat well.

I was peeking at the roast in the oven, hoping it would not be overdone, when I heard the stationwagon growl up the long driveway. Oh, it was good having Joanne coming home again. I had wanted to do something special so I'd taken tall candles from the buffet and placed them in the center of the big dining room table. Diane had shot me a quizzical glance, but never said a word, which was unusual for her. Now I was pressured to find a reason acceptable to a young mind.

Joanne and her father entered the kitchen with much ado. "M-m-m, smells good," Dan said, shedding his jacket and hanging it on a peg. He sniffed about with a theatrical air.

"Oh, it's so good to be home again," Joanne said, as she dropped her books on the booth's table. Then, while still unzipping her parka, she went to the swinging doors and peeked in. "Wow, candles. What's the occasion?"

I glanced at Dan just as he, also, raised an inquisitive brow.

Now I was really pressed for an explanation. "I'll tell you later, when we're all seated," I said, with a haughty air, and turned to tend the food. Everyone scurried then to wash hands and become presentable at table.

After we gathered in the dining room I struck a match and ceremoniously lit the candles. "It's graduation time," I said, in a lilting manner.

"Huh?" Diane cried, crinkling her nose.

"Yes, Diane graduated today, from crutches to walker." I said it with a flourish of hand, presenting her like a class valedictorian. Then I turned to Joanne. "And it's a home-coming, too," I smiled and clapped. Then we all enjoyed a great chuckle and clapped some more.

Diane swung her head about, her long blonde hair fanning out with the swift movement, and flashed a grin to me alone. Then her eyes fixed to mine. I knew in an instant she felt that the secret of the night before was completely safe now—with me.

Dan reached out and patted her shoulder. "I'm glad things are working out so well." I sensed a tremendous relief in his voice. "You'll be back to school in no time."

"I can hardly wait," she said, smiling very prettily.

"I'm glad, too," Joanne chimed in, "and Cathy's anxious, too. She's always talking about it."

'Well—but I'm sure going to miss the chess games," Dan interjected. "Oh, by the way, sport, how about one tonight?"

Diane beamed. "Sure."

After the meal was finished, the dining room table soon became a game table as Joanne and I quickly cleared away the dishes. When we had the dishwasher locked up and safely gurgling and swishing, Joanne picked up her books, including one giant physics book. "I've got lots to do."

I grinned and nodded with understanding. It hadn't been all that long since I'd had another student under my guidance. Oh, Kenneth, I miss you. And his face flashed before me as Joanne retreated to her room, the guest room newly emptied of Helen.

I flicked the kitchen to darkness and went to my room, feeling an exquisite rush of contentment. In the bathroom,

I stripped off my clothes and ran the deepest, bubbliest bath I dared. I slithered down under the foam and uttered a luxurious sigh, admitting exhaustion. But I didn't care. It was wonderful being a part of a happy family once again.

{CHAPTER 26}

Morning brought brilliant sunshine spreading over the
now bare treetops in the valley below Diane's windows. It
warmed the crisp, late October air. "Welcome, new day," I
said, adjusting her curtains to allow her the best view.

"I call a sunrise a *promise*," Diane said, beaming as she
slid out of her bed. (She needed little help now.) "I'll never
get tired of it, never, ever."

It's the poet in her, I thought. I liked that. Going to
her bureau drawer, then, I pulled out a hot-pink sweatsuit.
"How about this?" I asked.

"Neat," she said, catching my toss.

"See you later." I left the room, anxious to get to the
kitchen, to get on with the new day.

Soon the entire room spoke of tart, chilly grapefruit, of
spicy sausages sizzling in a pan, of thick maple syrup oozing
across steamy pancakes. Jed came into the kitchen earliest
of all and ate his breakfast with relish. Hah, I thought, who
could resist a breakfast such as this? I felt so smug.

Jed rose from the booth at the precise moment Dan's dressing room door popped open. "Morning, Dan. I'll be takin' some salt licks up the south slope," he said, taking his hat from the pegged rack.

At that moment both girls entered the room, greeting the men with cheery comments. The smiles reflecting all about the room then, like rays of sunshine, warmed me to the point of wanting to giggle. I turned back to the griddle pouring on new rounds of batter, all the while coveting a quiet contentment.

"I'm going out with Jo this morning," I heard Dan say. "She's going to limber up old Boots. Di's doing so well now it won't be any time at all and she'll be out roaming the hills again." He was beaming.

I brought a platter of new cakes to the booth just as Diane slipped onto the bench beside her father. Dan gave her a quick one-armed hug. Joanne, meanwhile, sprinkled a light coating of sugar across her grapefruit,

Diane cut her pancakes into tiny squares. "Oh, Dad, I just like to look for new things to draw and paint." She immediately stuffed a forkful into her mouth, chewed and swallowed quickly. "Hurry up, Jo, I'm really anxious to see . . ."

"Oh, slow up, I'm not going to gulp down my food."

"Ump, ump, now, girls," Dan said, tapping his fork gently on his plate.

I slipped into the booth beside Joanne then, and we ate

quietly, only short, polite phrases interrupting our breakfast. What's with these two this morning? Something's different.

Dan finished his food and drank his coffee in quick draughts, then excused himself. As he dressed for the outside, he stepped nearer the booth again. "I'll be getting the horses saddled, Jo," he said. She looked up to him with a broad grin.

Honestly, I thought, sometimes those two are of one mind. Then I saw the syrup bottle had been emptied and got up to get a new one. As I searched the pantry shelf I noticed Dan had taken his denim jacket from the peg, put it on and was slowly fingering the silver snaps. He had seemed in a hurry, but now he dawdled. I felt his eyes follow me as I moved about and was drawn to glance at him when he reached for his hat. He was still looking at me, studying me, it seemed, as if I were a curiosity.

I couldn't help but for our eyes to meet. He smiled, then, a most warm and intimate smile, yet with the shyness of a schoolboy. But before I could respond, he turned on a sharp heel and left the house, easing the door behind him.

When we finished eating, Joanne quickly cleared the table, depositing all things on the kitchen counter and left the room. An impending feeling filled the air. She returned with a large, square box, plopped it on the table and stepped back. "Surprise, Charlotte, we have something for you." She giggled and glanced at Diane.

"What is this?" Is this what's been behind Diane's

anxiousness, Joanne's quiet intentness, Dan's mysterious glances and secretive smile?

Diane sang out, "Open it, open it."

"Ssssh, Di, give her a chance."

Piqued to my limit then, I snatched off the cover. "Boots! Oh, girls, how nice." I had to sit. "How beautiful!"

"I hope they fit," Diane said, pressing her fingers to her temples.

"We peeked at your size," Joanne confessed. "Well, actually Aunt Mary did. We even have another pair if these don't fit."

I gasped as I pulled a boot from the box and turned it around. "I *like* them." They were dark brown with about an inch and a half of heel. Intricate cut-outs showed a tan underlay that went across the instep and again around the top of the boot forming a V in the front. I turned the boot slowly around, feeling the fine craftsmanship. "Quite fancy, I'd say."

"Try them, try them on," Diane urged.

I kicked off slippers and pulled the pair on and got up and sauntered about the kitchen floor, the heels clacking importantly. "Wow," I said, "They certainly give me—a lift."

But before I could say thank you, Joanne laughed and grabbed my arm and led me to the bay window where movement caught my eye. Dan was standing by the gate with three saddled horses: Baron, Boots and—Patches. I whirled around to face her.

"Yes, really. Dad and I want you to come riding with us."

Diane was behind me now and I turned to face her, too. She was smiling only slightly, her eyes now a cool blue.

"Will you, Charlotte, please?" Joanne's voice was soft, begging.

"Certainly." I laughed and gave each girl a quick hug.

Returning from my room where I'd dressed in jeans and sweatshirt, I entered the kitchen, my heels tapping smartly. I stopped and turned a foot this way and that, admiring the well tooled leather.

When I looked at Diane she cast her eyes downward. "They weren't my idea, Charlotte. Jo deserves the credit," she confessed. "At first, I didn't want to, then I did." She glanced up. "But would you like to wear my fringy jacket? You'll look really cool in it—and it's warm."

"Why, yes, Diane, I'd love to."

"I'll get it, Di," Joanne said, and disappeared down the hallway, returning with a handsome jacket of soft, ripe-yellow buckskin, its long fringed trim swinging about. She had also slipped into her own, one several shades darker, more like the carmel used on apples.

I slipped into the jacket and twirled around admiringly, then tied a red kerchief over my head. "So? Your father knew this all the time, did he?"

They answered in one voice. "Right."

Diane turned on the radio as we left the house, twisting it to top volume. It must hurt her a lot not to be able to join us, I thought, but she's doing so well it won't be long before she will be able. The way she studies she certainly doesn't lack determination. Yet I couldn't help feeling a twinge of sympathy as Joanne and I hurried to the gate.

Chase bounded ahead of us, barking his own anticipation. The skies were sunny, but huge mashed-potato clouds slowly moved across the endless blue space above. The wind blew strong and steady out of the northwest and I had to force my steps for I felt a little weak and a bit giddy from all the excitement. Lord, I need a little more resolve than this, I thought. Well, you were quite able—once. I know.

We reached the gate and I looked at Dan. "A real surprise," I said, trying to show a bit of annoyance at being tricked into the compromising situation.

He returned the look with a smirky grin. "Ready?" He'd grasped Patches' bridle and held her steady.

"Okay." I gripped the horn and lifted my foot to the stirrup with a slight hop. I felt as if a hundred pair of eyes, including the horses, were watching me. Patches moved sideways at the first pressure of my weight. "I don't blame you," I said, in a reassuring voice as I bounced backwards on the other foot. "That time in the corral hardly counts."

Dan chuckled and held the horse snubbed as I tried again. That time I executed a perfect mount, but my pulse raced all the way up to my throat.

Joanne had already taken her horse through the open gate on a slow trot. When I was firmly in the saddle, Dan handed me the reins, but the moment I turned the horse around to follow Joanne, I heard him give Patches a firm slap on the rump. No! The horse lunged ahead and I heard him roar with laughter, but I stayed easily in the saddle.

Patches trotted after the other horse, which was far ahead now, so I gave her her lead and soon she began to gallop. I heard hoofbeats gaining on me, and presently the rider was beside me. I turned to see the powerful bay, bearing the still-laughing man to almost touching range. And above the thunder of hooves, I heard him shout, "I like your boots."

Such nerve! I wanted to return something brash, but instead, I yelled into the wind, "Thanks." But the wind only caught the word and threw it over my shoulder. My kerchief was blown from my head, and it clung around my neck, my hair whipping out behind. Exhilaration sent a sharp tingle all the way to my toes, snug in the stirrups in my new boots. It felt wonderful.

Dan took the lead then and slowed the horses to a walk as we came to an easy climb up the first hill. We followed the trail down into a little valley, then up another hill. The trail now was narrow and the horses kept to a single file, gingerly picking their way. Nothing to it, I thought, seems like only yesterday since I've done this. Then why had you been so nervous?

Over that hill we rode, then down once more into a deep gulch. We stopped to look around. It was a secluded spot, out of sight from any mortal eyes, I was sure. I felt a little edgy. Relax, Charlotte Foster, you're in safe hands. I peered wonderingly about. All the deciduous trees were bare of leaves now, but many still clung to the shrubbery. A rustle sounded beside me and I started. A rabbit had jumped from a willow thicket and scurried into its burrow, flashing its plump, white tail in the sunlight. Patches was startled, too, and I patted her shoulder. "Easy. Easy, now." Dan smiled sympathetically as I soothed the horse. She calmed quickly and I sighed, feeling confident my riding skills of years gone by had returned.

As we rested the horses I marveled at the simple beauty surrounding us. A narrow stream flowed lazily, twisting and turning along its way, until it disappeared into a steeper part of the gulch. Shards of ice clung to the edges of the stream, shining like crystals on the clear water. Baron sought to drink and the others followed suit, as we talked about the ride through the hills.

Soon we went on, climbing to the top of the next hill, one considerably higher than the last. We stopped there to survey the view, for we could see for miles in three directions. But the mountains to the west loomed before us like another world. I retied my scarf and wiped tears from my eyes, brought there by the insistent wind, then I gazed about in awe. I chuckled to myself. Minnesota sure is flat, I thought.

As I peered to the north I saw an even higher hill. "How far away is that one?"

"Not too far." Dan urged Baron close to me. "It's just tough getting there."

"Do the cattle go all the way up there?"

"Sure do, several times a summer."

"Oh, what's that dark thing up there?" I pointed to an object near a stand of tall trees.

"That?" Dan asked. "Oh, that's the line cabin, a shack, really, on the property line. We use it when we hunt, or cut wood or look for our herds sometimes. All the ranchers around here use it."

"Oh, I see." But I left more questions unasked.

"Yup, it's my turn to check it before winter sets in. I'm a little late this year, but I'll get to it soon."

Just then Baron pricked his ears and snorted. He backed around sideways. Then Boots and Patches began doing the same. "What's wrong, Dad?" Joanne's voice was anxious.

"Well, I'll bet there's a cat over there in that tangle of brush by that tree," he said, calmly, "we may as well get out of here."

But my back stiffened and gooseflesh crawled under my collar. A mountain lion? Here? I reined up the horse and prepared to do exactly as I was told.

"Just follow me back down the trail. Easy does it. They'll be okay," Dan said, his words commanding.

I followed Dan, but stole a quick look at Joanne. Her expression was dead-serious. The horses walked steadily, only occasionally pricking their ears.

They're used to this, I reasoned. They're used to this, they're used to this. . . . I just kept repeating it to myself, gaining a bit of confidence as we moved down the hill.

Soon the horses calmed and we rode easily back up the next hill and all the way to the sloping hillside closest to the ranch. There the horses began to trot, but soon broke out into a gallop without urging. Sure, I thought, they know they're going home—to grain.

I tensed to keep control during the short, remaining distance until we came to a sudden stop at the closed gate. Whew! I had clung to the saddle like a seasoned rodeo performer, I thought, and mentally began to give myself a pat on the back. But then I leaned forward and gave Patches a few praising pats on *her* shoulder instead.

Joanne jumped from her horse and pulled the rails out of the gate. (Jed had replaced them behind us to contain the roving, but smaller herd.) Dan eased himself from the bay and handed her the reins. He took Patches by her bridle then and held her steady. I felt confident enough to dismount by myself, yet I liked his concern. I raised myself in the saddle and swung my leg over her rump. But when I stepped to the ground on both feet and turned to walk, my knees buckled. I began to sink.

Dan's hands shot out and caught me at the waist. I felt a current race through my body, weakening it further. He held me firm and we stood like that for what seemed to be an eternity—close—so close I could feel his breath on my cheek. Patches moved forward, straining at her reins. "You all right, Char?" he asked. I saw his eyes then, wide and bright.

"Yes," I answered, laughing weakly, "yes, I'm fine—now."

Dan released his hold and took a step backward, his eyes still on me.

"Well, I haven't ridden in a long time," I said, feebly making excuses for myself. I moved my legs but they were slow to cooperate. "Now I know how Diane felt." I began to giggle and moan at the same time taking a few steps, albeit with a wobble.

Dan laughed, too. "Well, you go straight to the house, we'll take care of the horses." He gathered in Patches' reins and began to take her to the barn, where Joanne had already taken the other two. I trudged toward the house. His voice, traveling on the wind then, said, "You did just dandy."

I waved at him with a disagreeing motion, and proceeded to the house, all the time remembering his strong hands at my waist. It clung in my thoughts until I reached the kitchen and faced Diane.

She had been sitting in the bay window with a book and she lay it in her lap. Then, with eyes squarely on me, she flatly stated, "You ride well, *Char*. I watched you ride out before. Dad must think you ride well, too."

"Thanks," I said, "maybe one never does forget how." But why did she emphasis my one-syllable name? Is she deliberately trying to mimic her father? I worked at the snaps of her borrowed jacket. She doesn't miss a thing, I thought, I'd better change the subject—fast. "It's sure nice out. Indian summer weather. In Minnesota we have lots of dreary, rainy days after our Indian summer. We always say, "Nice weather for ducks, but who wants to be a duck?"'

It was a silly old joke and she didn't laugh, either. I slipped off her buckskin jacket and hung it on a peg and went to the sink. "I'd better see to dinner," I said, and began to scrub my hands.

❧

Sunday morning arrived and snow arrived with it, just an inch or so. But then the sky cleared and the sun shone brightly, making everything sparkle as it spread across the hills. I watched the horses from the sink window. They would race around the meadow, swishing their tails and kicking up their hind feet. All, except old Sal. She would look around and shake her head as if to say, "Those kids!"

Late that afternoon Joanne readied herself for her return trip to school. Her father was outside with Jed, busy with their chores. Diane was absorbed with her painting again, now that Helen was gone. And I was building a layer cake.

Joanne came into the kitchen and leaned against the counter near me, her tall frame angled now, her blue-gray eyes solemn. "You know, Charlotte," she said, her voice wistful, "sometimes I wish I could just stay here and help Dad and Jed work the ranch. I really love it here."

"I'm sure you do," I said, wielding the spatula to create deep swirls in the frosting across the top layer.

"But—well," she continued, "ever since Mom died I promised myself I would study medicine. I want to work in research to help find a cure for leukemia. I want to do that for my mother."

"That sounds marvelous."

"You really think so?"

"Yes, I do." I paused with spatula in midair. "Sometimes certain events direct our paths, certain happenings tell us which way to go. I believe in circumstance. We must seize opportunity when it presents itself." I waved the spatula in emphasis. "Make your choices, Joanne, then never doubt your decisions. Doubt can be your worst enemy." I was spouting like an amateur philosopher.

"Oh, you sure can make a person feel good." She reached out, then, and took a swipe of frosting on her fingertip. I swatted at her with the spatula. "I've been thinking," she said, as she held the finger for close inspection, "maybe I won't come home next weekend. We have quarter finals coming up and I really should stay and study." She popped the frosted finger into her mouth, rolled her eyes and pulled it out clean, sighing appreciation. "I'll sure be glad when Di gets back to school." She was quiet for a long moment. "We don't come home near as often in the winter," she said, a sad note creeping into her voice. "Driving gets pretty tough, sometimes. But, gosh, I know Dad gets lonesome. He calls a lot."

"Yes, it must get really quiet around here in the winter," I said, giving the frosting a last swirl. Then I handed Joanne the spatula—and the bowl.

Diane came into the kitchen just then, managing her walker quite well. I felt her gaze brush by me. I told myself I imagined it.

I took dishes and flatware out of the cupboards and handed them to Joanne. She toted them to the table in the bay window and Diane helped her lay out the services. Soon they were chattering like the magpies holding forth on the corral fences some days.

The kitchen door burst open, then, and a cool breeze entered with Dan. "Sorry I'm late for supper, ladies. Jed wasn't feeling too well so I sent him back to the bunkhouse to rest a while. I finished up alone. He'll be in to eat about six, Char. Make sure he does, I'm getting a little worried about him." He turned to Joanne. "We'll have to hurry, Hon."

I'd made potato soup, lumpy with big pieces of ham, and I'd hoped to treat them to my layered spice cake, but now a new urgency had set in and we ate, hurried and silent.

Before long Dan and Joanne left for St. Anne's in Meadow Grand. Diane waved a book at me and faked a violent shiver. "I've got to read *The Scarlet Pimpernell,*" she said, and went to her room, her walker bumping down the hallway at good speed.

I heard the clock on the mantle strike six times, so I quickly reheated Jed's soup. He did come in, like Dan had said, and even ate an adequate amount. "It tastes just great, Miz Foster." (He still persisted in calling me Miz Foster, but from him it sounded special.) He declined the spice cake, though, only asking for a thermos of decaf, for later, he said. I noticed his big smile was missing and it saddened me.

Later, just as I snapped off the sink light preparing to leave the kitchen for the night, I caught a glimpse of the wagon's headlights coming up the drive. The shafts of light shone through the evergreens, still lightly crusted with the morning's snow. I watched for a moment. I'm glad he's home already, I thought, he needs more rest. And Jed does, too. We're all tired, I think.

I went to my room and undressed for bed, searching for warmer pajamas. I'm glad I had that nice talk with Joanne. She's such a sensible girl. I brushed my teeth and washed and creamed my face, examining it closely in the mirror. Not much summer sun remained on my skin. Well, I'll let California sun take over soon. And I'm glad Diane's over her suspicions of me. But, damn, now Jed worries me.

I laid in bed, coaxing sleep. I rolled over and hugged my pillow. Well, it won't be too long and that feisty child will be back in school, I thought, and I'll be on my way to California. California! I let the syllables of the word roll over and over in my mind. Cal i for ni a. Cal i for ni a. It sounded like waves whispering on a sandy shore.

I began to drift off to sleep when suddenly I was astride a racing horse, the wind strong in my face. I gulped the fresh air and felt my face tingling. Such a wonderful feeling. Then, just as suddenly, I relived the touch of Dan's strong hands at my waist, the nearness of him—how it warmed my skin. I liked it.

Now, look here, Charlotte Foster, he had to keep you from falling, didn't he?

{[CHAPTER 27]}

Several days went by and life at the ranch moved along smoothly. Then I noticed Diane getting restless and more irritable. Of course, that's it. Her father's been spending a lot of time away from the house doing chores or traveling to Red Hill for the mail, or Jackson Buttes for winter supplies. I suppose he thought my company was enough for her. Well, she'll hint to him soon, if not tell him outright and pout. She should be busier. Maybe she could do something for extra credits at school. I'll write a note to Sister Agnes. No, I'll ask Diane first. I don't want to risk any bad feelings. I took a deep breath and then another and dismissed it from my thoughts.

A chinook wind had come up and removed all traces of snow, but there still was a slight nip in the air. Jed was feeling much better, or so he said, and kept up with the tending of the horses and cattle. And he never failed to portion out Chase's food from the big bag on the porch. He even seemed to have a new bounce in his step and his big smile was back, the one that almost made his eyes disappear.

The men came in to supper later than usual that night and stayed in the booth long after their meal was finished. They were talking, figuring, making notes. I didn't offer any small-talk, just cleaned up the kitchen, set the dishwasher to work and went to my room. Diane had told her father earlier she had tons to read and had gone to her room, also.

I wrote a long letter to John, mentioning, of course, my fantasy of becoming a trick rider in a rodeo. More seriously, I wrote: Do you ever stop by my house anymore? You must know the three teachers that rented it? How's Mama? Have you seen Dorrie around? I admit, John, I miss you. Funny, though, I thought I'd be more homesick.

Later, when I stretched out in bed, I closed my eyes and tried to remember John's arms around me. They were comforting, warm arms. Then, a kiss. Sweet. Tender. I drifted into a peaceful, restful sleep, my head dreamily on his shoulder.

I awoke in the morning unprepared to view the dreary sight out my bedroom window. Misty rain was being thrown about by an angry wind. A few soggy snowflakes were mixed into the rain, but the moment they touched any earthly object they were obliterated by more whisps of rain. Several chickadees hopped about, seeking shelter in the branches of the big spruce outside my window. For a moment I imagined I could reach out and pluck them from the cold and hold them safe in my hands.

Diane, upon arising, and without a sunrise to watch, had gone directly to the kitchen. I'd heard her thumping down the hall. She was making good progress with her walker and would even venture a few steps without it.

"Good morning, Diane," I said, as I entered the kitchen.

She didn't look up. She was wiping coffee rings from the booth table and muttering. "Men. Spill. Mess." She turned and walked across the kitchen to the counter.

My, aren't we crabby this morning, I thought, it must be the weather.

She had something in her hand, and was, at the same time, trying to open a box of frozen waffles. "Here, let me help you," I said.

"Thanks. I can do it myself." She went to the booth to put the waffles into the toaster. I set coffee to brew and poured myself a glass of orange juice.

Diane still clutched the object in her hand. Then she went to the sink and threw it in the waste basket there. Her waffles popped up. She put them on a plate, laced them with syrup and began to eat.

"You're quiet this morning. Didn't you sleep well?"

"I've got a headache," she snapped.

I poured a mug of coffee and took it with me as I went down to the basement to start the laundry. I may as well stay out of her way, I thought. Although the minute I started down the stairs, I heard the radio flick on and the volume raised outrageously. Hmmm, I thought she had a headache.

When I came back up to the kitchen she was gone, but the radio was still blaring. I turned it down to a pleasant level. The booth table was sticky with syrup. Is this deliberate? I wiped it clean and set two new places. Then I began to prepare french toast.

Soon Dan and Jed came in together, bringing with them a chilly, damp breeze. They ate a hurried breakfast, gulped their coffee and mentioned they were going to Red Hill for supplies.

"We need engine oil," Dan said, almost apologetically and rose from the booth. I looked away, not sure if I should comment.

"We need Chase-food, too," Jed added, grinning as I glanced to him.

I had to look to Dan, then. "Oh, would you mail a letter for me, please?" I asked, retrieving it from the top of the fridge.

Dan took it from my hand. "Sure thing." He glanced down at the letter and a scowl creased his brow. I had written Mr. John Cummings in a rather large hand. Without a word, he slipped it into his pocket, took his hat from a peg and left the house. "Back soon, Miz Foster," Jed said, and followed, the grin still there.

While cleaning up the kitchen I was about to toss Diane's empty waffle box into the wastebasket when I discovered crumpled notepaper on top of the refuse. I could readily see my name on it. I picked it out and straightened it enough to see my name printed repeatedly and traced over and over again, amidst many other doodlings. Dan's writing. That's right. I noticed him marking the paper in that manner last night just before I left the room.

So! Diane has already made up her mind as to what it means. Lord, here we go again. I squeezed the paper with an angry fist and threw it back into the basket. My hands flew to my temples, wanting to blank it all out of my mind, but it couldn't be done. Damn, damn. First Mary. Then Helen. Then Diane. Suggesting, suspecting, resenting. Now—Diane again. Why can't they let me be? I can make my own decisions. I'm an adult. An individual—with a mind of my *own*.

Wait! Was that *only* absent-minded doodling, Mr. Garner? Stop it, Charlotte. But he did scowl at your letter to John. Only a curious reaction. Methinks your mind is playing tricks on you, dear girl. Better keep it on your work.

I struggled to obey a common sense order and spent the morning doing laundry. I even took down the bay window curtains and rewashed all the little panes of glass that Helen had done before. But, throughout the morning, Diane stayed in her room and played her record player, exceptionally loud.

She didn't appear at our normal dinnertime, obviously sulking, and, as the men hadn't returned from Red Hill, I let her sulk. She'll come out when she's hungry enough. I ate my lunch, cleaned up after myself and went back down in the basement. Only then did I hear her come into the kitchen. The radio blared again.

I put the last load into the dryer and lugged a big basket of folded things up the stairs. The kitchen was empty. But the breadboard was littered with crumbs, dotted with globs of grape jelly. And smears of peanut butter and droplets of milk were everywhere. I looked about. Even the hand towel was left in a damp ball near the sink. Well, I guess she wants me to know she still has control over the house at OUR Ranch.

What a spiteful child she can be, I thought, but I dutifully cleaned it all up. Should I have a talk with her again, I wondered. Well, maybe I'll say, "Soon I'll no longer be a threat to you, Diane, so go ahead and pout."

The men returned and it cheered me somewhat, but they ate their noon meal quickly. Then they went back outdoors to deliver a salt block to the cattle far up the slope.

That afternoon I spent my time tending a big pot of beef vegetable soup, thankful for a job to keep me distracted from Diane's unpleasant behavior. Soup, I'd noticed, was beginning to be a favorite meal and it was especially convenient to serve for our suppers.

As it was, Dan was late coming in for that very meal. His hands were smeared with something dark. He grinned. "In the garage, changing oil in the wagon," he said, holding out both hands like a little boy falsely accused. I had to smile a little, but I felt a slight irritation at the lateness of the meal.

Jed had come in behind him and we all ate quietly at

the big table in the bay. Dan noticed the missing curtains but he didn't comment. When Diane finished eating, she excused herself, got up and left the kitchen, her empty bowl remaining on the table. I knew it was hard for her to carry things while using her walker, but how did she manage that big science book earlier?

The men finished their supper and rose to leave. "I'll be out in the garage again, Char—till late," Dan said.

"Fine." I nodded.

He followed Jed from the house. "You get some rest now, Jed, you hear?" Dan's words were terse. So, even the steamy, rich soup could not warm the chilly atmosphere of the household.

The weather was still unpleasant, as it had been all day. The misty rain had turned the evening sky prematurely black, and even the usually bright yard lights were obscured in a cloak of gloom. And my mood was beginning to match the elements. The house was quiet, too, only an occasional burst of wind whistled through the tall firs above.

The phone rang just as I was putting away the last clean dish. It startled me and I almost dropped it. Calls were few these long, dark evenings. "Hello."

"Hello. Jack Colby here, is Dan around?"

"Yes, he is," I said, almost too weary to be polite, "but he's in the garage. Is there a message or should I go and get him?"

"No. No, it can wait. Just have him call me after awhile."

"I will."

"Thanks. Goodbye."

"Goodbye." I clopped the phone back on its hook. Charlotte, you were not very nice. I know.

I walked over to the sink and flicked off the light. Hmmm, I'll have to leave a note for him. No, he may not see it. Well, I'll have to tell him sooner or later. Good grief, I may as well do it now.

I took my parka from the peg and slipped into it, flipping the hood over my head. I was pulling on my gloves when I heard a faint rustle and then a thump. Turning, I glimpsed Diane leaning on her walker in the dining room doorway, the swinging door partially ajar. She glared at me with large eyes. Did she hear the phone ring, I wondered? No, not from her room. Maybe she was in the living room and heard it. Or is she spying on me? Oh, what's the difference? Now, I suppose she thinks I'm sneaking out to meet her father. Well, damn, let her think so. But it does look that way, Charlotte.

I looked at her again. "The phone was for your father," I said. But her eyes had grown even larger, flashing accusations, and her mouth was sourly drawn to a pucker.

Oh, think what you want, you spoiled, cantankerous child. But I didn't make a secret pact with your Aunt Mary to come here and steal your father's affections from you. And I'm certainly not the seducer Helen insinuated I was. I glared right back at her, but she never blinked once, I whirled around and went out the door, slamming it behind me.

As I ran to the garage in the darkness my hood slipped from my head. I didn't even care. The wind tousled my hair and bits of ice, hidden in the gusty rain, stung my face. I felt as wicked as the weather. My hair dampened quickly and I started to shiver, misery engulfing me.

I had seldom gone to the garage. When I arrived at the side door I reached out and grasped the knob. But before I could turn it, the door was jerked open and I was pulled inside. Dan jumped backward as I stumbled over the threshold, thudding against him. An ugly sound escaped my throat before I fell. Dan had reached out to catch me, but I'd felt myself slip through his arms, falling to the floor in front of him. He grasped my upper arms, at once pulling me to my feet. Pain burned somewhere. I was startled, embarrassed. I wanted to shrink to nothing. Then I felt his hands on my arms, supporting me altogether, while my legs seemed to dangle. I looked up and sickly felt my face grow hot.

"Char. Char, are you hurt?" he asked. "I didn't mean to hurt you. I'm sorry."

His words were like an embrace. I couldn't speak, my lips trembled so.

"I didn't know you were out there," he said, his voice pained now. "I was just coming to the house. Oh, damn, Char, I'm so sorry." He still held my arms. "Are you sure you're not hurt?"

"No. I'm not hurt. I—I'm fine." Then his hands loosened. But I was hurt. Everything flashed through my mind again. I was damn hurt. Hurt by the tension between Diane and I all day. Hurt by being used as a pawn by however well-intentioned Mary Kane. And damned hurt by being branded a seducer by jealous, rejected Helen Lucas. It was then I burst into uncontrollable sobs.

Dan gently gathered me into his arms and ran his hand down the back of my head, stroking my tangled, wet hair, all the while murmuring soft words, soothing words in my ear. "I'm so sorry—are you okay—I'm so clumsy—so sorry."

Wants flooded my mind. I wanted to go home, back to Spencer, back to John, and Dorrie, and Mrs. Nelson. I wanted to go home to my old house on Grant Street, back to my room papered with the serenely-blue morning glories. Where the maple trees stood over my house, fiercely protecting me from the lashings of the storm.

But, oh, Dan's arms felt good. I found undeniable comfort in the circle of his arms and I buried my face in the warm, wooly fibers of his shirt. The tears finally washed away the hurts and bathed my senses to a new calm.

Slowly, I pushed away from him. "I'm fine," I said, but I had to sniff. "Really, I am." I turned my head aside and took a deep breath. "It was stupid of me to trip. Jack Colby wants you to call him." I finally delivered the message.

"Thanks, but are you sure you're all right?" He held fast.

"Yes, Dan, I'm really not hurt. I was just kind of shocked for a minute. It surprised me." My voice trembled with the weak excuse and I felt a stinging in my knee. I bit my lip. For a fleeting second I wanted to feel his strong arms around me again, strong arms that held me hard—and safe.

He hesitated, then released my arm and I walked ahead of him out the door. I hoped he didn't notice my limp. He pulled the door shut and tested the latch, but he kept a considerable distance, allowing me to reach the house before him.

Once in the kitchen, I took off my parka and hung it on a peg, then hurried to my room. I could see, under the bathroom door, that Diane's light was already out—but I didn't care either way. I threw myself across my bed, miserable and confused. Damn, why did it feel so good in his arms? His arms, I thought again, enfolding me like the protective branches of the maple trees, his body against mine, hard and strong. I hit my pillow with my fist. What's wrong with you, Charlotte Foster? I'm just tired, I thought—but I have to admit, I am homesick, too. I'd had my eyes closed and I wanted to open them to see morning-gloried wallpaper. Instead, I saw the painting of the black and white horse above the desk. I squeezed my eyes shut again. I reasoned for a long time. Well, it has been a demanding day alright, but there was something bothersome about that man—the strength of his jaw in the dim light, the concern in his deep voice, the warmth of his closeness.

Suddenly, without plan, I rolled over and sat up. Charlotte, you're more than a grown woman—you're a sensible, experienced woman, damn near middle-aged.

You must get back to the matters at hand, you must write to Joyce.

I had to force myself, though, to get up and go to the desk and take out pen and paper. "Dear Joyce," I wrote, "I can hardly wait to leave here. Does the sun really shine every day in California? Is the beach sand always warm? Are cabanas inexpensive to rent? I dreamed all this was true."

Valiantly I tried to transplant my thoughts, but it didn't work. I tossed the pen onto the paper and hurriedly readied for bed. I crawled into it then, huddling in the dark, until I began to shiver. Groping for another blanket to pull over me, I curled to an almost fetal position. I had a miserable night's sleep.

❧[CHAPTER 28]❧

Morning came without bringing any improvement in the weather; it was still depressing. I bumbled about the kitchen, mechanically preparing pancakes. I served Dan his breakfast, offering little conversation. What more was there to say?

I busied myself at the sink and from the window, I watched Jed filling the horses' bunker. He seemed to have a renewed vigor. He could swing the bale, cut the twine and spill the hay over the rack with one smooth motion. And when he came into the kitchen for his breakfast, he still had the pleasant odor of wild hay clinging to his clothing. He looked at me and grinned. "Morning, Miz Foster."

For a second I didn't want to look at him. He can't know about my clumsy, humiliating performance last night—can he? Of course not. I had to believe it. "Good morning, Jed," I said, lightly, "It's pancakes this morning." I did smile at him, then, because it was very easy to smile at Jed Simpson.

He seated himself in the booth and poured a cup of coffee.

Dan glanced up quickly. "Jed. How're you feeling?"

"Aw, hell, Dan, I'm fine," he said, "I feel just fine. Strong as a bull. Whatever was ailin' me is past." He spoke convincingly. Besides that, he ate an unusually large helping of pancakes and ham.

Dan turned his attention to me. "We have to go up to the line cabin, Char. Remember the shack you saw when we were out riding the other day?"

"Oh, yes," I said, nodding slowly, "You did mention it that day."

"We have to check it out, make sure it's ready for winter. We always take some supplies up there, too. Hard telling just who might happen along and need them."

"It's quite a distance to travel—I mean on horseback, isn't it?" I felt a sudden apprehension.

"Yup. It is. But that's 'cause it's pretty slow going. Anyway, we've decided to go tomorrow."

"Oh, I see." My stomach muscles tightened. Now, Charlotte, these men certainly know what they're doing.

Dan produced a list of provisions they would need for the three days they would be gone. Besides a store of staples to stock the cabin for emergencies: tins of dried meat, crackers, beans, rice, coffee, they would also need materials for repairing possible damage to the building. That list included nails, putty, panes of glass, and a roll of asphalt roofing. Firewood had to be gathered, too, they'd said.

Wait! This notepaper looks familiar. My mind began backtracking. So that's what all the planning and figuring was all about that night. But why was my name marked so deeply on the paper's edges?

I tried to keep my thoughts organized. "But how are you going to manage all . . ?"

"Oh, we're goin' to take our trusty pack horse, old Sal. She likes that kinda work," Jed said, and grinned. "Mighty good at it, she is."

"Shouldn't take us more than three days," Dan said, "we'll get up there and start right in, check everything over. Hopefully we can finish up the next day, then come home the next." He finished the last dregs from his cup. "Yup, we'll be home Wednesday afternoon, for sure." He paused. "Don't like this weather, though."

"Aw, the radio says it's goin' to get better," Jed said, "maybe a chinook will come along. They usually do."

"We'd better hope," Dan replied, slapping an open palm on the tabletop. He rose. "Well, let's go, Jed, and pack up."

Early the next morning Andy came. "You'll need someone around to help you, Char," Dan had said. The men ate a hearty breakfast of ham and hashbrowns, and that pleased me. They discussed their plans once more until they concluded everything was in order.

Diane, having already nibbled on ham and toast, was

reading at the bay window table, not offering any visible concern, yet, not entirely devoting all of her attention to the book. She's still pouting, I thought. I suppose she's peeved about her father leaving again. Well, chores must be done, and I did believe she understood that fact.

"I grained just our horses," Jed said. "They're all saddled and ready. Andy, you'll have to take care of the others."

"Oh, let me, Andy, please?" I needed reasons to leave the house now and then.

"Sure." Andy grinned. "They'll like that."

Diane's head bobbed up from her book, her eyes assessing the scene. Then she rose slowly, went to her father and hugged him. Her eyes were wet. I couldn't discern what she said to him, but he responded quickly. "Help take care of things around here, Di, and maybe, when I get back you can whip me at a game of chess."

She crinkled her nose and backed away. "Hah, I wish I could," she quickly retorted. But it was easy to detect the great love between them.

The men dressed warmly, donning rain gear of leggings and rubbery ponchos. I put on my parka, too, snugging the hood about my face. After all, I reasoned, I had chores to do, too. But what I really wanted was to be a part of the bustling excitement taking place in the yard as they left.

A bone-chilling damp hung in the air, but the three horses tethered to the porch rail didn't seem to mind. The men tied packs, rolls, and bags of various description onto the old piebald mare. She looked incredibly burdened and it took all three men to assure me she was not.

Jed mounted his sturdy sorrel and affectionately slapped its shoulder. Then Dan hoisted himself to the saddle and the big bay snorted and stomped, eager to be on its way. Andy went ahead and pulled the gate rails aside as the horses and riders moved out across the yard. Dan blew a kiss to Diane, who was seated in the curtainless bay window and I saw her rise from her chair, waving both hands.

I walked with them toward the open gate. "Take good care of Sal," I called.

"Don't you worry none, Miz Foster," Jed called back, "I'd never mistreat that fine lady." He grinned, waved and rode out, Sal following him dutifully.

"Well, Char, see you in a couple days." Dan had moved his horse close to me. "I'm counting on you to take care of things, you and Andy, that is." I looked up to him, and even in the dreary light of the sunless day, his eyes were arrestingly-blue. For a wonderful, but fleeting moment, a rush of warmth swept through my entire body, fending off the chilly breeze.

"Oh, I will," I said, but the cold had stiffened my lips and I was sure no sound came out. I could only offer a taut smile.

He grinned and waved a jaunty salute to me, then reined Baron around so tightly the mighty horse stood high on its haunches. And, as they passed through the gate I saw small clods of dirt tossed into the air by eager hooves.

Chase was caught up in the hub-bub, too, and Andy had to restrain him from following the group. The dog seemed not to know where he was needed most, so I had to hold his collar then as Andy fitted the rails back up on the gate.

We watched as the horses began to climb the slope, for once over the rise they would be out of view. I took a deep breath and turned away, not wanting to prolong the sight of the bay and its rider leaving the homestead. I felt Andy's glance as he walked near my side. Lord, I thought, does he know about the awkward incident in the garage? Does he suspect anything . . . ? Of course not. How could he?

I became instantly annoyed with myself for even letting it enter my mind. "A-a-h," I quickly said, "I love the fresh air."

Andy tipped his head toward the hay barn. "I'm going to gas up the tractor."

"Well, I'm off to visit my friends," I returned, yelling into the wind. And I hurried toward the corral. I was fingering the two carrots I'd stashed in my pocket earlier, one for Patches, as usual, and now one for Boots, who had intuitively discovered our covert operation.

The girls' horses were feeding at the bunker with the newly trained cutting horses, but when they heard my voice they trotted eagerly to the barn's far open door. I hurriedly doled out the grain, for the three chestnuts were not far behind, having become quickly domesticated. I hope they don't catch on to the carrot bit, too, I thought guiltily, as I watched them move in haste to get to their prized rations. Now look what you've done, smarty. You're playing favorites. I walked slowly back to the house trying to think it through—sensibly.

Diane, who could take care of all her needs now, was at the bay window table doing schoolwork. I walked near her. She was drawing a map of the mountainous regions of Mexico. Suddenly she threw her colored pencils into their box and yowled, "I hate earth science." But then I think she realized she'd actually spoken to me, and she quickly gathered up all her things and retreated to her own room.

Well, Diane, I thought, how long will this go on? I felt my patience as thin as tissue paper. Then my father's voice came to me from the past. "Don't stir a hornet's nest, Lottie."

Noon came. Diane entered the kitchen on cat's paws and slipped onto a chair nearest the window. Andy came in, hung his hat on a peg and sauntered to the table, shirt neatly tucked and hair plastered damply to his head. He seated himself next to Diane and tried to engage her in silly banter. She couldn't help but grin at him. He *is* a wise old fox. Yes, I'd discovered *that* shortly after arriving at OUR Ranch.

I had made a big, spicy meatloaf and we sliced it to make fat sandwiches. Diane picked out all the onion she could detect, bit by bit. That's curious. I thought she liked onion.

Andy bit into his sandwich. He chewed and swallowed. "Gee whilikers, Charlotte, this is a mighty fine tasting lunch, I'd say." He took another bite.

"Well, thanks, Andy. My meatloaf never turns out the same way twice in a row, though," I said, laughing to his aside.

Diane suddenly got up and went to the fridge, returning with a bottle of ketchup. Her meat was promptly laden with a thick coating of the bright red sauce.

Charlotte, hold your tongue. I seemed to be gaining in volume to an impossible size when I felt Andy step on my toe under the table. I looked to him. His point was quickly taken and I smiled a sugar-coated smile. Still, I felt a scowl tight across my forehead.

Diane ate less than half her food, then excused herself, and left the kitchen, gingerly picking her way down the hall devoid of any aids. But my scowl remained.

"We've been real busy at George's saddle shop," Andy said, offering conversation, I was sure, to fill the sudden void. "I like to help out there, gives Ruby—that's George's wife—more time to spend with Helen. They're sisters, remember?"

I winced at the sound of Helen's name.

"Oh—oh, just as I figured," he said, "she didn't make herself too popular here, did she?"

"Well, no, she didn't."

"You know, Helen's been helping out here ever since Dan's wife died. What, three years now? Helen needed the work, she'd just gotten divorced."

"Yes, I understood that."

"Oh, she's a bold one, that Helen. Wow-ee. She's tried every way in the book—and a few that weren't—to get Dan to tumble for her. But I knew he never would." He paused. "Heck, I ain't too smart, but, I had that one figured out right off the bat." Andy drained his cup of coffee, and paused again, maybe waiting for a comment, but I kept my gaze on my dessert dish, lest I say more than I really wanted.

"She's a poor loser, never knows when to quit," he continued.

"Well, I just wished she hadn't involved Diane," I said, quietly.

Andy must not have heard. "Now, take you, Charlotte. . . ." He rapped his knuckles several times on the table and leaned forward a trifle. "Dan sure would be makin' a big mistake if he lets you get away."

"Andy! Stop!" I jumped to my feet and began to clear the table. "Now you sound just like Mary." Oh—why did I say that?

Andy got up, too. "Better get that wagon into the hay barn," he muttered, reaching for his jacket on the peg. "Yup, he's noticed you. I'm sure of it." He turned to me. "I'd catch him lookin'." Then he pulled his mouth into a straight line—not quite a smile—and rolled his eyes.

"Shoo. Go now," I said, waving him off with a dishtowel. "I don't believe you. Not a word."

The door shut hard, but I heard him on the porch—chuckling.

What is this, anyway, Charlotte? Looks like a game

everyone here is playing. Yes. It's called Let's Marry Off Poor Dan. I shook my head. "Incredible," I muttered, "what nonsense."

❧

The next day passed slowly. Andy was good company; Diane was not.

My alarm clock sounded Wednesday morning with a raucous jangling, jolting me out of a deep sleep. A-a-h, I thought, they're coming home today. I rolled over and tossed off the covers and swung my feet to the floor all in one swift motion.

Later, when I glanced out the sink window, I found the same dreary conditions that had hung on since Saturday.

Breakfast was uneventful, so I eagerly went to the barn to give carrots to all my friends, and to portion out their grain. When I'd finished I sat down on the pile of bagged feed just inside the barn door. I'm sure going to miss you guys, I thought. It's almost cruel to make such good friends knowing full well I'll be leaving here soon. What are you really saying, Charlotte? That you'd like to stay? Certainly not! I'm going to California, I reminded myself quite smugly, to begin my long-awaited vacation, and I may not even go back to Minnesota until spring.

I heard Chase whining outside the door. "Coming, Chase," I called, and, with that, I whacked my hands down hard on the bags of grain and jumped to my feet. But a restlessness had already begun to gnaw away inside me.

I pushed the heavy barn door open and stepped out. I drew back, startled by darkening skies. Then, brushing aside silly fears, I walked toward the house. Chase circled me several times and I patted his head. "Oh—oh, Chase, is that drizzle I feel?" I roughed his thick fur, then turned my face to the sky. "Yes—it is."

Once in the kitchen I shed my damp parka and hung it on a peg. It's chilly, I thought, I think I'll turn up the thermostat a bit. I hurried to the sink to wash my hands. I passed the radio on the fridge just as it spit out, "Warning!" I stopped and twisted up the volume. "Stockman's warning!" I *did* hear it. My heart plunged to the pit of my stomach. I looked out the sink window then to see tiny bits of ice, accompanied by little clicking sounds, already pelting the glass. I wheeled around to face the radio again. With my eyes glued on the dial, I listened to the entire forecast. A storm, with possible blizzard conditions was about to hit Peace County.

Andy said he'd be in the garage. I must tell him. But then Diane entered the kitchen, her hesitant gait muffled by fluffy slippers. I didn't know which way to turn. She poured herself a glass of milk and took a donut from the big glass jar and settled into a chair by the bay window. Her eyes were reddened.

"I don't need a lecture, Charlotte. I'm sorry for the way

I've been acting. I'm a brat, I know it." Her voice was quiet, calm.

I walked over to the table and sat down in the chair opposite her.

"I just don't know why I act that way." Her gaze lifted to mine. "But I really, really am sorry—for everything."

I saw repentance in her face—and fear. She's scared, I thought, she's heard the radio, too. "Well, now, Diane, that's all right. I understand how you must feel." I was truly in sympathy with her. "You're going through a rough situation. But it won't last much longer. You'll be back in school soon, and I'll be on my way to California. I have family to visit." I purposely emphasized *family*. "I wrote to Joyce, my brother's wife, a few days ago to tell her you're walking well now, and that things are going along as scheduled." I sighed heavily. "Oh, I'm so anxious for sunshine." I said, waving my hand at the window where sleet was collecting and sliding down the panes.

I glanced back to Diane. Her eyes were downcast now, and she only picked at her donut. "I heard the warning on the radio a few minutes ago," she said, quietly. Then she sucked in her quavering breath. "But Dad and Jed'll be back soon, won't they?"

"Oh, yes. Yes, I'm sure they will be." I reached across the table and patted her hand. It felt cold and I rubbed it a little.

Before long the sleet turned to snow, and, in what seemed like only a matter of a few short moments, the snowfall intensified. The wind caught it and blew it in white swirls across the driveway. Beyond the dooryard I glimpsed Andy in the hay barn door loading bales onto the wagon. "He's taking hay to the cattle, Diane." I jumped to my feet. "I'm going to help him."

After dressing warmly, I raced to the barn. Once on the wagon, I helped lay the bales in an orderly fashion until Andy signaled enough. I hurried to the gate and pulled out the rails and Andy drove the tractor through. Back on the wagon again, I rode with him up to the south slope, the most sheltered area, where the herd had gathered for refuge.

Together we broke open the bales and spread the hay among the cattle. But they only milled about, too agitated by the storm to feed. The wind caught the hay and blew it into drifts, but we knew it would be there when the storm subsided, even if we had to dig it out of the snow.

I clung to an upright pole on the empty wagon as Andy headed the tractor toward the gate. Some of the gusts of wind were so strong they seemed to steal my breath away. When we passed through the gate I jumped off and put the rails back in place while Andy drove on. After unhooking the wagon near the barn, he put the tractor in the garage. The wind was blowing the snow into angry white clouds and I could hardly see my way back to the house.

Andy called to me, found me and grabbed my hand. He pulled me along until we reached the porch. When we passed Chase's lair under the shrubs all I could see was a big, dark furry lump covered with a dusting of white. Our burly watchdog only opened one eye as we hurried past.

{CHAPTER 29}

It was well past our dinner hour. I found some sloppy joe mixture in the freezer, thawed it and reheated it. Piled onto small buns, it looked quite appetizing, but the food seemed to stick in our throats. We were exhausted—and worried. Even a plate of brownies didn't have much appeal, but we drained the coffee pot.

We searched each other's faces, it seemed, for a sign the men would be appearing soon, while the hands on the clock moved sluggishly. And as time wore on one or another of us would get up and stand next to the glass and peer into the blowing snow, hoping to see the outline of horses at the gate. "Not yet," we'd say, and slouch down onto our chairs again.

"Oh, Diane, get a deck of cards or something, and let's sit in the living room for awhile."

"A right smart idea," Andy said, getting to his feet, "and I'll build a fire in that big block of rock."

Diane brought out checkers, too, and we spread the game out on a small table near the huge split-rock hearth. Andy arranged the logs and struck a match. The flames on the kindling pieces drew furiously from the strength of the wind across the top of the chimney, but he soon had the blaze controlled, with lively tongues of fire lapping out from under the big, pungent ponderosa logs. It did provide a small degree of comfort.

"The men will surely enjoy this fire when they come," I said, but I knotted my hands between each checker move. Soon not he, the checker game or the fire's warm glow could keep us from worrying aloud, so we moved again, back to our bay window station.

"Oh, Andy, why didn't they have a better forecast when they left?" I grumbled and set about to make a fresh pot of coffee for their arrival.

"Best they can do," Andy answered, "these storms come up mighty quick. But at least it's not too cold yet."

"Yes, it is," Diane said, whining, "I'm freezing." She got up then and hobbled away on legs getting stronger daily, returning with a sweater pulled about her shoulders and my new green afghan bundled in her arms. She fluffed it and draped it about my shoulders.

"Thank you, I needed that," I said, reaching out and patting her arm. I glimpsed a faint smile on her face, and her eyes seemed to brighten for a moment. I was startled by the attention, but pleased.

"Andy, I'm going to deal you in, too." I picked up the cards and began to shuffle them. We're going to play King's Corner.

"But I don't know how . . ."

"Oh, you'll catch on—fast," I chided, and began to deal. We fanned our cards and studied them.

All of a sudden Diane flung her cards on the table. "It's getting dark out there," she wailed.

Andy touched her shoulder. "Honey, even if we called the sheriff," he said, "they still wouldn't go out there 'til the storm lets up, whether we like it or not." He tried to hide the tremors in his voice by coughing, then he got up and turned on the yard lights. But the glow was barely visible in the blowing snow.

Diane clasped her hands together under her chin and began to sniffle. I went to get some tissues from the box on top of the fridge, but before I could return she'd burst into sobs. Snatching the tissues from my hand, she dropped her head onto her arms on the table. I stood by her, rubbing her back, stroking her hair. "Well, we can all pray, can't we?"

Swiftly Diane blessed herself with the Sign of the Cross and began: "Hail Mary, full of grace, the Lord is with thee . . ." She mumbled the words as I formed prayers of pleading in my own mind. Andy rested his forehead in the palms of his hands, elbows on the table. We sat like that for a torturous time.

A stark new urge forced me to get up again and look hopefully to the gate under the yard light's glow. I saw dark forms outlined in the swirling snow. "They're here!" I screamed, "Oh, God, they're really here."

Andy jumped to his feet and was instantly by my side. "But there's only two horses, not three," I cried, "I only see two horses."

Andy groaned and raced to the peg board and started to dress, knocking clothing to the floor in his haste.

I looked to Diane. Her tear-stained face had turned ashen. "Stay where you are, Diane." I pulled the afghan from my shoulders and tossed it about her.

Rushing to dress, I snatched my fallen snow pants from the floor and pulled them on, shoved my feet into my sno-paks and managed my parka on in what seemed only seconds. I was still tugging at my gloves when we raced from the house, my heart pounding a sharp, pain deep within my chest.

Once outside, we heard the dog's frenzied barking. He would come close to us, then disappear into the blinding, white cloud a few steps ahead, his howls lost to the wind. We trudged behind him, stumbling and falling in the snow in our frantic effort to reach the gate.

Then, with a fierce struggle, we shoved the gate's rails aside and snatched for the horses' reins. Andy grabbed Baron and I managed Sal to the porch, where we tethered them to the rail. I could see Dan slumped in the saddle, his chin resting on his chest. Jed was lying across the saddle of the old mare, his hair blowing in the wind.

"Andy!" I screamed, the wind tearing the words from my throat, "Andy, what's wrong with Jed? Where's Duke?" Useless questions. My mind was flooding with dire thoughts, and, while the icy snow pelted my face, my heart rose to my throat and almost strangled me.

The mare pulled at her line and I tried to steady her, and while pushing against her, I touched Jed's leg. "My God in Heaven," I wailed, "no, God, please, no." I felt myself beginning to crumble.

"Help me get Dan," Andy yelled, and I could see him trying to pull the motionless shape from the horse. Together we tugged at him until we got him to the ground, but Dan couldn't stand and we all went down in the snow. I thrashed about in the whiteness, groping for an arm to tug at, and, at the same time, trying to regain my own feet.

Andy struggled to stand. "Take that arm," he yelled, and we began to drag the unwieldy form to the house and into the porch.

The kitchen door flew open, and Diane stepped back, her face aghast, both hands pressed to her mouth. We pulled Dan to the middle of the kitchen floor and brushed away hard clumps of snow from his clothing. He was making strange, guttural sounds. I dropped to my knees.

"J-J-Jed's d-d-dead." Then he was still, his face pale and encrusted with snow and ice. His kerchief had slipped to his chin and I untied it, feverishly working the damp knot.

Diane, her eyes wide at the sight, was shaking frightfully.

Andy moaned, "Oh, God—oh, God," and began to work off Dan's boots.

I pulled his gloves from his hands. "Diane, get some towels. Dry his face and hands. Careful." I gasped for breath.

She hurried on clumsy legs to a kitchen drawer and pulled out a stack of towels. Returning, she fell to her knees beside him. His hat had fallen off by the door, but she unwound the wool scarf from his head and neck and patted his face with the soft warmer towels.

I ran to the hall closet and yanked several blankets from the shelves. When I returned Andy had gotten Dan's boots off and was struggling with his heavy, sheepskin coat. It was stiff with ice, but together we pulled it from his limp body.

Diane had taken the afghan from the chair and had put it under her father's head, and was, now, pathetically trying to warm his hands with her own. I dreaded that she may be near hysteria. No time for that now. Keep her busy, I thought.

"Diane, listen closely," I said, "get the electric blanket from the closet. Put it on his bed, plug it into the outlet by the bureau and set it on LO. Hurry!"

Andy had undone Dan's belt buckle and we slid his jeans from him. By the time Diane returned, we had moved him to a dry place on the floor and had him wrapped in several blankets. He began to shiver, slightly at first, then commencing to a violent shudder.

"Good," Andy said, "he's coming around." We hovered over him for a time, watching until his shuddering subsided.

Andy stood up. "Diane, we're going out to care for

Jed." He moved close to her. "He's dead, honey. But he's still on the horse. We'll be back in as soon as we can. While we're gone, wring out some towels in hot water—not too hot, now—and warm his hands." He moved to the door. "We'll hurry." Andy's words were terse and I jumped to my feet. Diane, still speechless, was moving about knowingly.

Once more we were outside facing the icy, biting wind all over again. I followed as Andy led Sal to the bunkhouse and snubbed the rein to a rail. The old mare moved from side to side, extremely nervous under her woeful burden. That horse knows, I thought, she knows. I felt sick.

We didn't talk—there wasn't any point. Jed was tied across the back of the horse and Andy took his knife and cut the ropes. We lowered him to the ground. I don't remember just how we got him into the bunkhouse and onto his bed, but we covered him with his wooly, red blanket.

"Oh, Jed, Jed," I cried, groaning with a hard pain, and I pressed my hands to the blanket covering his head.

Andy tugged me away. "We have to see to Dan."

We made our way back to the house, Andy leading Sal. Tears rolled down my cheeks and quickly turned to ice. I hurried ahead and untied Baron.

"These critters are exhausted. I'll see to them—you go in the house," Andy shouted.

And between the blindingly-white gusts, I saw the dog dutifully carrying out his chores—accompanying the staggering trio to the barn.

Back in the house, I tore off my outer clothing, my

heart beating like a bass drum. I thought it would burst. I leaned for a moment with my back against the inside door, my breath coming in painful gasps.

Diane was kneeling by Dan's side, tears spilling down her cheeks. She looked up. "He said my name—he *knows* me." Then I gained a new strength, for the terror that had been in her eyes had disappeared in the brief time I'd been gone.

Dan shivered only slightly now. I unbuttoned his shirt with trembling hands and we pulled it from his body, rewrapping him in the blankets. I wanted desperately to hold him in my arms, to warm his body with mine, but, instead, I went to ready his bed.

Andy was in the kitchen removing his outer clothing when I returned. We stood facing each other for a seemingly endless time. We knew the facts: Jed was dead, Duke was missing, and now Baron and Sal were safely in the barn. We could turn our complete attention to Dan.

Andy and I pulled him to his feet, and, half walking, half dragging, we managed him to his room and into his bed. Diane rushed by me to his bureau and began to rummage in a drawer. She pulled out a neatly-folded article and shook it out, revealing brown-striped flannel pajamas. "Will he need these," she asked, timidly. "I gave them to him for Christmas one year. I thought he'd like them, but I guess he didn't."

"Well, he doesn't have much choice now, does he?" I said, in a wry tone, and took the pajamas from her. "Now go fix him a big mug of warm milk, and put coffee in it—for taste."

It was no time for propriety. While Diane was out of the room, Andy and I quickly removed Dan's long underwear and dressed him in the flannel pajamas. Then we covered him with the warmed blanket, draping it loosely over his feet.

Diane brought the mug of milk on a tray, with spoon and napkin. Steam curled from the mug's surface into little whisps. I stirred it to a soothing degree of warmth.

"Dan, I have coffee for you. Here, drink this." I put a spoonful to his closed lips and tipped it, but it ran to the corners of his mouth. I caught the drops with the napkin and tried again. I coaxed. I pleaded. Finally he opened his mouth, took the liquid and swallowed it. "That's good, Dan. Here, try again." And he did. I fed him spoonful after spoonful of the warm milk. Diane sat nearby, twisting her hands and smothering a whimper, while Andy paced the floor at the foot of the bed.

Once he left the room and returned. "It's stopped snowing. Even the wind is dying down." He took a chair and placed it at the foot, dropping into it wearily.

Dan had stopped shivering and was swallowing the warm milk without hesitation. Soon he finished the entire amount. He seemed to be relaxing. Good. I'd planned it that way.

His eyes fluttered open, then closed again. Soon he calmed and slept. Relieved and exhausted, I sat back in my chair and looked to the others.

"He's better now, isn't he?" Diane asked.

She was anxious for a solid sign, I knew, yet she maintained her composure remarkably well.

"Yes, sweetie, I think he's going to be fine. He just needs a long rest." I reached out and put my hand on top of hers. She put her other hand on top of mine and squeezed it—hard. I liked that.

"Thank the Lord, he's okay," Andy said, getting up and walking up the side of the bed. "But Jed, poor Jed, I just can't imagine what happened." He hit his fist into an open hand. "And where's Duke?" He threw both arms outwardly as he spoke. "Damn, we'll just have to wait 'til Dan can tell us." He scratched his head with a big swoop of his hand. "I've got to call the sheriff now." And he went to the door. "I think I'll have myself a cup of coffee while I'm out there." He disappeared through the dressing room doorway, his shoulders hunched in his grief.

I turned to Diane and touched her arm. "You were just super. Your dad will be proud of you, and grateful, too, I must say." I was beginning to unwind. "Joanne told me how he helped you the day you had your accident in Yellowstone—how he almost carried your stretcher by himself." I gently clasped her arm. "There's a lot of helping each other in this life." I found myself whispering, but I needn't have. Dan seemed to have drifted into an even deeper sleep.

Diane eased herself to the floor by the bed and touched her father's hand. "I love Daddy so much—I thought I would just die if he'd fall in love with you—or with that darn Helen, even." She rubbed her palms together. "I couldn't stand it when she'd *hit* on him, you know what I mean, stand close to him and giggle. Then I could see he didn't like it, either." She was speaking low, almost whispering. "Then you came. I felt scared and I'd worry a lot, about dumb things. I know it's not right to be—jealous." She covered her face with her hands for a few seconds

I reached over and rubbed her shoulder and gave her hand a quick squeeze. "You worry too much."

"But, Charlotte, I almost lost him today in the worst way of all. He could've died in the storm, too, like Jed did." She began to sob. "Poor Jed, I'll miss him so much. And Chase liked him better than any of us. Poor Chase." The sobbing ceased but she rambled on. I knew it was good for her to say it all—to someone. "From now on Daddy can do whatever he wants. I'll never treat him nasty again. Oh, I could be stinky. I'd even spill the games on the floor just so he would have to stay in my room longer. That was horrible of me, wasn't it?"

"Well, yes, it was."

Then tears brimmed in her eyes again and her voice began to break. "Oh, Charlotte, I'm sure going to do stuff a lot different from now on."

"Things will work out just fine, Diane, you'll see." Then I knelt beside her and hugged her with a tenderness that I hadn't felt for any child, save my own little boy when I'd thought I'd lost him at the county fair one time. Funny how that popped into my mind just then.

I stroked Diane's hair and spoke softly. "I think you should go to bed now, sweetie, and give those legs a rest. Have a snack first, though, if you're hungry. I know none of us ate."

The tears in her eyes had washed out over her cheeks, their wetness glistening in the dim light of the bed lamp, before she brushed them away with the back of her hand. She got to her feet, bent over, and kissed her father on the forehead. "Good night, Daddy, I love you." she whispered. He didn't respond. She came to me. "Goodnight, Charlotte," she said, and kissed my cheek. As she left the room, I noticed how well she walked.

Andy tiptoed in and stood at the foot of the bed. His steel gray eyes had misted over, too, and a weariness clouded his expression. "It's okay, Andy, he's sound asleep." I offered a faint smile of gratitude. "I'm going to sit with him for awhile, yet, though." I paused. "Did you get through to the sheriff?" I found myself whispering, the words coming with a painful effort when I thought, again, of Jed.

"Yup, I did. He'll be here soon's he can. Roads are drifted pretty bad in some places. He's bringing Doc Freeman, too."

"Oh, good," I said, my hands clasping themselves over my chest. Then I remembered. "Oh, Andy, do you want something to eat? I can heat some soup."

"Maybe. I feel hungry, then again, I don't. Anyway, you'd better have something, too."

Then I detected heavy snoring rising from the bed. "Yes. Yes, I will. He should be just fine."

{CHAPTER 30}

Andy and I sat at the table in the bay window sipping hot soup, waiting, watching for the snow plow's blinking blue lights. We could see the drifts of snow now, under the yard lights, and, in the sky, the thin clouds as they scudded across the moon. Several times I got up and tiptoed back to check on Dan. He was blessed with a deep sleep.

I felt painfully weary, as though my entire body, and soul, too, were a mass of bruises. I reached across the table and caught Andy's arm "Tell me about Jed, Andy. I want to know all about him." I somehow thought it was important to know more about a friend—even a friend of such short duration. "You said his wife, his bride, actually, was killed in an accident?"

"Yup," Andy said. He poured himself a cup of coffee from the carafe. "They'd been on vacation to the Oregon coast. Hadn't been married long—five, six months, the most. Comin' back Jed'd insisted on driving all night to get home sooner. Well, up in the pass—over the mountains, I mean—there'd been a rockslide. Jed didn't spot it soon enough. Drove right into it and flipped his old jalopy clean over." He paused, cleared his throat, sipped from his cup, then continued. "Well, she was killed outright and Jed wasn't hardly hurt. To make matters worse, she was in the family way. His heart was busted. Never could figure out the why of it all—poor fella. That big smile of his was only a front." Andy stopped and stirred his coffee, forward and backward, then took another sip. "Jed had lots of pictures around his bed, just like a shrine, you'd think."

"Oh, how sad," I said. "And I was in there tonight and never saw them. But then I don't remember seeing anything. Oh, that's really awful." I could feel the heat of the tears as they slipped down my cheeks.

"Yup, it sure was." Andy nodded and went on. "He'd talk like he'd seen her ever once in awhile—just like he'd say he'd seen Prince—that big, old black stallion. Dan's wife's horse, you know. We all knew different but we didn't say much. Hell, what was the point, Jed was contented, thinkin' that way."

"I'd wondered how he filled his evenings. Here I thought he just read a lot." I said, catching tears on the back of my hand.

"Nope. Jed couldn't read." Andy shook his head. "I mean, he wasn't good at it."

"Did he have any family?"

"Well, yeah, his mother lives in Wyoming. He'd get a letter from her once in awhile, askin' him to come home. But he said he just couldn't, not with Sissy bein' so close—

that's what her name was — Sissy. We didn't know if he meant up where she's buried, up near Red Hill — or if he meant seein' her up there, up on the high hill." He heaved a sigh. "No doubt his mother will take him home now."

I jumped to my feet, blinded by tears. Well, you had to ask, didn't you? Now you will never forget it. "I'm going to sit by Dan for awhile. Let me know when you see the plow coming." I just had to leave the table. I grabbed a handful of tissues as I passed the box on the top of the fridge. Lord, I should be dry of tears by now.

Before going to Dan's room, I hurried down the hall to peek in at Diane. Her drapes were open and the moonlight streamed across her bed. I brushed a long strand of hair from her face, then tucked the covers in around her. You're growing fond of her, aren't you? Yes. Yes, I am.

I slipped through the study into Dan's room and eased myself onto the chair by his bed. He seemed to sense someone near and after a short time he began to stir. He tried to roll over, but failed. Then he began to mumble and I listened closely. "Jed, J-J-Jed, don't go . . . no . . . no. . . ." And his arms began to flail.

I jumped up and pressed my hands down on his arms, but he pushed against my hold. Oh, Lord, should I call for Andy? Then, just as swiftly, he relaxed and was still. I stroked and patted his arms and his hands. "It's all right, Dan, you're home now. You're safe at home. Oh, Dan, try to rest."

Dan. Dan. I sank to my knees by the side of the bed. A

moment later he opened his eyes and stared blankly at me. I put my face close to his. "It's me, Dan, it's Char." I tried to make my voice sound comforting.

He sucked in a deep breath and gave an agonizing moan. "Oh, God. Char—Char," he mumbled. His mouth jerked to one side, and I wondered if it was a smile. Then his eyes fell shut and he slept.

He knows me, I thought, he actually knows it's me here beside him. I flushed and reached out and brushed a lock of hair from his furrowed brow, a brow that now felt gloriously warm to my fingertips.

I sat for a time listening to his steady, rhythmic breathing. Then I went to find Andy again. He was at the bay window, the window where, not eight hours before, we had watched for the men's return. I stood at the window with him hoping to see the plow's blue lights blinking through the bare trees beyond the meadow. All the clouds had been swept away. The moon's liquid silver shimmered on the pure, new snow, while millions of bright stars studded the dark heavens like diamonds strewn on a jeweler's black velvet.

A strange chill climbed my spine. I caught my breath and gave out a cry. Then I saw whirlwinds of snowdust rise up out by the gate and almost obscure the yard lights. Wild, mixed emotions welled up inside me and tore at the very fiber of my being. The immense beauty of the night pitted itself against the stark reality that Jed Simpson was lying in his bunkhouse—so cold. My bones ached dreadfully with a helplessness I'd never known before.

Sinking onto a chair, I put both arms on the table, lay my head on them and let the sobs come. Oh, I tried to be strong, and I was for Diane's sake, but now I had to let go and grieve for Jed. But when I thought of him I could see only the big smile, the one that would make his eyes almost disappear behind the beard. I felt much better.

Andy patted my arm. "They're coming, Charlotte. I see the blue lights, and some others, too. Must be the sheriff's truck right behind 'em." We watched the plow push a big swath around the loop of driveway, then leave. A Ford Bronco appeared, stopping at the corner of the porch. The sheriff, a big man, got out first, a sliver of moonlight glinting from his badge as he turned to walk to the porch. He was followed by a tall, thin man carrying a large bag. Oh, thank heaven, the doctor was able to come.

Chase sniffed the doctor's bag and, as Andy opened the door, I heard the dog growl his protest. He was quickly restrained. Poor Chase. He knew something was frightfully wrong at OUR Ranch.

Andy ushered the two men into the kitchen. "Charlotte, this is Sheriff Churchill and Doc Freeman."

I nodded. "This way, please," and the gangly man followed me into Dan's room. I explained our treatment, step by step. The doctor examined Dan swiftly, and, it seemed, thoroughly, all the while nodding and mumbling, "Uh-huh, uh-huh, good." Dan had seemed to sense the concern for him, and had cooperated with the doctor, although the loud snoring soon afterward was all the assurance I needed.

"Well, he seems to be in pretty good shape," Doctor Freeman said, closing his bag, "but he'll need a few days rest." He turned to leave the room.

"I'll see to that, Doctor," I said, following him to the kitchen.

Andy and Sheriff Churchill were sitting in the booth, their hands clutching coffee mugs. "He'll be fine," the doctor said, then he wagged his head. "Damn, but he was lucky."

Andy jumped to his feet. "Thanks, Doc, thanks a million." He poured the doctor a mug of coffee, the steam rising in a plume. Then he slipped into his parka.

"Thanks," the doctor murmured as he took the mug. He went to the sink, cooled it with tap water and gulped it down. He dressed again in the heavy topcoat he'd hung on a peg.

Sheriff Churchill rose to his feet and soberly doffed his hat to me. "Good night, Ma'm, mighty sorry about the man, Simpson." Then he dressed, too, in a heavy sheepskin jacket, and the three men left the house, making little sound.

From the sink window I glimpsed the tail lights of the sheriff's Bronco move to the bunkhouse. I hoped they'd kept Jed wrapped in his wooly red blanket. Then, with numb fingers, I began to load the dishwasher with soup bowls and coffee mugs. A short time later the Bronco rolled through the dooryard and down the drive. I hurried to the bay window just as it disappeared below the rise. My hands gripped the back of a chair and I waited and watched until I could no longer see the flickering of its lights through the bare trees. "Goodbye, Jed," my heart called after the burdened vehicle as it drove away into the cold, moonlit night.

Andy came back into the house. He looked drawn and chilled. "The sheriff'll be back tomorrow, about eleven," he said, "to talk to Dan." He shivered and hunched his shoulders.

'Oh, Andy, stay with us. I mean, stay in the house with us tonight. You can have the couch, or even Joanne's room, if you'd like." I patted his arm.

"Shucks, I'd rather just sleep in the recliner in Dan's office room. That way I'd be near if he should wake up."

I took both his hands in mine and squeezed them. "Andy, you're such a dear." He looked at me for a long moment, returning the squeeze, and a wan smile settled onto his mouth.

Finally, with mixed emotions and total exhaustion, I climbed into my bed. The sheets were so cold I had to get up and add an extra blanket. Still, I tossed about.

Lord, let Jed be at peace now, with his Sissy. And bless Diane, she handled it all very well. I thought of Dan, then, and I wanted to speak to him. Whatever happened out there today, Dan, how lucky you were. Such wonderful animals, to have brought you home under such conditions.

I patted and plumped my pillow to gain more comfort. Then I punched it. "Damnit, Dan Garner, don't ever do that again." When I had realized I'd said it aloud, I buried my face in my pillow to blot up the tears.

Suddenly the big clock on the mantle began to peal midnight. I bolted upright in my bed. Charlotte, relax. You are not Cinderella. Things will not change that dramatically. I lay back an snugged the covers under my neck. But you will be leaving for California soon, maybe only about two weeks from now. I tried to feel warm sand under bare feet, tropical sunshine heating my skin, frothy waves against my legs. I'd heard so much about it all.

I tried desperately to feel uninvolved with all the people at OUR Ranch, yet an inner voice whispered, "But you are involved, Charlotte Foster, whether you want to be or not, as long as you remain in this house." A battle brewed inside me and I found myself fighting a strange feeling of permanency when sleep came to me on a rolling black cloud.

CHAPTER 31

It was by far the most restless night I'd spent since I came to the new land and when I woke I felt as if it had all been a nightmare. I crawled out of bed and peered out the window, blinking back the daylight. Miniature drifts of snow on the big spruce sparkled brightly, even in the gray dawn, belying the stark events of the night before. I blinked again, hard.

I thought then of the poem I'd found under Diane's bed when I cleaned one day—the poem I'd been compelled to save. I found the crumpled paper and again read the words:

THE MYSTERY BIRD
I peer through glass
Glass shielding me
From bitter cold.
I wonder at the sight of you,
Fragile little creature—
Snowbird that you are.

Puffy ball of gray feathers
Belly turned white
Reflecting the new snow.
Heart of fierce determination
Alive with enduring bounds.
You hop about on brittle little sticks.
Don't you feel the cold?
What sustains you, little mystery?
God endowed you with gifts
The nature I shall never comprehend.
Will you take these offerings,
These seeds, these crumbs?
Take your fill and fly away,
But bless me with your return—
Give me hope for tomorrow.

I folded it and laid it away. Diane, it's beautiful, I hope you won't mind that I kept it. And, just then, I spied a Junco sitting on a lower branch, wondering, I supposed, just where to look for the day's sustenance.

I dressed and went to the kitchen, and as I entered I caught the aroma of freshly-brewed coffee. Andy! What a guy! Then I noticed tiny clues that he'd had toast and coffee in the booth. Now, as I looked out the sink window, I could see him spilling hay into the bunker. Whatever would I have done without you last night, Andrew Wallace?

Turning from the window, I went to Dan's door and

tapped on it. No answer came, so I entered. I went through his dressing room and tapped again on his bedroom door. Again, no answer. I peeked in. The tall man, now rolled onto a side, appeared to be sleeping soundly. I looked at him for a moment, then turned and walked toward the door. "Good, he needs all the sleep he can get."

Someone was behind me. I jumped and gasped. It was Diane. She had entered his room through the study, and, without wheelchair, crutches or walker, she could move about in almost total silence. "I wanted to see Dad," she whispered, "I can't believe he's still sleeping." She followed me into the kitchen. After a moment, she asked, "Do you always talk to yourself?"

I turned and smiled wryly. "Yes, I do, once in awhile. It's a habit I can't shake, comes from living alone, I guess." It felt like a confession.

Suddenly the seriousness of the past night's events clouded the homey atmosphere of the kitchen. I felt a chill seep into my bones, knowing we had to find out what had happened to Jed, and to his horse.

We tried to make and eat a breakfast, but it was difficult. Diane wanted to talk, yet she didn't seem to know how to express herself. She'd stumble and stop speaking, but she kept right on making cinnamon toast until I insisted she'd made quite enough.

The kitchen door popped open and Andy hurried in. "Whoo, sure cold out there," he said, and waved his arms about in the clouds of vapor that circled him before he could close the door.

"Andy, Daddy's *still* sleeping. Oh, I just can't believe Jed's, ah, gone," Diane said, all in one breath. She got up from the booth and moved away. "I—I'm going to my r-room. Let me know when D-Daddy wakes up, w-will you?"

"Oh, sweetie, I sure will," I said.

With that, she burst into tears, swiping at them with the sleeve of her robe. "Oh—I'm going to miss Jed so much," she wailed, the sound trailing off as she scurried down the hallway on legs more agile each day.

I bit my lip and began to prepare Andy's breakfast.

"Stop, Charlotte, don't bother. I'll just eat some of this toast, I'm not a bit hungry." From the corner of my eye, I saw him sit down in the booth and rub his eyes with the heel of his palm. "I was just by the bunkhouse. Damn, but it feels empty." He shook his head and bent low. "It's gonna take a lot of gettin' used to."

I went to him and patted his shoulder. "I know, Andy."

"I'll get his things together, send them back with Churchill."

"Oh, I hadn't even thought of that."

When Andy dressed and went outside again, I heard him call Chase into the porch. And a blow struck my heart when I heard the rustle of the dog food bag. Yes, Chase, I know you'll miss him, too.

I loaded the breakfast dishes into the washer, what few there were, and began to bake a batch of cookies. I always baked something when I wanted to compose my runaway thoughts. Besides, the aroma of fresh baking always could do something nice for the weariest of souls.

I was taking the last sheet of cookies from the oven when I heard a commotion in Dan's doorway. Startled, I whirled to look and tipped the pan, causing several cookies to slide off and fall to the floor. Dan stood motionless and watched it all with a helpless expression. I stooped and picked up the warm pieces and put them in the waste-basket. He remained still.

He was wearing a navy terry robe, and it was hanging crookedly from his shoulders with one end of the long tie-belt dragging on the floor. His feet were bare, as were his legs, halfway to the knee. It was plain to see the gift pajamas did not fit well. And his hair was a tousled mass. I wanted to laugh, but the urge passed quickly, and I went to him and stood close. I looked up to him. "I'm so glad you're all right, Dan." I hesitated. "But—but, dear Jed. We're all so sorry." I reached out and carefully wrapped his robe about him, slowly straightening and tying the belt, smoothing and patting the lapels.

He seemed confused, more like he was half-asleep. Then his eyes began to focus on mine. "Char—Char," he stammered. Slowly, he reached out and cupped both my shoulders with his hands, holding me at arm's length, his eyes searching mine—wonderfully searching mine. "Char— what can I say? How can I ever . . . ?"

I stood mute, waiting, wondering. My heart stumbled.

"It's alright, Dan, it's alright," I managed to say, with barely enough breath to form the words. At first, I wanted to put my arms around his waist, to comfort him as if he were a little boy. Then, contrarily, I wanted to take his face in my hands and kiss him and tell him how happy I was to see him looking so wonderful. But the terrible sight of his pale, icy face returned to haunt me for the moment. My jumbled emotions left me quite numb, and I remained wooden.

Suddenly he dropped his hands from my shoulders and shuffled to the booth. He sat down, heavy in body, and rested his forehead in his hands. I poured a cup of coffee for him, then slowly raised my hand and let it rest on his shoulder.

"Thank you, Char," he said, and grew quiet.

I went to his room to fetch his slippers, and to renew the hold on my senses. When I returned to the kitchen, Andy was there, the sharp odor of hay mixing with the warm kitchen smells.

He clasped Dan's hand for a quiet moment, then eased himself into the booth opposite him. They didn't speak; there was no need to verbalize their sorrow.

I hurried to Diane's room. "He's awake now," I said, "looking pretty good, too."

She'd been standing by her window, almost trance-like, and didn't seem to hear me. "Snow can be so beautiful," she said, choking with emotion, "and yet—yet—so scary. It's just so hard to understand it all."

I walked to her side. "Yes, Diane, nature is quite complex."

"I wrote a poem awhile ago about it, but I threw it away." After a pause, she said, "I wish I still had it."

I drew a deep breath. "I have a confession to make. I found the crumpled paper under your bed and I kept it. It was so nice, I just couldn't destroy it." I picked up her robe and helped her into it. "Come," I said.

I stopped by my room, retrieved it and handed it to her. She pushed it into her pocket. "I'll make you a nice neat copy," she said, and tapped my arm.

We walked to the kitchen together.

Dan had been using the phone. He hung up the receiver. "Sheriff Churchill wants to talk, he'll be out about eleven," he said, somberly. Then he turned and saw Diane and gathered her into his arms. "Good morning, my Di."

"Dad! Oh, Dad," she cried, and further words were smothered in his shirt.

I waited for some moments before I gave the order, "Sit down, Mr. Garner, and drink this." He slid into the booth and Diane snuggled in beside him. I placed a steaming mug of beef broth before him.

"I'm not hungry," he said, and began to push it away.

"I know you're not, but drink it anyway."

He looked irritated for a few seconds, then grinned sheepishly and sipped. Diane's eyes widened and she looked from me to her father several times. I smiled at her, shrugged and poured Andy a cup of coffee. Before long Dan had finished all the broth. Then he went to his room and returned dressed warmly in working attire.

"I've got to see to the horses—they'll be needing their grain." I knew he itched to return to his normal routines. Dan and Andy left the house, walking to the barn side-by-side. Dan looked like a giant next to Andy, but Andy proved to me he had a spirit as big as the mountain I could see from the bay window.

After a time I saw the men emerge from the barn. They must have heard the sheriff's truck grind up the drive, retracing its tracks from the night before. When the sheriff clambered out, they shook hands all around, then walked to the door. Wagging his tail, Chase welcomed the man, but still sniffed and circled around him, perhaps not quite sure what he was about.

{[CHAPTER 32]}

I opened the door. The men stomped the snow from their boots, then trooped into the house. Dan led the way into the dining room, and as they seated themselves, I followed with a fresh pot of coffee.

Diane had set out saucered cups, as well as the sugar and creamer, and spoons and napkins. Then, quite conspicuously, she placed a large, glass ashtray at the sheriff's elbow.

"Thank you, Miss," he said, in a deep, rumbling voice. He promptly used it to tap a small ash from the tip of his newly lit cigar.

Diane and I seated ourselves at the opposite end of the table from Sheriff Churchill. Dan sat at his right, still looking peaked, and Andy his left. The sheriff puffed his fat cigar into billowy, little white clouds as he took a notebook and a pen from his breast pocket. He glanced to Dan.

Dan heaved a tremendous sigh, clasped his hands together on the table, and leaned forward in his chair. "It was raining a little," he began, "we were just about done closing up the place. We weren't bringing back much, but it was all packed. We were just about ready to go down and get the horses when we heard a terrible ruckus out of them. We'd put them down in a deep ravine by a stream. Plenty of forage there. 'Course, we had them hobbled." He stopped and squinted his eyes as though trying hard to remember. "Well, Jed grabbed his rifle and went out the door ahead of me. He ran down the side of the ravine, stumbling and slipping. Then he yelled, "'Cat! Big cat!' When he got to the bottom, he yelled, 'Going up the other side.' He shot twice, but didn't get it. Then I saw it in the trees, up the other side. A real big one." Dan paused for a moment while the sheriff, taking notes, caught up to him.

"Go ahead," the sheriff said, and puffed his cigar until it glowed.

"Then Jed came part way back up and handed me his rifle, and went on down again to get the horses. They were really spooked. Duke was the worst." Dan stopped then and unclasped his hands and rubbed them together in a grinding motion.

That poor man, I thought, having to relive it all so soon. I wanted to go and stand by him, to pat his shoulder, to take his hand—anything to comfort him. I swallowed hard.

"I know Jed didn't think Duke would run," Dan said, "but he just bolted and flew, the moment he was loose. Jed ran after him but couldn't get him. I stashed the rifle in the cabin and ran down to get the other two horses." He paused again and cleared his throat. "Jed gave up on Duke and came back to help me get them up the side. It was really steep. That's when he fell. I grabbed Sal's rein, too, and tried to help Jed up. The horses were real skittish so I tied them to a little tree." Dan suddenly put his forehead into his cupped hands, his elbows on the table, and remained motionless for a time.

Sheriff Churchill puffed at his cigar and tapped a huge ash into the dish, and, all the while, Andy seemed as if he were carved of stone. I felt Diane nudging close to me, her eyes glued on her father.

"Yeah?" the sheriff urged, nodding and scribbling.

"Well, Jed didn't try to get up, so I let him rest. It was raining harder then, turning to sleet. Then I tried to help Jed up again, and right away—I knew. I think it was a heart attack. I—I couldn't believe it. I was yelling and hollering at him, but he slumped over in my arms, never said a word, never moved again." Dan stopped, ran his fingers through his hair, coughed a bit, and wiped his eyes with the back of his hand.

I crossed my arms tightly to keep from shivering, and I heard Diane suck in a quavering breath. I expected her to burst into tears, but she did not.

"I held him for awhile," Dan began again. "I had to figure out what I should do. God, I couldn't believe it. The snow was starting up pretty good. I pulled Jed up the ravine and went down for the horses. I put Duke's saddle on Sal and put Jed up, tied him real good. I saddled Baron and tied as many packs to him as I could. I left the rest there. I looked again for Duke but he was gone." Dan choked up then, and I saw tears glisten in his eyes, but he blinked them back.

My heart twisted at the sight of him hurting so badly. I wanted to scold that sheriff and tell him to go away and let Dan be, but I was helpless to do anything.

He continued. "The snow was getting heavier and the wind'd sprung up good, picking up damn hard by the time I headed home. Fine snow—ice in it. It stung my face, so I pulled up my scarf and turned up my collar, that was about all I could do. Baron kept up a good pace, though I couldn't see much ahead of me coming down the high hill. I knew Sal was right behind, though. After awhile I couldn't see anything at all. I thought of turning back, but I wanted to get Jed home so damned bad. So I just gave Baron his head—and that's about it." He puffed his cheeks and blew his breath out slowly, then went on. "Damn, but that storm came up fast—and out of nowhere. I was getting cold, but I wasn't too wet. Hell, my rain gear was in the packs back at the cabin. It wasn't raining much when the horses first screamed, and I just never thought later to put it on. All I could think about was Jed." He cleared his throat again and rubbed his brow. "Yeah, I was pretty worried, thought a lot about my girls." He looked at Diane. "Just prayed I'd stay in the saddle. God, it seemed slow."

Then he very quickly caught my eye. My heart tripped.

"Baron just picked his way along, even stopping now and then." Dan leaned back in his chair, and, with a tired sigh, he concluded, "Don't remember getting home at all. This morning I wondered if I'd dreamt it all." Sadly he shook his head. "Now, it's all too damn real."

Andy got up from the table and walked around behind Dan and gripped his shoulder, then turned his face away as if to hide a moment of weakness.

Sheriff Churchill had only nodded, time and again, during the telling. He took a deep breath and got to his feet, grinding his cigar stump into the ashtray. "Damn," he said, clapping Dan's shoulder, "that's a tough break, Garner. Damn tough. I know Simpson was here with you a long time. Sorry—damned sorry." He shoved his notebook into his breast pocket and carefully clipped the pen in beside it. "I got hold of his mother in Cheyenne. She'll be here tomorrow. Anything you want to send along, I'll take it now."

"I've got it all ready, Sheriff," Andy said.

"Well, thanks for the information, Garner, I'm satisfied." He moved into the kitchen and toward the door, then extended a hand to Dan. "Sorry—mighty sorry," he said and shook his hand vigorously. Then he nodded politely to Diane and me, and Andy followed him out the door.

¶[CHAPTER 33]⅌

It was almost noon. None of us had eaten much breakfast, but now I sensed appetites returning. Before long we sat down and ate mountains of golden-yellow scrambled eggs and cords of delicately-browned sausages, while Diane kept busy at the toaster. Afterwards, the men lingered at their coffee. Diane systematically nibbled at a cinnamon donut stuck on her index finger, while I scolded that everyone should have eaten more applesauce. "It's good for you," I said, but no one paid heed. Conversation, in general, was at an ebb.

Diane helped me clear the table and load the dishwasher. Dan watched her closely, a look of wonder clearly etched across his rugged features. He sure can look handsome at times, I thought, then I hurt for a moment remembering the pale, cold face of the night gone by.

But Diane's involvement surprised me, too. Both of us worked amiably together in a small space, and conversed quietly with the simple pleasure we had found in our new-born relationship. Yes, Dan was visibly pleased.

My mind traced again over all the little happenings that had taken place since I'd come to this ranch. I wondered if he'd been aware of any of it? He'd be amazed if he knew how much he's been the center of attraction for all the women who have been in this house recently. But, it's best he not know. He's had his own problems, Diane's long healing process, the roundup, the cabin work, and then —losing Jed. And almost losing his own life. Well, he won't hear any more from me, I'll not add an ounce to his problems. In fact—I'd like to help ease them. Now, Charlotte, you've gone and let you mind wander off much too far.

Dan sat for a long time looking out the bay window to the mountains in the west, I assumed. Their greatness was enhanced now by the new snow, and the diminished winds and cold temperature had brought out a clarity not often allowing those giants to be viewed with such majestic grandeur.

I felt, too, that he had thoughts of Jed, as I had, fleeting or persistent, sure to be with us for quite some time. Jed Simpson had left a huge space to be filled, and it would not be an easy task. With a gnawing guilt, I realized we did have simple warnings of Jed's illness—his occasional lack of appetite—a tired spell. Lord, why didn't we insist he see a doctor? I knotted my hands. My eyes grew moist.

During all that time Andy sat twisting his spoon in his coffee cup, staring at the miniature swells and eddies created by his hand. It was a long, quiet period for all of us.

Finally, Dan rose and made his way to the big leather couch in the living room. Diane, alert to his every move, was by his side. Later, I noticed she'd tucked him in with the new, wooly green afghan, while she was curled up in the rocker with a time-thinned blanket. Diane's simple gesture touched me deeply, and it brought thoughts of Mrs. Nelson clearly to mind. I could see the pale green yarn flying across her fingers and I longed to see her. My eyes moistened again, and I rubbed them with the heel of my hand.

Andy had gotten up, too, and dressed in his outer clothing. "I'll be gettin' a bit of rest, myself."

Oh, I thought, now he has to face the emptiness of the bunkhouse. Well, at least, it seems, he has the courage to cope with it. Andy was a sensible man, experienced by age far beyond my comprehension, I'd discovered. Even so, I'm sure it will take a long time for him to adjust comfortably to the void.

With leaden feet, I walked to my room and lay down on my bed, pulling a spare blanket over me. But I wasn't really sleepy. No. I was weary—weary to my bones, drained as dry as a desert breeze.

I thought of Jed and his lonely life, after taking all the blame for his wife's death onto himself. One should not grieve so, but I suppose he didn't have many occasions to talk about it with anyone at length. But making a little shrine, like Andy had said, was not good, either. One dwells too long. Life is for the living. I didn't have time to grieve for my lost husband. Remember, yes. But not grieve. I had my son, and my father to live for—they needed me.

I moved on. I did see John, though not a lot at first. Still, I think we have a good, sound relationship. I'll go home in February, maybe March. Or even not until spring, but I'll take up my life in Spencer again. Oh, John, I could use your arms around me about now. I rolled over, pulling in the covers over my hands. I felt warmer. You were so comforting that night, John, after the storm. We sat on my couch. Oh, John, I miss you.

Waking with a start, I jumped from the bed. My clock told me I'd actually slept for two hours. I went into the bathroom and splashed cold water on my face. Odd—I hadn't even been sleepy.

I went to the kitchen, but as I passed the door to the living room, I peeked in. It was empty. They *were* there, I know—or did I dream it?

I'd put a roast in a slow oven, earlier, and now I started to peel potatoes. But I drew a mental blank when I tried to plan a salad. My sense of time was all turned around.

From the sink window, I found Dan. He and Andy were loading hay onto a wagon. Then they took it out to the south slope and spread it on the crusted snow. By the time they'd finished, it was dark.

I could see the moon as it cast a sheen on the new snow. It excited me. It was a new moon building, like a new dawning in an altogether different measure of time and place.

Diane came from her room and set the big table in the

dining room, taking extra care to nicely arrange the settings. Her mood was pensive, complimenting my dreamy nature of the moment.

Suddenly I heard footsteps on the porch and the door burst open. "Duke's home!" It was Dan. "Duke came home!" He was almost shouting. "I found him standing at the gate. He made it home." He jerked off his gloves and rubbed his hands together.

"Oh, Dan, how wonderful," I said. Then I had to lean against the counter for support.

And Diane, holding her cheeks in the palms of her hands, squealed, "Oh-h-h, Daddy, I'm so glad."

"He had a slash, though, a deep one—on his left flank. I knew that cat must've got him, otherwise he wouldn't have run off like that."

We listened, quite speechless, then Diane began to tremble.

"He's okay, though, Honey. I cleaned it and salved it up good." Dan smiled. "I gave him extra grain tonight, you can be sure of that. Sal, too. She's got a bruised foot. Poor old Sal."

"They're all heroes," I said, "I mean heroines. Well, I mean both, I guess."

Diane giggled softly. Dan's eyes darted to me, then his look softened and warmed my skin like a hearth fire would. It disturbed me and I had to look away. Come now, Charlotte, you're a grown woman—act like one.

❧[CHAPTER 34]❧

A week went by. Life adjusted slowly to more pleasant routines. We surely missed Jed, though—God, how we missed Jed. Occasionally someone would speak of him, and suddenly develop a catch in their throat. Even Chase whined a bit more than usual when I petted him.

Then one day Diane and I drove to Red Hill. It was her first outing since her accident (except for her trip to the hospital to have her casts removed) and now used only a cane.

We shopped for groceries at Mitchell's General Store and I let Diane's preferences run wild. She gleefully snatched up items that had eluded my shopping lists, and I felt pleasure, too, watching her enjoy herself. But I could see lots of chocolate chip cookies in my near future. I shall encourage her to bake, I thought, with a cunning twist of mind.

We were loading the wagon with the bags of groceries when Diane asked, "Oh, do we have time to stop in to see George and Ruby? You know, George is Andy's brother."

"And Ruby is Helen's sister, right?" I glanced at her.

She nodded, a plea in her eyes.

"Sure we do, let's go," I said.

We crossed the street and I pulled open the creaky door beneath the ornately painted sign, the one that read Saddle Shop. A bell tinkled as Diane limped over the threshold and across the dusty floor to a counter. I followed. The room reeked with the smells of oils and acids and leather, but beautifully-tooled saddles hung about on various display poles. A woman was seated behind a counter, reading a newspaper.

"Hi, Ruby, surprise!" Diane said to a short, plain-looking woman with dark,graying hair.

She looked up. "Diane! My, you're looking wonderful."

"Where's George, is he here?"

"George! Ge-or-ge!" she called through an open door to a back room. "Come see who's here."

A man appearing to be a clone of Andy came through the door and stood by his wife. Were they twins? I must have smiled. Another? As nice as the first?

"Well, hell-o-o-o there, little girl," he said to Diane, "sure glad to see you up and around again."

"I want you to meet Charlotte Foster," Diane said, quickly. "You know, she's been here since September." Diane turned to me. "This is George and Ruby Wallace."

"Nice to meet you," I said, with sincere cheerfulness.

"Hul-lo, Missus Foster, I hope you enjoyed our part of the country," Ruby said, "when will you be leaving?"

"Soon," I answered, quickly. Well, you can hardly wait

to run me out of town, too, I thought. Not unlike your sister. I smiled but my face felt stiff, like cardboard.

"Nice to meet you," George replied, smiling broadly. He reached across the counter and shook my hand. "Andy's said some nice things about you."

"Thank you," I said. And after a few brief words to Diane, he returned to his back room.

Diane chattered happily with Ruby, but I had to draw on my patience to remain there. After surveying some of the wares of the shop (with true admiration), I nudged Diane it was time to leave. Yes, I was still smarting from the brush-off.

We walked slowly across, then down the wide, sunny street, dodging small tumbleweeds tossing in the wind. Our next stop was the mail-order store where Helen worked. Upon entering, I found the simple showroom to be filled with vividly colorful merchandise. Helen's hand, I knew. She was arranging a display of soaps and cremes and lotions on a shelf in the corner, and the air was heavy with flowery fragrances.

She looked up, "Oh, hi, Diane, honey," she cooed, "How're ya doin'?" But her voice became crisp when she turned to me and said, "Hell-o, Charlte."

"Hello, Helen. Has my order come in yet?" I said, with all the nonchalance I could muster.

She sniffed and turned and retrieved a large, bulky package from a shelf and placed it on the counter. I handed her several bills and smiled.

She snatched them from me and made change. "Thank you," she said, with barely enough voice to be heard.

Diane patted the package. "Wow, what is it?"

"I'm not telling," I said. I didn't want Helen to know or guess anything. So, Charlotte, you're still miffed at her, right? "I probably won't be seeing you again, Helen, so this will be goodbye." Then I turned my back to her. I really did enjoy my stay at the ranch. It was a wonderful experience." I walked to the door. "Take care now," I added, smug with my polite words. Let her squirm, I thought, as I waited, outwardly patient, for Diane to say her goodbye, too. I was very happy to walk out of there.

The post office was our last stop and it produced quite a stack of mail, piled up since the blizzard. As I pulled the wagon out onto the main road and picked up speed, Diane sorted through the letters, calling out names all the while. Then she was quiet for a long time, thumbing through the local newspaper and various flyers.

We were nearing the ranch. Suddenly she blurted out, "I'm sorry for the way Ruby was rude to you. It's my fault, too, for going there. I don't know why she's like that, but don't be mad at her. I'm really sorry."

I looked to her, smiled, and offered her the palm of my hand. "It's okay, 'cause we're friends, remember?"

She gave my hand a smart slap, then laughed with a gaiety I'd never before heard from her. "Friends—forever," she said. And then the two of us laughed all the way up the drive, until I stopped the wagon by the porch.

Much later, with all the groceries put away, and Diane
off to her room to read some Shakespeare, I sat at the
table in the bay and began to read my mail. I opened a
greeting card from Kenny, an early Thanksgiving message
with a big turkey on the front, but inside he wrote a short,
cramped letter. It was newsy, at first, then I read, "Poor
John. Mom, why did you leave him for so long? He's got to
be really lonesome for you."

Okay, Kenny, I thought, it's just for a while. You let us
handle it.

He went on to tell of more experiences at Bailey's farm,
and I realized, then, he'd spoken of Beth, here and there,
throughout the entire letter.

"Mind your own business, Kenneth," I'd said on the
phone the night of the storm, and he really took me at my
word. Now, it was like a painful, final severing of the
maternal cord. I laid the card aside and bit my lip to stem
the stinging in my eyes.

I tore open a letter postmarked Seacove, California.
Joyce said she was busy rearranging Larry's den until it
looked like a dormitory. "Lena and the girls," she wrote,
"will be coming for Thanksgiving." (Oh, how I wish I could
be leaving here, then, too. Well, maybe it will work out
that way.) "Tom's already in Hawaii, finding a house for
them." (Lena, what next? You've already lived in just about
all of the most romantic, exotic places in the world. Well,
Sis, I just may come to visit you there.) "They'll be leaving
here right after Christmas, but, Lottie, you can stay on—

and on—and on. And yes, the sand is warm, the sun shines almost every day, and cabanas are reasonable." (Finally, I thought, I'll be a real tourist.) I leaned back in my chair, stretched my arms high above my head for a moment, then resumed my reading.

A letter from John. It was long and warm and humorous. Yes, he'd been over to my house—to fix a leaky faucet in the kitchen sink. "You remember Arlene Krammer," he wrote, "she's that junior high social teacher that moved in with the two new teachers. Arlene said, 'You know the house so well.' What could I say? So, while I was there I put a new spring in the back porch door and changed a couple light bulbs." (Well, Charlotte, you had to ask.)

Of course, he had to tell me that 'Lover-boy Martin' got a black eye from an irate husband at the harvest festival street dance. (Touché, John. I laughed.)

Then I read his postscript. "I miss you most, Lottie, when I walk by your house and see your empty rocking chair. It looks so forlorn." I folded his letter and wiped away a tear or two. Don't dwell, Charlotte. But it was hard not to. Arlene was *there,* and I was *not!*

Thankfully, the phone rang. I jumped up and put the letters on the bay window sill in the order in which they were read, John's letter on top.

I picked up the phone. "Hell-o?"

"Hi, Charlotte, it's me, Jo."

"Hi, dear." Lord, she sounded blue.

"Will you tell Dad I'd like to come home tomorrow night? Can someone come?"

"Oh, I'm sure."

"How's Dad?"

"Seems fine."

"Is Andy there all the time now?"

"Well, he has been."

"How's Diane, still being a brat?"

"No. She's fine, I mean, we're fine."

"Well, see you then."

"Okay, honey, someone will be there. Bye."

It was decided at breakfast that Friday morning that Diane would ride with me to St. Anne's. I flew through the housework. The trip had the promise of excitement, making the hours pass swiftly. Diane finished her lessons remarkably quick, then spent an hour primping and changing outfits.

We acquired a new hand at OUR Ranch this day, and I wondered if it had anything at all to do with her sudden attraction to her mirror. Andy brought his grand-nephew, Joe Berg, to the ranch. I met him briefly, but Diane was busy—dawdling in a bubble bath. I was surprised to find family resemblance still running strong, for he was a younger version of the veteran cowhand. Andy settled him into the bunkhouse, and, from time to time, I saw the two of them going in and out of the barns.

Hmmm, I wouldn't think they'd need an extra hand here through the winter. Well, maybe he can cook. Now,

Charlotte, mind your own business, you'll be gone from here soon enough. And I almost glided around the living room, dusting, dancing, and singing, *California Here I Come.*

It was time to leave for the school in Meadow Grand, and the wagon had been parked by the porch. Diane and I were on either side of it, about to get in, when Dan hurried from the garage. He went to her side, put his arm around her shoulder, and gave her a squeeze. He must have whispered something in her ear for she giggled.

Then he walked around the wagon and stood quite close to me. I looked up. Our eyes met—and held. "Drive carefully, now, Char." His voice was deep and soft—almost pleading.

"I will, Dan," I said, simply, and got into the seat. We fastened our belts and Diane settled back against the cushion. I started the engine, shifted into gear, and began to roll the vehicle down the drive. But my hands felt weak. What unnerved you, Charlotte? I don't know, but I hope Diane doesn't notice.

Seconds later she glanced to me, smiled impishly, and said, in a sing-song voice, "I think—he—likes—you."

"Well, heavens, I hope he does." I laughed, but I looked away quickly lest she detect other clues from my trembling form. Wait. Had I seen a twinkle in those know-it-all blue eyes?

But she added at once, "You know very well what I mean, Charlotte."

I did. But before I could comment, we were distracted when a flock of magpies flew in front of the wagon toward the corral.

❧[CHAPTER 35]❧

The trip to Meadow Grand was pleasant, but uneventful—not even a herd of antelope to startle me. The radio spewed out lively tunes and Diane hummed or sang along. She had not been back to her school since her accident, and she spent the last five miles brushing her hair until it floated about her shoulders like a cape of gold.

Arriving at St. Anne's, we drove up to the front door and parked, (we were allowed to do that when picking up students) but I was drawn to glance over to the parking lot. "That truck—that rust-colored truck, I've seen it somewhere before," I stared.

"Beats me," Diane said, and began to climb out of the wagon.

"Well, I just know I have, but I can't think . . ."

I had to hurry to follow Diane into the building's main lobby. There, Sister Agnes rushed from her office and folded her arms around Diane, giving her a crushing hug. "We missed you, dear," she said.

Diane's face reddened and her lips began to tremble. Finally, when Sister Agnes released her, she gained her voice. "Gosh, I'll be so glad to get back to school."

At that same time Joanne came into the lobby with a bulging book-bag clutched in her arms. The bag tumbled to the floor releasing several volumes, as Joanne, crying out, wrapped her arms around both Diane and me. "Oh, I'm so glad to see you two," she wailed.

I saw a rush of tears. (And I always thought she had such unusual composure.) She's thinking of the blizzard, and Jed, and her dad, and maybe the horses, too. I clenched my teeth as I felt myself come close to breaking.

"Hi, Jo. I missed you," Diane said. She backed away, then, seemingly uncomfortable with her big sister's show of affection. "Wow, it seems strange to be back here." She peeked into the office. "Where's Janet Lonetree? I was hoping to see her."

"Oh, you just missed her," Sister said, quickly. "She has a new beau now, and I can't get an extra minute's work out of her on Friday nights. I just don't understand it." She grinned at me and rolled her eyes upward.

I chuckled and said nothing.

"Well, dear, I hope this is your very last lesson packet," she said, then, handing Diane a large, brown envelope. "We're all looking forward to your return. God bless you, and have a safe trip home, all of you."

"Goodbye, Sister," we returned in unison, and stooped to help Joanne gather up her books.

When we went outside, I became dumb-struck. Standing in the parking lot by the rust-colored truck was Rod Price—the Rod Price I knew from Spencer, Minnesota. And Janet Lonetree was sitting *inside* the truck with a complacent smile on her face. Facts, like pieces in a jigsaw puzzle, quickly fell into place. Cathy Price. Uncle from Minnesota. Has an interest at St. Anne's. We hurried our steps to meet. "Well, look who's here," I called.

"Lottie Foster, I don't believe it," Rod blurted, then gaped.

I grabbed his hand.

After a moment, he regained his voice. "I—I thought you went to—to Jackson Buttes. That's quite a way from here."

"Oh, the plane did drop me in the Buttes, but then, I do get around," I said, letting go his hand and laughingly smoothing my hair. The girls stood by and grinned with amusement while Janet climbed out of the truck, her expression curious.

After I made the introduction, everyone talked at once. But it was Rod's turn to explain *his* presence. "I won a contest," he said, "and I'm using the prize money to go to school—here—in Meadow Grand. Great photography school. The good part of it is my brother lives here. But this is the best part of all," he said, lifting Janet's hand high in the air and grinning.

I caught Janet's eye. "Oh, how nice," I said, with a mixture of surprise and pleasure. But the girls giggled and shuffled from one foot to the other, and I sensed their uneasiness dealing with love. "But, tell me, Rod, did you sell the old clinic building? I mean—your studio?" I felt a stab of melancholy.

"Yes, Lottie," he said, "I had to. It's a fast-food joint already." And his eyes turned away from mine.

I felt like ice water had been thrown on my soul. Pieces, one by one, were being stolen from my past, my heritage, and this one was as painful as the others. The near solitude of Lilac Lane, that quiet street that ran by the side of my house, where I'd taken many a pleasant walk with my little dog, Pepper, would be no more.

I strained hard to regain my composure, and we exchanged phone numbers and promises to call, then went our respective way. But homesickness clawed at me for quite a few miles on the way back to OUR Ranch, and part of the time I imagined I was rocking peacefully on the cool, open front porch on Grant Street, in my father's old, white wicker rocking chair, my thinking chair.

After some time the girls' chatter brought me back to the present. Diane was talking. "Oh, there's a new man at the ranch, Jo. He just came today. I haven't met him yet, but I saw him outside. O-o-h, is he ever cute. Wait'll you see him. Oh, but he's too old for you. I heard he's twenty-six, that's really old."

"What do you mean—that's really old?" I demanded, grimacing with a comic air.

"Oh, I—I . . ."

"I thought we were friends," I said, scowling and laughing at the same time. Then I held up my palm to her and received a loud smack, her giggle resounding throughout the stationwagon.

I glanced in the mirror at Joanne in the back seat. At first she rolled her eyes and smiled questioningly, then she, too, burst into laughter.

Soon after we arrived home and the girls unwound a bit, they began to help me with the evening meal. We were quite busy when Andy brought Joe into the house to meet the girls. Moments later we heard the Jeep pull up the drive and circle around to the porch. The men excused themselves and hurriedly went back out to meet Dan.

The girls had behaved quite properly during the introduction, but the moment the men were out of the room, they began to bubble giddily—"He's cute. He was watching you, Jo. No, he wasn't, he was watching you. He's got dimples. He's got neat hair—long. I don't think he smokes—his teeth are too white. Ooh, those eye lashes." And so, the girls had a new subject of interest.

We had a late supper at the big table in the bay window. Conversation was plentiful, but rather awkward at times due to the new man, Jed's absence and Joanne's return. So the meal was over in a short time and Joe and Andy bid their goodnights.

Dan, seated next to Diane, turned and said, "How was your visit at school today, honey?"

"Oh, great, Dad. Sister Agnes squeezed me so hard I thought my face would blow up. She's anxious to have me back, she said."

Dan chuckled. "Well, we have to go see the doctor one more time. I made an appointment for next Wednesday."

"Oh, okay, but I'm sure I'm all healed—perfectly."

"Good, then it will be back to school the Sunday next."

"I can hardly wait. It's sure been a drag being home all this time."

I frowned at her—an exaggerated frown.

"I'm sorry, Charlotte, I didn't mean to . . ."

I winked at her then, and suppressed a grin.

Dan had started to rise from his chair, but sat back down and looked at me. "Oh, Char, how about coming with us to the Buttes that day? You need a trip in another direction for a change, I would think."

Before I could speak, Diane did. "What a super idea." She clapped her hands, and Joanne joined in, too, smiling broadly, eyes wide.

"Oh, gosh, I don't know. . . ." My neck was scorching inside my collar and I tugged at it.

"Why not?" Diane groaned.

"Well, I—I—ah . . ." What had come over me?

"We can stay the evening, too, have dinner at The Golden Nugget." Dan said, quickly. His eyes were on me, then, holding, searching, and all the while speaking directly to Diane. "We can take in a movie, too, Di. May as well make a night of it once we're there." He looked to Diane once, then quickly back to me. "Live it up a little. Don't get to do that very often."

"Neat-o," she said, squealing and clapping her hands again. Diane *always* clapped her hands when thrilled. "Oh, Charlotte, please come with us."

I sat silently while pesky little thoughts grappled inside me. My lips parted to speak, but I sat, still tongue-tied. Should I go? Yes—go. No—maybe you'd better not. But it may be the last chance you'll have for an opportunity like *that*. Like *what?* To be with them both. Then maybe you *should* go. It's not as if it's a date, or anything like that.

My throat was so dry it hurt, but I managed to say, "Yes, I'd like that." I paused and swallowed hard. "I suppose, while we're there, we may as well see about my flight to California." I looked away, then back to Dan. "It'll save some calling, don't you think?"

I saw him flinch. He looked down, and slowly placed his napkin on the table. "Yes, I suppose you would like to he moving on." He stood up quickly. "Yes, we should do that."

He glanced at each girl. "I have some book work to be doing tonight, then I'll be turning in. Good night, gals." He turned to me and nodded. "Good supper. Goodnight." Then he disappeared into his room.

How could such an exciting conversation get so far off track, Charlotte Foster? Boy, you really blew it. You could have acted as thrilled as you really are. But he might get the wrong impression. So? What *is* the wrong impression? Oh, I don't know.

࿔

Some time ago I'd spied an old sewing machine on a closet shelf, so, the next afternoon, Joanne helped me set it up in the dining room. After some cleaning, oiling and tinkering, it began to purr like a contented cat. I unwrapped the large bundle I'd picked up at the mail-order store as the girls stood waiting, their eyes wide, anxious. Yards and yards of pale-blue morning glories born on an airy white material cascaded across the dining room table. "New curtains for the bay window," I exclaimed, "do you like it?"

"Yes, yes," they chorused and fingered the crisp yardage.

"Well, Mary had suggested I'd do something about the old curtains. And I just love blue morning glories," I added dreamily.

Diane clapped as she always did when pleased. Joanne helped me measure and cut the goods and we worked industriously all afternoon, while Diane, from the kitchen, moaned over her algebra lessons. And, all the while, a simmering pot of ragout sent a mouth-watering aroma about the house, and I told them stories about my own home with the bedroom papered in pale-blue morning glories.

We put the perfectly-pressed and puffed new curtains

in place just before it was time to set the table for supper. After exclaiming clumsily over the new curtains, Andy and Joe ate a hurried supper and then rose to leave. "Sorry, we're in such a rush, Charlotte, no time for dessert. Joe, here, has a heavy date tonight." Andy said, giving Joe a sporty clap on the back. Joe turned red and looked away.

"Yes, by all means, don't be late," I said, laughing. Then I wanted to slap myself for showing such an indifference to my *date* for the next Wednesday in the Buttes.

Shortly after the men left for Red Hill, Dan came in from the garage. He noticed the curtains immediately. "They're nice, he said, "you sure did a good job."

"Thank you," I said, "but Joanne helped a lot."

Joanne just grinned and scurried around the kitchen helping me with the next session of meals.

Dan held up his hands, darkened with stains. "Doing some work on the tractor," he said, and disappeared into his room for a few minutes. Then he returned to sit at the table in the bay, giving the new curtains another once-over.

It was a typical meal with the girls; Joanne saying how pleased she was to have learned something of sewing curtains, and Diane fuming over having such long algebra lessons.

After Dan finished his ragout, he leaned back in his chair. "Damn good eating, Char," he said, "whatever it was."

"Yes," Joanne agreed, "I really liked it, too."

"Um-hmm, sure better than Helen's cooking," Diane sniped. "Hers was getting bor-r-ring."

"Di-ane, that's no way to talk. Helen did her best and we were lucky to have *had* her here."

"Sorry, Dad." She dropped her head. "I know."

Dan seemed to handle his girls with loving discipline. But why did he use that past tense though, I wondered. It sounded so-o past. I shut it out of my mind—until dessert was over—then I wondered some more.

Dan got up and walked toward the pegged rack, then turned around again. "Girls," he said, "maybe we can all get together and play some cards when I get back in. I have to do a little more work in the garage, then check on Sal and Duke again."

We all smiled a willingness.

Dan reached for a light denim jacket. "Dandy out now," he said. "We got a chinook wind this afternoon. It'll make short work of the snow—melt it in a day or two." He went out the door, but he'd looked at me longer than it took to say the words.

I had a wild urge to follow him. Really, Charlotte, you'd better make more of an effort to control your thoughts.

The girls helped me clear the table and load the washer and the kitchen was tidied in the shortest time ever. Then Joanne filled two glasses to the brim with fizzy root beer, and, snatching up a large bag of potato chips—"In case we get hungry later"—she disappeared through the swinging door, chips bag fast in her teeth. Soon, the music in the living room was turned up to a raucous volume.

Hmmm, looks like that's the end of our card game. I may as well get busy and plan the menus for tomorrow. But the catchy tunes excited me and I began to dance about the kitchen as I peered into the pantry, the fridge, and the freezer. I sensed a deep joy and my heart wanted to race.

❦[CHAPTER 36]❧

The phone rang, its jangling interrupting all thoughts of food. I glided across the kitchen floor and picked it up. "Hello-o," I answered, fairly singing it.

"Charlotte? Ben Cloud here. Dan around?"

"He's in the barn."

"Will you give him a message?"

"Yes, I will."

"Tell him if he needs any alfalfa on Monday to call me right back. If he can wait another week or so, call later on. I'll be home here for another twenty minutes or so."

"Okay, Ben, I'll tell him right away."

"Thanks, Charlotte. Goodbye."

"Goodbye," I said, and replaced the phone with a flourish. I slipped on my boots and parka and left the house. I didn't bother to zip up when I felt the warmer winds, and my gloves stayed in my pocket. Chase ignored me when I passed his lair, preferring to guard the dooryard with one partially-opened eye.

The night was beautiful, the moon so bright it cast my
shadow on the snow with sharply-defined lines, and the
heavens were alive with millions of glittering stars. I drew
in a delicious breath and walked slowly to the barn, feeling
the heels of my boots crushing into the softening snow,
liking the breeze rippling my hair. I wanted to walk
forever—enjoying the perfectness of the night.

When I reached the barn I found the door slightly ajar,
a long, narrow shaft of light shining out into the inky night.
I approached with caution, remembering the ill-fated trip
to the garage a few weeks before. I even giggled a little at
the thought of the silly collision. You can laugh now,
Charlotte, but it didn't seem so funny that night.

"Da-an? Oh, Da-an." I heard my voice changing notes
like a diva.

The door opened slowly and I saw the tall man outlined in the dim glow of the inside lighting. I took a deep
breath and spilled out Ben's message.

"Oh, it can wait a week," Dan said. "Got a good supply
yet. Don't really use much."

"Okay." I turned to leave. I'd only taken a few steps
when I felt his hand on my wrist.

"Char?" He tugged at my arm. "Wait—please."

I turned around and looked up, feeling dwarfed by the
bulk of the man. He put his other hand on my shoulder
and we stood very close. I saw his face in the shaft of light
and he appeared almost frightened.

"Don't leave. I—I mean don't leave me." He spoke

earnestly, yet his voice held a tenderness. "I don't want you to leave me, Char."

I stared up at him, unable to utter a sound. Oh, God, what am I hearing?

"I'm sorry, but I—I know you got a letter from that John Cummings again. What does he mean to you? Were you going back to him?" The moon shone full on his face now and I saw his jaw muscles working. "I don't want you to go back to him. Hell, I don't even want you to go to California."

I still couldn't find my voice.

"Oh, damn it, Char, what I mean is—I love you—I want you to stay here—with me, with us."

Then I gasped. "You can't mean that, Dan. You can't really—mean that." Then my senses reeled and my heart felt as if struck by storm.

Slowly he pulled me closer to him, drawing me out of the moonlight and into the shadows. I moved with him. I felt purpose in his arms as they went around me, and his lips brushed mine, then lingered. There was a subtle questioning, begging to be answered.

I didn't resist, I couldn't resist—I was paralyzed with joy. My heart began thumping in my throat, yes—yes—yes. My hands crept up his chest until my fingers slipped behind his neck and tightened altogether. I returned his kiss and his response was immediate, full of a hungry love, and, at the same time, I knew the ardor in his arms strong around me.

A long, long moment later he released me. I was stunned, but I found enough voice to whisper, "Oh, Dan, I—I never thought you felt like this. I—I can't believe this is happening—to me—to us. I think . . ."

Before I could finish he kissed me again, and again. "I love you, Char," he murmured, "Oh, God, I've loved you from the first minute I saw you. It *must* have been the first minute." There was an anguish in his words then. "Damn, but it scared me."

His nearness brought a warmth that flooded over me, as before, yet now increasing until I felt as if I were aflame. "Oh, Dan, I—I . . ."

A gust of wind blew around the corner of the barn, interrupting my words and tumbling my hair into my face. He brushed it away and kissed my cheeks and my forehead. "Char, Char, my darling," he murmured, and, at the same time, he led me into the barn, pulling the door close behind him.

We sat down on the broad pile of bagged grain just inside the door. Then his arm circled my shoulder. My parka fell open and his other arm slid inside and around my waist. As his lips found mine again, he gently put me down on the soft, sweetly-musty sacks, our bodies hard against one another.

I ended the kiss and moved my mouth close to his ear. "I love you, too, Daniel Garner. Oh, I do love you, and, yes, I'll stay with you—forever." I took a fresh, deep breath.

"Oh, yes—yes, I will," I whispered. But my heart sang joyfully, the notes rising up until I was almost deafened, and I did not know for sure what I was actually saying.

Then the tears came. Our arms tightened about each other and I knew our thoughts were merging, blending, melding into a new-born unity. His mouth found mine again and I felt his emotions surging through every fiber of his body, as well as my own. He kissed my cheeks as the tears spilled over them, and then I sensed he was shedding tears, also, and soon our faces were wet with our love.

After a time we lay quietly on the bed of grain. My lips found his ear. "Dan," I whispered, "is this all true?"

He pushed himself up on one elbow and peered into my eyes. A thin slice of moonlight, shining through the partially opened door, spread across our faces. The light from a single bulb reflected off the inside barn door, bathing us in a soft, warm glow. He put a gentle hand on the side of my face, caressing it lightly for a moment. Then, with a curled forefinger, he lifted my chin to meet his gaze. He searched my eyes with an intensity that caused my heart to burn. Slowly he lowered his lips to mine and kissed me—tenderly, sweetly, reverently—a kiss that left me totally committed to him with every bit of flesh and bone and breath of my being. He moved his mouth close to my ear, then, and gave a soft, quavering sigh. "It's true, Char, really true. I give you my word."

All anguish had disappeared from his voice, and now it

was deep, soothing and positive. He lifted his face and let his lips brush mine, and I knew we'd found something rare and special to jealously guard from that moment on.

But then we shared a kiss that kindled a sudden new fervor consuming the both of us until our passion began to burn almost out of control. "Dan! Oh, Lord, Dan, no." I struggled to sit up, and, at first, he wouldn't let me. "Please," I said. Finally, he gave in to my resistance and slowly pulled me into a sitting position.

He sat quietly and began to rub my back, gently, in circles. "I know, sweetheart, we have things to do, like tell the girls," he said, in a soft, choking voice. We sat on the grain pile now, our legs dangling over the edge, holding hands like children. He heaved a deep sigh, then, "Charlotte," he said, (he'd never called me Charlotte after the first day), "I want to do this right, so—well—uh—Charlotte, honey, will you marry me?" He had a comedic lightness in his voice now, a drastic change from the heat of the preceding moments.

I clasped his face in the palms of my hands and held it in the shaft of moonlight. "Yes, I will, Daniel Garner," I answered, solidly, "and you'd better not change your mind—not ever." I put my lips to his and our marriage promise was sealed.

Jumping to his feet, Dan pulled me to mine and held me at the waist. My hands pressed to his chest. "Oh, Dan, you know—that darn Mary. She was right. She admitted to me that she had this in mind all the time—that she'd planned it that way. She would say to me, "Whatever will be, will be." I shook my head. "She was absolutely uncanny." Then I told it all to him in a rambling fashion, still trembling, still reeling with the intoxication of bliss.

Dan chuckled softly. "Well, the other night when I saw Di helping you with the dishes, and getting on so well—then I had hope—finally. I know my daughter. She's been a little firecracker all her life. I knew what I was up against the whole time." He stopped talking and kissed my forehead—twice.

"M-m-m," I said, "go on."

"Coming home in that storm, Char, I thought of you and prayed I'd get a chance to at least tell you how I felt." He paused, took a deep breath and pulled me against his chest, holding me firmly. "I knew you were near me that night. I just knew it. You were, weren't you?"

"Yes, Dan, I was. Oh, Lord, how I prayed, too."

"But the next morning I got worried again. God, Char, I'm so glad we found our chance. I'm sure glad old Ben called tonight." He threw his head back and laughed almost wildly. "I didn't know when the time would be right that I could *ask* you if you cared anything at *all* about me. But I made up my mind that I wasn't going to let you get *through* next Wednesday."

"And I—I was actually afraid to go to the Buttes with you. I guess I was afraid of having my feelings found out, somehow. Oh, but I'm glad Diane convinced me to say yes." I started to laugh, too, then. "That morning—the morning after the storm—you looked so pathetic, kind of funny, too, standing there with your robe half off, and in your big, bare feet—you do have big feet, you know—I felt then I loved you, but I was still trying to deny it. I wanted to protect my *pride* I guess." I felt chagrin. "I'm just not the seductress Mary hoped I'd be."

"You could try, baby," he said, doing a wonderful Bogart, then he laughed again.

I reached up and pulled his head down and planted the most sultry kiss I knew on his unsuspecting mouth, one I'd hoped he wouldn't soon forget.

"Damn, woman," he groaned, "you could get arrested for that." He began to tighten his arms around me, but I wrenched free, turned, and bolted from the barn, pushing the door wide with one forceful shove. He followed me out, closed the door and latched it.

I ran toward the house, but he soon overtook me and caught me up in his arms. And he laughed with the roar of a grizzly. Swinging me around and around, he danced in a large circle, there, in the dooryard in the slushy snow. I laughed, too, but the whirling motion made me dizzy and I began to shriek. Chase shot from his cove under the junipers by the porch. He joined us, barking wildly, and ran in even larger circles around us.

"Put me down, you big oaf," I cried.

He obeyed, staggering and breathless. We stood for a few minutes in the moonlight, gazing into each other's faces, smiling joyfully while allowing our breathing to return to a more normal rhythm. Then slowly, and arm-in-arm, we walked to the house.

Dan opened the door. Both girls were standing in the middle of the floor, motionless and wide-eyed. We entered and stood, arms linked.

"Dad, what's wrong?" Diane asked, "Chase was barking like crazy." Then she scowled.

Joanne just stared, her mouth dropped open. I knew we were a shocking sight. I glanced to Dan.

His smile was gigantic. "Well, we just asked him if we could get married and he was just saying *yes*."

Diane's eyes popped wide and her mouth dropped open, too. They looked almost comical. But then Joanne recovered quickly and rushed to her father and me. We held her close and I said, "It's true, it's really true," over and over again.

We three spread apart and looked at Diane. She moved forward—cautiously at first. Then she let out a piercing screech and hurtled headlong into her father's open arms. I beheld her painful, heart-wrenching moment when she surrendered her father to me, and being the true lady she'd become, she did it honestly and graciously, with a most beautiful smile. Dan kissed her forehead three times.

She hugged me, then. "I think I do believe in first stars," she said, softly. "Aunt Mary's wishes sure came true. I called her Peter Pan once, and she just laughed and said we'll see and grinned like she had secret powers."

I nodded, laughing. "Yes, she was quite the busy-body matchmaker, wasn't she?"

Joanne observed everything in her quiet way, then motioned for us to sit in the booth as she poured each of us a fizzy root beer. We toasted each and all for quite some time before Joanne ran off to fetch the big bag of chips from the living room.

"Dan, let's call Mary," I said, "I think she should be the first to know."

"Yeah, we can tell her we'll be seeing her in about a month. If we can get married in the chapel over at St. Anne's, we can fly to Florida right after, on—ah—a little trip."

Diane frowned and shook her head. "Dad, it's called a honeymoon."

"Oh, yeah. Well, I'm so old I forgot what it's called." I saw him wink at Joanne, but when he turned to me, I saw a mischievous glint in his eye. His smile was shy, though, almost school-boy shy. (And oh, how I loved him.) In a moment, he brightened. "Char," he said, "can we all go to California for Christmas? You *said* it was a family reunion, didn't you?"

"Yes!" I clasped Dan's hand in mine. "Oh, yes. What a reunion that will be."

We settled down then to the seriousness of marking dates on the large calendar, the one with the yellow-breasted birds on it, hanging on the wall above the booth.

[CHAPTER 37]

Waking even before my alarm sounded, I rolled over, brushing hair from my eyes, and stretched both arms above my head. Wednesday morning. Glorious Wednesday morning. You have such an exciting promise in store. I tossed off the covers and sprang from my bed and went directly to the window. We'd had a light dusting of snow in the night and it seemed to have touched everything with magic. Charlotte, say it—magic has touched you, too. And the beauty of all of it was almost enough to stop one's breath.

We all had an early, but pleasantly relaxed breakfast, then set about to do our chores. As I cleared away the remnants of our meal, I watched the horses frisking about in the corral. You're waiting for Joe to call you for grain, right? I missed my little forays to the barn with pilfered carrots. I saw Andy loading salt licks onto the wagon to be delivered to the herd up on the south slope, while Chase warned several jays in a juniper by the gate not to come any closer.

Joanne had been back at school since Sunday, but I wished so much she could be with us for our outing to the Buttes. Even so, it was a beautiful morning, and I was tingly with anticipation. I wrapped my arms about myself and offered a silent prayer of thanks.

Dan returned from the barn after tending his ailing horses. "Well, what do you know, Sal doesn't limp anymore, and Duke's scabbed over really good." He grinned.

"Oh, Honey, I just knew they'd be alright," I said, cheerily, "they just *had* to be."

"That's one more thing I love about you—your optimism." He kissed me then, lightly, sweetly, and disappeared into his dressing room.

I searched my closet for a nicer dress to wear on this special occasion, and, finding a fawn-colored cashmere shirtwaist, I laid it on the bed. Selecting a green and gold scarf, I tossed it on top. I liked it. Then, snatching up my atomizer of Charlie, I misted it about my shoulders and throat. Ah-h-h, Dorrie, you always did come up with that extra special something at the right time. And yes, pal, you'll be getting a long letter from me quite soon.

Suddenly, I felt a strong urge to tell it all—everything—to Lena. Yes, sister, my life could never compare to your exciting travels, your three nice daughters, your loving husband, but now I think *I've* been so truly blessed, I could never ever envy again. I love you, Lena.

Then, I thought of John. I'll have to write and tell him I won't be coming back to Spencer, Minnesota, at all soon.

I felt sad about hurting him, but then I realized he'd mentioned Arlene Kramer more and more in each succeeding
letter. Oh, John, no—I don't think you'll hurt for long.

Fully dressed now, I retrieved my coat from the closet,
plucked a gold chain bracelet out of a box, and went to the
kitchen. My soul was singing an aria.

Dan was waiting there, leaning against the counter,
resplendent in a smooth, white wool shirt. A leather bolo
tie sporting a silver pull, with an enormous turquoise
stone, lay at his throat. And his rich brown hair was
brushed and smoothed until not one strand dared stray.
Just the sight of him added mightily to my already full
heart, and now it was near bursting. Dan drew in his breath
and whistled softly.

"Flattery will get you—everything," I said, laughing,
but then I held up the chain, my eyes seeking assistance.

He fastened the chain around my wrist, his fingers
clumsily working the delicate clasp. Then I slipped both
arms upward and twined my fingers around the back of his
neck. "Thanks," I said, offering my lips. His kiss was tender
at first, then, I thought—Lord, it could melt all the snow in
Peace County. I noticed a scent of a new cologne. Oh, yes,
Charlotte, there will be many things to experience, joyfully
as before, and I began to tremble. Yet, there in his arms, I
knew there was nowhere in the world I'd rather be.

Diane swished into the kitchen then, and plopped her
coat on a chair. She was wearing a navy pleated skirt and a
wooly sweater of a pink so rosy it put a delightful rouge on

her cheeks. Besides, she must have brushed her hair a thousand strokes for it fell from her shoulders like a golden waterfall.

"Do I look alright, Dad?" she asked, twirling around. "I don't limp anymore, do I?"

She did, a little, but he said, "No, sugar, you look just grand," and smiled adoringly.

Take good notice, Charlotte, of the competition you will always have around here for Dan's attention. But, inwardly, I swelled with satisfaction remembering the slapped palms.

"Let's go, Dad," Diane said, handing him my coat. She giggled, her sparkling eyes glancing from her father to me.

The phone rang, startling the three of us.

"Don't answer it," Diane said, "we'll be late."

Dan did, though. "It's for you, honey," and he handed me the phone.

"Hello."

A voice came. "Hello, Lottie, this is Rod."

"Hi, Rod."

"Just thought I'd let you know I'm driving back to Spencer for Thanksgiving vacation. Anything I can bring back for you?"

A soft thud hit my heart. Then, "Yes. Oh, yes, Rod. Well, it's quite a long story, but do you suppose you could bring back my father's wicker rocking chair?"

"Sure thing. Glad to do it," he said, "plenty room in that old truck."

"Oh, Rod, that would be wonderful. I have just the place for it—here at the ranch. From our back porch you can see the south slope—and the high hill—and the mountains. . . ."

Then I felt Dan's strong hands come from behind and firmly cup my shoulders.

ॐ

About the Author

Audrey Brown, a native Minnesotan, began writing seriously in her later years. She was a student in the COMPAS Literary Post program for five years and had a short story published in one of their first anthologies. At the same time, she either won or placed in all five of the smaller writing contests she entered. She also was accepted into a writer's group, which she still attends.

Widowed now, Audrey and her pilot-husband, Michael, later disabled, raised five children and have ten grandchildren.

She is currently on the board of directors with her late husband's army reunion association and enjoys traveling to the yearly reunions.

She is presently working on another novel.

About the Story

Charlotte Foster, a gentle person, widowed early, is approaching middle age in the small town where she has lived her whole life. Now, with the death of her father, and her only child, a son, away at college, she finds herself free of responsibility to others for the first time in her life.

When a sudden violent storm blows into her life, changing the familiar landscape, it gives her a new view of her situation, including a long-standing romantic relationship.

She makes an impetuous decision.

But has she made the right choice, she wonders as she admonishes herself:

". . . Lord, Charlotte Foster, maybe you should have listened to Dorrie. Maybe you should have thought things through a little longer and not have jumped at the chance to bring a little excitement into your life. There could have been other ways. Whose advice did you seek? No one's. Well, damn, damn, it's too late now."

Follow Charlotte as she tells in her own words, with stirring detail, the events of her journey in search of a more fulfilling life.

For additional copies, write to:
Gently Press
P.O.Box 2555
Inver Grove Heights, MN 55076